AFTER THE

DASH

Lynda Abernathy

Dedicated to my mother, the kind of woman one could only ever aspire to be. I'll never know how you've had the patience, vigor, tenacity and wisdom to consistently remain the wind beneath so many wings. Thank you for growing my roots deep and my wings strong.

Many thanks and lots of love to my brothers, whose blood, devotion, support and scars we all share. *All for one and one for all*.

And to Don. Thank you for you.

AFTER THE

DASH

"This life is but a brief tenure, one of many perspectives a spirit must experience in the quest for eternity."
— Brian Rathbone, *Call of the Herald*

PROLOGUE

I could not breathe. I could not scream. No help was coming. No one even knew. My skull and my lungs ached to explode as the darkness closed in.

Terror seized me. My limbs thrashed helplessly, as heavy as concrete in quicksand. Liquid shadows strangled and suffocated me. The realization that I was dying draped over my thoughts like a thick velvet curtain. This was not my time. I did not belong here. But here I was again, in the same illusory anguish to which I was drawn night after night.

I forced open my bulging eyes and gulped in big breaths of air. Awake. My lungs were on fire, and my head was splitting. The dream was nearly forgotten once I awoke; however, there was that same old nagging sensation. It had always tugged at the back of my mind like a whisper. There was more. An answer to a question I couldn't remember to ask and couldn't recollect, but something that had hovered in the shadowy corners of my mind for as long as I could recall.

Somehow, the thought terrified me. I was not sure why, but I implicitly understood that the answer, and even the asking, would forever change my life and all that I thought I knew.

CHAPTER 1

I am born of the first people. I am the flesh and DNA of she who tasted that forbidden fruit. That same curiosity courses through my blood. The irreverence to the rules. I have evolved and descended. I have lived through everything. I have lived despite everything. And I have changed. I was made in the likeness of light, but I have swum in cold pools of darkness. My story is not black and white; there are reasons and motives and explanations. Circumstances are ever-changing. We must change with it or we will be swallowed up by - and disappear into - the browned, wispy, rusted pages of history.

CHAPTER 2
Aiyanna

I am just like you. I order fast food and curse at traffic while eating all the french fries from the greasy paper sack before I even get home. I despise crowds, early mornings, and humid, hot weather. I un-wrinkle my clothes by running them through the dryer. I read stories while tucked into my favorite chair, my dog curled at my feet, sipping coffee and living vicariously through the characters and their tales of greatness. I am not that. I am not greatness. I am a great mess.

You're probably wondering, then, why you should even keep reading. Good question. While I may not be particularly notable or heroic, I do have a magnificent story to tell you. A big story. A story that took me on unimaginable journeys. A story that changed me forever. Perhaps you will find something in these words that changes you, too. It may shed some light on parts of yourself you have kept in the shadows. Or perhaps it will pose questions you had never considered before. Maybe it will alter your life. At the very least, I hope my words reflect the concept that we are all here for a reason. Your reading these words is not arbitrary. You are here. You exist. You matter.

Living up to a name like "Aiyanna" has been something of a challenge. We don't spend a lot of time considering those things, do we? Names are powerful. They are an outline for what character is to come. Funny people have funny names. Lawyers and murderers have three names. Shakespeare was wrong. If roses had been named Hooker's Lips instead, fewer folks would stop to smell them, I think.

The meaning of Aiyanna is heroic and beautiful: *Eternal Blossom*. Oh, how whimsical and romantic! Growing up, I couldn't figure out why my grandmother would have chosen such a majestic and mysterious name for such an awkward, ordinary wallflower like me. Granted, I am sure I wasn't born awkward. Surely. I always thought, especially in my gloomy teenage years, that my grandmother must have been disappointed to have wasted that name on someone like me. Of course, there were no other options, so I win by default – my favorite way of winning.

This is what I am getting at: I always sought love from external sources, like so many of us do. I felt undeserving and odd, like I did not really belong anywhere. I was a puzzle piece, always searching for some other's ragged-cut edge to align perfectly with mine in order to create a lovely picture. I discovered, on this journey I am sharing with you, that I needed to fill my own self with love. I had incessantly been so busy giving it away, I'd never thought to save some for myself. It became clear to me that I was a culmination of history itself. I was important. I matter. So do you.

While I will never save the planet from a dark-caped villain or the gray cloud of human pollution, perhaps I can spare it from a few dark forces whose aim is to infect minds and cast shadows upon our little candle lights.

With that disclaimer of ordinariness out of the way, allow me to properly introduce myself. My name is Aiyanna Burns. I am in my thirties, married, childless, and I still have yet to find a hair product that can do anything to control my crazy tresses.

So, now that I've introduced myself, I would like to share something with you: how a strange and sensational string of events led to an understanding that my normalness is, in fact, extraordinary.

CHAPTER 3
Estienne

He was born in the Kingdom of France in the early fourteenth century. It was a terrible time and place to have been born. He was a happy boy with thick, honey-colored curls atop his head and a constant smile upon his face. At least for the first three years of his life. Ignorance, as they say, was bliss indeed. Then, as it does from time to time, the earth decided to cleanse itself.

His feet, the tiny feet of an ill-fed toddler peasant, splashed in the puddles and mud pits about his cottage. It was springtime. He should have been spread out in a field of grain, hiding from his chores and imagining the different shapes of clouds in the bright blue sky to be various farm animals. Instead, it was raining. It was always raining. It remained that way through spring and summer that year. That was the beginning of the end.

The crops could not grow in such wet conditions. The tiny cottage in which Estienne and his family lived was filled with pots and urns of grain. His mother began to talk to it, urging it to grow. His grandmother sadly shook her head. He did not understand what was happening. Then, as if the misery of disappointment were not laden thick within the cottage walls already, it rained straight through the next harvest season, too.

He could not forget those months of desperation. The poorly-veiled terror on the faces of his family. What were they to do? There was a constant, deep line of worry on his father's forehead, his lips always pinched in the same worried expression. They were hungry. So hungry. They fell asleep hungry and woke hungry the next day. His father did not know Estienne was watching when he slaughtered their last farm animal. Estienne had named the undersized goat Louis. Blood spat and sprayed from little Louis's neck like the rain beating upon it. The scariest part to Estienne, though, was what he thought were tears in his father's eyes. He had never seen his father cry before. But perhaps it was just the incessant rain.

The family ate on Louis for several days, portioning out meager bites and rationing what was left, despite their animal instincts to desperately gulp it down. His grandmother nobly refused to eat in order to allow the rest of the family to consume her portion. No one argued.

When their cheeks were sunken once more and the color of the leaden clouds above, Estienne, his father, and his sisters walked to the village gates to beg for scraps of food or any spare livres. They were never successful but once, when another poor farmer whose family had all just been taken by famine gave them the feet of his last chicken, which he had hidden from his dying family and under which the weight of his guilt he could no longer live. The fingernails scratched as they went down, but Estienne was grateful for dinner.

His grandmother was gone the next morning. She was so thin Estienne could have lifted her alone. She was indignantly buried, as he and his father and brother lacked the strength to dig a proper hole between the pressure of the rain from above and the weight of the earth in their hands.

They had truly given up whatever may have remained of their hope when they were forced to eat the seed grain they should have been planting for the next season. It only bought them a little time, though.

Estienne's sister, Henrriet, was the next to go. She slept beside him that night, as she always did. She would run her fingers through his curls to distract him from his hunger and soothe him to sleep. She had done the same that night, but in the morning, she was not breathing. Her lifeless hand was frozen in place atop his head. Her rigid fingers would not let go of his curls. She looked as light to lift as the cat they once had, despite being two years older than Estienne. She was his favorite sibling, and yet, their father did not have the energy to bury her. He left her on the small plat of land that should have been grain. If it had just grown some grain, her body would not have had to rot away upon it. Estienne watched as the crows ate out her eyeballs. They ate better than his family had in months.

Next was his brother, the strongest of the siblings. Estienne could not understand why he went before himself, a wee little nothing of a boy. Then was his other sister. In absolute desperation, his mother placed the tiny body of his smallest sister, Margot, into the fire. She did not go into the pile for feasting from the birds. The family consumed her flesh with tears falling from their faces. It was never the same after that. When he awoke the next morning, having slept better than he had in weeks, his parents were gone. They were not dead – they were just gone. He was another mouth to feed, and he supposed that was one too many. He assumed his sister's body provided them the strength to travel and leave him behind.

He survived, though. He lived. He vowed to himself that he would do whatever had to be done to live. He would do anything to have food in his belly and enough coin in his purse to keep food in his belly. Money. It all came down to money. Those who had it got the privilege of survival. Those who didn't had to die. Estienne found himself with no family. He could have no identity. He could be anyone he chose, and he chose to live. He lived for years afterward, in whatever ways he needed. He stole. He lied. He manipulated. He even killed. But he lived.

***

He was a grandfather, a ripe age of thirty-four years. He had nine children. He named several of them after his siblings and his grandmother. They were good, and kind. They had not known the sort of hardships Estienne had survived. They had only known peaceful lives and family. For that, he was grateful.

He attempted to be a good man once he was wealthy enough to no longer know hunger. He helped his neighbors and discretely spared a livre or two for the sickly beggars when they passed him in the village. His children were good, too, but genuinely so. The kind of goodness one can only be when one hasn't experienced the true terrors of the world. In all of his years of sinning, Estienne had done at least nine good things. That was until it all ended.

His family encouraged him to buy a batch of minces and hand them out to the hungry. He was not able to tell his bébés no, so that is exactly what they did. The hungry, though, they were strange. Their eyes screamed of death even as they hid behind oily strands of hair. They writhed in pain and spewed vomit onto his family's feet. Estienne slapped the hand of his baby girl, who was kindly grasping the palm of the sick, and pushed his children to hurry along. Something was not right.

That was when it happened again. Everything was taken from him.

Black Death.

It swept in, killing everyone.

He knew it was he who had brought it upon them. He sold his soul to the devil when he was but four years old. It was his time to pay the penance. He had not been good enough or tried hard enough. He had not prayed to the Virgin enough or repented for his sins enough. He had not been enough.

It began with his baby girl. She developed enormous boils on her neck and in her armpits and private parts. Each were as big as a piece of fruit, and they oozed and spread. His son stopped breathing next, struggling for air between bouts of vomit. Within a day, most of his children had boils all over their bodies. Their house was acrid with the stench of vomit and pus and blood. Then his baby girl died. He wept over her tiny, ruined body. He cradled her little hand in his. Her hand was not even big enough to cover his palm. He buried her properly, by himself, where he put a carved wooden cross with her name beneath the finest tree. That used the last of his strength. He cursed the Lord for taking her from him when he had tried to do good. He had tried, and he was punished for it. He cursed God for killing his daughter.

That night, Estienne had the same boils that covered his family's bodies. Over the next week, in an all-too-familiar scene, he watched as the rest of his family died. Too weak to help or even move their bodies, he could do nothing but watch their eyes frost over with death. They stared at him, accusing him of their demise. He did that to them. He killed them thirty years before when he promised his soul to darkness.

That was the last thought he had before he perished from the Earth.

CHAPTER 4

The moment may be an eternity for how slowly it unfolds. But it is just a blink of an eye. A shower of scratches falling upon a beautiful face, twinkling shards of glass sprinkling and shooting like precarious confetti. It is a glittery rainfall of fear and failure and finality. The sound of tires screeching and metals contorting, scraping and bending in unimaginable ways. Screaming. Hot spikes of pain stabbing into flesh. One second, one beat in time.

One second. One choice. It can change everything. The end is not always the finale and forever is not so long. Love is not just black or white. Change is not impossible. Villains are not all bad, and goodness has its flaws, too. We do not have all of the answers. We are each just making our way in the world and doing our best, and every single day we have the chance to rewrite our stories.

A wisp of smoke ascends and dissipates into the sky. The scent of kerosene stings the nostrils. Gasoline rainbows spread and crawl across the black asphalt. Scenes spanning a lifetime like a reel of film on fast forward, moments popping and clicking like photos from the shutter on an old camera. It was all for this. It was always for this.

CHAPTER 5
Aiyanna

Me again…

I know I haven't introduced myself in the grandest light, but I want to give you a basis for the story I'm about to share with you. We are all taught not to take candy from strangers. I'm pretty sure there is something similar about inherently trusting some random narrator to properly unfold this story for you. Let us take a peek behind the curtain, so to speak.

Let me clarify: I'm not a wizard. I've read the same books you have. The ones where the seemingly nerdy or insignificant kid has special powers or abilities that eventually make him stand out in the world. His peers and parents and everyone around him just don't recognize and appreciate his gift at first, but because he is such a humble and good person, he continues to save the planet and winds up a hero. Let me reiterate that this is not me.

I am a regular woman stumbling clumsily through each day. You wouldn't know me if I passed you on the street. I'm not a showstopper. I like to think, however, that you might relate to someone so nondescript. Not that you are nondescript, but there is something soothing about a wallflower, is there not? My incredible story exists within the confines of the ordinary. Isn't that just like life, though?

I have spent the majority of my life as a shy, chubby kid with frizzy hair and an addiction to stories. I never quite fit in. Let's be honest — I still don't. I watched my peers develop talents and passions they pursued wholeheartedly, while I gathered and disposed of hobbies like they were paper plates after a meal. There was nothing I found particularly fascinating, other than history, books, and people. I was restless. I felt pulled toward something I couldn't put my finger on — some invisible, unidentifiable pursuit. I had wanderlust for somewhere I had never been, a place without a name. I wondered if I had been born in the wrong time or the wrong country.

History, however, enveloped me. I had a keen understanding of it, and an ability to remember certain dates and timelines. I was fascinated by stories of people throughout the ages and how they helped shape the way of the world today. You could always find me with my head buried in a book about wars or witchcraft or madmen or the sinking of the Titanic.

Reading was not just a hobby. It was a passion. I never quite felt like I was attached to this life in any tangible way. Most days, I felt like my real self, my soul, whatever you want to call it, was trapped within a skeleton with some suit on top (one I wouldn't have picked for myself), like some marionette performing a play. My mind never matched the body into which I was born, and I never felt like I belonged. Thus, I would escape into other worlds through the written word. A fantastical beast that breathes a fire that burns the entire world could be found in the pages of some nondescript novel sitting quietly on a shelf, tucked between a romance and a self-help book. It was amazing. It was like I belonged in those lives just as much as I ever belonged in this one. I could be a knight in a suit of armor, instead of a lonely kid with a tattered old book on my lap as I sat cross-legged on the grass at recess.

I was invisible, and thus never a threat nor an attraction. Interacting socially always felt like a performance, like I was reading from some imaginary script. I was quite good at it, when I turned it on, but I would need time to myself afterward, exhausted, like a starlet with three shows a night. There was some unseen glass wall that prevented many real connections. I could never tell if that wall was some the societal norm, or if it was just me.

There was always an inner battle, of sorts, to hate or to love the people and the groups to which I would never belong. I felt I could easily go either way, but with the guidance of my grandmother, I stayed in the lane of goodness for the most part. When I would seethe at some hurtful phrase flung thoughtlessly from a classmate's mouth, like word diarrhea, my grandmother would soothe me with reciprocal kindness. She would softly remind me of how it felt when I was tempted to cut them down with razor words of my own.

Don't get me wrong. I was not unhappy or an angry person. Quite the opposite, in fact. Observing life from the objective stance of an outsider made me all the more passionate about it. Instead of being wrapped up in myself and the daily dramas that consume some people, I learned to appreciate the primitive privilege of being alive. I was glad to open my eyes every morning and thankful for every sunset I got to see.

I was a good kid. A nice person. My grandmother raised me on her own. She taught me to be kind, even and perhaps especially, to those who weren't. She instilled in me a desire to do what I thought was right and to keep a very loving heart. There were times I resented her for that – like the terrible boyfriends who never got their comeuppance because I didn't want to hurt them…even when I knew I could. However, for the most part, I was grateful to have had a happy childhood and a loving guardian.

I had one friend in my childhood years, Daisy, who was a roller coaster ride unto herself. We were the on again-off again sort. She was difficult to describe. In some ways, she was the most laid-back person, coolly uncaring, but in others, she was quite anxious. She cared very much what others thought of her, but you would never know it to look at her. She was lovely and outgoing, and it was obvious to me why so many gravitated towards her, like a moth to a flame. However, like fire, she could sometimes burn you without notice. She was alluring, like a fireplace, as long as you remembered to keep a safe distance. Still, she was my best friend. She helped keep some of the ever-encroaching loneliness at bay. For that, she would have my loyalty and friendship for as long as she wanted.

I will admit, though, that there was always some whisper of absence. Something missing. Like some fairytale princess, whose infant head a dark queen had waved her staff above as she gleefully promised to rip those who might love me from my life, like pulling weeds from dry ground. It was difficult being such an introvert while spending my days dreaming of a prince who would ride in and love me eternally or a best friend who understood my humor and loved me unconditionally. I didn't feel empty, per se. No one could feel that way around Jamma. But I did feel like no one else could love me or even wanted to.

There were numerous examples of failed relationships to illustrate that. Granted, I had (mostly) stopped caring by the time I was an adult. I had been disappointed too many times. I'd been taken advantage of, lied to, used, belittled. I had invested everything of myself into relationships that took it all and gave nothing back. I allowed some people to steal my spark, to snuff the light inside of me. It was at this point in my life our story begins. I was destroyed, depressed and all of the light had left my soul.

***

My mother left when I was a baby. Talk about a blow to one's ego. I was never clear on the specifics of her leaving, but my grandmother raised me from infancy. Jamma, as I referred to my grandmother, usually tried to avoid the topic. It was actually kind of infuriating. I don't know if she thought she was protecting me or if it was something she didn't know how to say. She rarely even mentioned my mother, her own daughter, so I understood there must have been some history there that Jamma thought I wasn't ready to comprehend. She did keep a picture of my mother and me on the mantel above the fireplace. It was tucked slightly behind the array of photos of me, from kindergarten school pictures to my senior portrait. I was very small in the photo, with blonde curls that matched the natural beachy waves of my mother's. We had matching dimples, as well. It was a bright day. We looked happy. That's all I know.

Once, in my early teens, I did snoop through Jamma's bedroom in an effort to find more information about my mother. Generally, we respected each other's privacy and personal space and tended to stay out of the other's room unless asked or otherwise granted permission. But I was rebellious and frustrated that she wouldn't just tell me things. I felt like I was old enough, and it angered me that there was always an air of mystery about my own mother. Didn't I have a right to know?

She was out that day, gone to the grocery store buying supplies for a spaghetti dinner. She was one of those people who like to smell the produce and squeeze the fresh bread and read every label, so I knew I had plenty of time. Her room smelled like baby powder and lemon Lysol. She kept it meticulous, with but a few small knick-knacks and necessities. She had a round, maroon-colored velvet ottoman between the dresser and the closet. She obviously used it to put on her shoes, as there was a well-worn pair of house slippers placed neatly beside it, the edges fraying to expose the white rubber of the soles. I dragged the ottoman to the closet and stood on it to snoop through the top shelf above her clothes.

There wasn't much: a plastic bin filled with various Christmas cards and thank you notes, a pair of kitten-heeled pumps that hadn't been worn in quite a while, stacked sweaters sealed in vacuum bags. Then I spotted a wooden container about the size of a shoebox. It looked like a jewelry box. I lifted it from its hiding place beneath the sweaters and plopped myself upon the ottoman to rifle through my spoils. I ran my fingertips along the swirling flower carved into the wooden top. A Forget-Me-Not, with its stem winding and whirling like the skate marks on an ice rink. I lifted the thin metal latch and lifted it open. Letters and photographs were piled upon each other, different colors and ages stacked like paper strata.

There was a black and white photograph of a woman. She wore dark lipstick and a Mona Lisa smile. There was a simple locket around her neck.

Her eyes were happy. Winged mascara framed a pair of light eyes. I could just make out the bursts of dark splatter in her irises, like a fireworks display. I recognized those eyes. It was my grandmother. She looked completely happy and so *young*! Since when did my Jamma wear lipstick? Below that was a locket with a thin, plain chain. The same from the picture. I wedged it open with my fingernail. A handsome young man's face looked back at me from inside. Neither smiling nor frowning, he had a pleasant look about him. I wondered who he was. The next layer was another photograph. The original print of the picture on the mantel – me and my mother. On the back, in Jamma's flowing handwriting, it read, "Three generations." I slid the photo into my jeans pocket. She surely wouldn't miss it, and I had nothing else of my mother's. There were other pictures of the same blond woman, my mother. Her as a teenager, clearly uncompliant with having her picture taken. Candids of an even younger girl, presumably still her, one in a pretty dress and the other in a Halloween costume as a witch, posing dramatically for the camera.

All I knew was that my mother's name was Amara (yes, my grandmother had a penchant for unusual baby names) and that she had never been a part of my life. My grandmother spoke of her as if she were dead, but she wouldn't tell me when or how. I never knew my father.

I placed the box back upon the shelf, slid the ottoman into its original position and walked to my room to hide the photo beneath my pillow. Perhaps osmosis would provide some answers.

I never really knew my backstory at all when I was growing up. In truth, the only family I ever had was my grandmother, Jamma. No cousins, no siblings, no parents. Whenever I brought up the subject of abandonment, Jamma would dismiss it with a slight wave of her hand and warm smile, offering me a snack instead. She knew exactly what would distract me – food. But I never felt at a total loss for love, not with someone like Jamma around. Her warmth and affection filled in any gaps I might have had in having no parents. She made me feel treasured and alive and unique, and she showered attention and affection upon me. Most days, that was enough.

CHAPTER 6
Ronnie

He took a long drag, inhaling deeply on the homemade cigarette. There wasn't much else to do in prison. The smoke from the cig made of spinach and toilet paper smelled terrible, but it staved off the shakes he got when he went without. The wretched smell did not earn him any extra friends in the pen, but he did not care. The intimidation was present, despite his build. Even the fearless felons could see something in his eyes that left him alone for the most part.

The inmate in the cell next to him shouted profanities.

He puffed and released, watching the wisps disappear into the bunk above him. Of course, his cell mate knew better than to complain.

He was going to be there for a long time. They were not lenient in his sentencing.

But it didn't matter. He would never be deterred from his purpose.

He would find that girl, and he would kill her.

CHAPTER 7
Aiyanna

Glass raindrops cut my face. The shadowed world spinning into oblivion.

I awoke, trembling, to what I thought was blood running from my eyes, tickling my cheek. It was actually a mixture of perspiration and tears. I sat up, soaked in a veil of cold sweat, my t-shirt sticking to my back and my hair matted to my forehead.

The grief was consuming me in the day and invading my dreams as I slept. It permeated my every thought, blocking me from any hope or positive deliberation or decision-making. I didn't understand what it was about that one event that shredded me or why I couldn't seem to recover, but I was entirely defeated and despondent. I was just so tired.

I fell back into my swampy sheets and gazed at the first glimpse of sunshine sneaking through the window of the bedroom Jamma kept immaculate. It used to be my room. I supposed it still was, since Jamma had left everything the way it was the day I moved out. My trinkets and old perfume bottles were carefully dusted, the vanity beneath thoroughly cleaned, but everything put back in its original place. The old pink shag carpet and matching faux llama fur pillow. A corkboard with printed flowers, pinned to which were drawings and honors awards from school.

The stuffed teddy bear I slept with as a child stared down at me from bookcases filled with everything from Dr. Seuss to Dickens.

It was comforting, in a way, to be surrounded by memories from when life made sense. In another way, it reminded me that I would never have that again. I would never be that bright-eyed, hopeful child. I studied, with dewy eyes, the particles of dust dancing in the rays of the early morning sun. They floated softly, glistening, in their spotlight, like delicate raindrops. I tried to trace their descent with my gaze.

I lay unmoving and unrested, the blankets on the bed nothing more than a wad wrapped around my legs. I watched with scalded eyes and a broken spirit as the world warmed from the blackness of night to the soft glow of the morning sun. Another day. It felt like a weight of oppression and obligation upon my chest.

***

The tangle of bare trees swayed with a breeze, and I saw a solitary leaf let go and dance down, surrendering to Nature's will. What had once been green and thriving had painted itself a beautiful crimson color before browning and turning crisp with demise. The death of something beautiful. I felt my chest caving in with sorrow. I was imploding.

The gritty salt of tears that fell effortlessly throughout the night scratched my eyes with every blink. I didn't know if I was happy or not that I could still feel something, be it the sting of swollen eyes or the pile of bricks on my chest that made every intake of breath a conscious effort. Feeling meant I was still alive, and I could no longer conceive of why that should be. Feeling, even living, had become a burden.

If the nightmares had been bad before, they could be categorized as brutal at this point. My sleep had been plagued with them off and on for as long as I could remember. Scenes so real, they sparked my senses, even in sleep. Smells and colors, fantasies mixed with reality when, as often happened, something in life played out exactly as I had dreamed. Never knowing if it was a memory or made up or reverie, my brain lost in some infinitesimal cycle of recalling a memory of a memory. I always referred to them as nightmares, knowing no one would understand that it was a whole other life playing out in the wrinkles of my exhausted mind.

I kicked the quilt to the foot of the bed and pulled the sweat-dewed sheets back over me, allowing myself the sweet indulgence of living cerebrally in those dreams instead of actually in reality.

"Good Morning, my beautiful blossom." I had heard the soft shuffle of my grandmother awakening, and the clicking of the dog's toenails on the hardwood floor, but I could not muster the energy to respond.

She watched me with worry. I knew I needed to say something, but it was impossible to pick words from the swirling cloud of thoughts traveling ceaselessly in circles about my mind.

I only had two modes. I was either overwhelmed with flashing vignettes and glimmers of ideas that darted from one thought or another too quickly to capture and coming through all at once, like several people trying to walk through a doorway at the same time. Or I was…nothing. I suppose it was a survival mechanism, but I experienced long periods of a numb sort of stupor, my mind cleansed of the exhausting dark thoughts.

A deep, consuming depression had taken my energy for a couple of months. Life had won; I had put forth my best efforts and battled her fiercely, but I was the weaker of the two. I was broken. I could not sleep while the world rested. I lay awake all night, listening to the silence and watching the shadows from the moonlit windows move across the room. Just me, alone with my thoughts, all through the darkness. It was as if I were on guard against the shadowy demons who pierce the night to invade their prey. If I slept alone, I would hear them whisper how useless it all was. How I should just give up and be done with trying. It was only once I heard the sounds of Jamma waking in the early light could I feel the weight of my eyelids, swollen and wet with tears. I may not have known how to handle her presence, but there was something comforting about knowing she was up, and I was safe, that finally allowed my vigilance to falter into sleep.

My Jamma shuffled into my room and softly finger-combed the nest of tangled hair away from my face. I was curled in a fetal position, my eyes bloodshot and heavy, my body aching and exhausted. I could feel the exhaustion in my eye sockets, pressing my skull and urging me to rest. She began to hum a familiar lullaby as she eased into the rocking chair at the foot of my bed. My dog, Cooper, gazed curiously at me over the edge of the mattress, only his honey-colored eyes and pointed ears peeping over the edge. He licked me square on the nose before circling three times and curling up next to Jamma. He calmly gawked at me, as if assessing the situation and how he should proceed. Cooper could always tell when something was wrong.

Evelyn Elizabeth Burns, my Jamma. Known to those around her as Eve. Known to me as my guardian and closest compadre. She had been the one to hold me when I awoke in the middle of the night with nightmares that periodically tortured me throughout my childhood and adolescence. She would make me a warm cup of milk and sing the same lullaby she had always sung until I drifted back to sleep. On bad nights, she swayed softly in that same rocking chair, and I would wake to the gentle creaking of wooden legs pressing against the hardwood floor. I selfishly never even considered, until after I was grown, that she had spent the entire night by my side.

I wanted to say something to her, to speak some phrase of confidence and hope that would comfort her and let her know that I was going to be okay. But the words wouldn't come. In truth, I wasn't sure I would ever be okay again. Too much had happened, too much taken away.

I remembered myself as a chubby-legged toddler being bounced in my grandmother's lap. I don't know how I recalled it since I was so young – perhaps it was the memory of a story my imagination made real. My grandmother was bouncing me and I was giggling at her as she exaggeratedly pronounced the word *grandma* over and over in an attempt to get me to speak it. I recollected, or I remembered being told, that I was trying to make my soft little mouth and tongue move around the word, but what was produced was *Jamma*. She has been Jamma to me ever since.

I recalled that carefree kid, and I felt myself ache for the simple joy of childhood. Each new day was met with smiles and promise, bounding out of bed in search of that day's adventure. My heart was alive and unmarred. That feels like a lifetime ago.

Fat tears welled up once more and fell softly into the pillow beneath me, disappearing into the fibers of the pillowcase. Cooper let out a low whimper. Jamma patted his head reassuringly. With wet cheeks and a very heavy heart, I closed my eyes and drifted off to the creaking of the wooden rocking chair and soft hum of Jamma's song.

CHAPTER 8
Eve, aka Jamma

The hand-stitched quilt Eve had pulled back over Aiyanna rose and fell with each breath she took. The stitched flowers looked as though they were blooming with every intake of air. Eve had unconsciously timed her rocking to the rhythm of it. Inhale, rock forward, exhale, rock backward. The chair creaked as she leaned over to pat Cooper on the head, his tail thumping once in recognition. It was midday, but Aiyanna was still sleeping. She had not been getting enough rest. Eve knew that. She could hear Ai's soft sobbing through the night. She had to stop herself from going in to hold her and rock her like she did when she was a baby. Eve prayed for God to help her see the light, to take away her pain.

Though her hips were killing her and her legs had been asleep for some time, Eve did not want to start moving about for fear she would wake Ai. She would make them both some lunch or dinner whenever Aiyanna naturally woke. She needed the rest. Eve recognized her poor, sweet baby girl had experienced so much pain and so much unfairness and disappointment in her short time in this life. She had had her own share of devastation, so she understood Ai and wanted more than anything for her to be okay again. Eve reasoned that her dreams would help her with that.

We are sometimes able to go to certain places in our minds which allow us to break free of what binds us in our everyday lives. That freedom, even in fantasy, can be a remarkable healer and nothing is more potent in killing pain than hope.

Eve's throat tickled. It was highly irritating. She had not been able to shake the persistent cough since her summer cold decided to bless her with its presence. She squelched the tickle with a cup of what-was-once hot tea set on a doily on the dresser.

She could feel the wear of her seventy-three years. She was still young, as far as she was concerned, but she was so tired. That cold had really taken it out of her. She couldn't clean or even cook without running out of breath or wearing herself out. She was beginning to lose her balance at the most mundane things, like the curb at the grocery store. She wondered, when, exactly, she had become such an old lady. It is funny how age creeps up on us. Well, at any rate, she had to muster the strength to be the rock her sweet Aiyanna needed. She was going through hell, and Eve would be there beside her until she got to the other side.

Aiyanna was not eating. The plates of food Eve fixed for her were left untouched, and the nightmares were worse than ever before. When she was a child, they were just dreams. Sometimes she would tell Eve about them, then, with whimsical stories and fantastical friends. However, since the devastation that she could tell already was going to change her forever, Ai had nightmares every time she tried to sleep. Eve imagined she was wrestling with some pretty dark demons in those dreams of hers. Wrestle away, baby girl, she thought, and I'll be here to help you recover.

Ai had her grandmother turn away her best friend, Daisy, earlier. She had actually been awake, which was unusual for early afternoon. But when Eve told her who was at the door, she just shook her head, her bottom lip trembling. She was gaunt and weak, with dark, puffy pockets beneath her swollen, disengaged eyes. Daisy was disappointed, of course. Poor girl, Eve thought.

She was relieved Ai was finally resting, though. She had been there before herself, when it felt like not a soul understood what she was going through. When the words weren't sufficient, whether she was explaining herself or listening to others try to convince her to be okay. How lonely it had felt. How her destruction seemed so unimportant to the rest of the world, as it carried on every day as if nothing had happened. Sometimes, all you can do is put some time between yourself and the heartbreak, like treading water. You just breathe in and breathe out, and every ragged heartbeat brings you closer to closure. At the very least, you wake up one morning a week or a month or a year later, and you realize that you survived so far. Sometimes that's enough inspiration to survive another day still.

She was sad for Ai, and with her.

The whole situation of her heartbreak left Eve paralyzed with indecision; should she protect her and guard her from the things she knew, the things she had experienced? In doing so, she was committing her granddaughter to a lifetime of regret, with only her memories to forever flip through, like a dusty, wretched old photo album with yellowed pages and worn edges.

The alternative was to expose her to more than she might be able to assimilate. There would be no coming back from that knowledge. If handled incorrectly, it would ruin her. If managed, though, and perhaps with Eve's guidance, she could navigate the waters of her depression, with her at the helm. She could understand so much more and have so much more power over her life.

What was Eve to do?

Ai was still so young. Eve had not anticipated telling her before she had a better handle on life. She wanted her to be settled and secure before giving her a proverbial bomb she could potentially use to blow herself up. Like her mother had done. And yet, she certainly didn't want to run out of time. When would she be settled enough? Especially without knowing?

Eve knew what it was like to have to learn something so important on her own, and she wouldn't wish that on her girl. The timing was what concerned her. Would she ever figure it out for herself? And if she did, who would be able to guide her through it if not Eve? With no guidance, would she turn out like her mother? Or would it just be better if she never even knew? She could live a normal life if she never told her. But she wouldn't, would she? Her world had just been destroyed, and only Eve (and possibly time) had any solution for it.

No, Eve told herself in a frustrating inner dialogue. It must happen, and you, Eve, are the only one who can help her. And so it was decided.

CHAPTER 9
Daisy

She cut the tip of the stems from the bouquet of daisies and set them in the window. She bought the brightly-colored flowers to try to cheer up her friend, but she had her grandmother turn her away again. Daisy guessed she sort of understood, but it still stung to just be ignored by her best friend. How was she supposed to be there *for* Aiyanna if she wouldn't allow her to be there *with* Aiyanna?

They had had a falling out over the whole Ethan thing, but that didn't mean Daisy didn't love her friend. She wanted to show Ai that she could be there for her when she needed someone. And Daisy wouldn't even say she told her so! That's real friendship.

Daisy met Aiyanna in the eighth grade. She was a military brat, moving from town to town every couple of years until her father retired and her parents finally decided to settle on this place. For some reason. She missed the lights and noise and excitement of city living, and the small town offered her nothing interesting. But then she met this girl whom she felt she had known forever. Although, it wasn't exactly friendship at first sight.

She went through the regular rigmarole of paperwork, in-processing, the awkward introduction to her homeroom as the new girl. Phony friendliness as a front for the teachers, but totally ignored throughout the day and avoided like the plague in social situations. The usual. Especially for small towns. They didn't want to upset the social hierarchy already in place. The new girl, with her knee-high boots and pink highlighted hair could definitely do that. Daisy was used to the process.

She wasn't concerned. She had learned to hold her own from a young age. She knew how to be alluring and mysterious. She could portray herself as apathetic. For some reason, apathy is intriguing to people. Like a mystery to be solved. She understood that psychological behavior, but she personally found it infuriating. If anyone ever acted disinterested in her, she would have nothing to do with them. How's that for apathy?

She was leaning against a tree at break time (what they called "recess" for the older kids), wishing the day would go by faster. She was trying to arch her back like she saw actresses do onscreen, but she kept her head tucked, self-conscious of the birthmark on her throat. It was an attempt to look appealing to the group of boys playing kickball in front of her and to appear mysterious and sultry to the girls who were whispering about her so obviously. Maintaining a look of bored indifference (mostly because her smile was full of metal from her braces), she surveyed who had noticed her pose, since it was really starting to make her back ache. But the only person she caught staring was a small girl looking at her like she had killed her cat or something. Daisy stared back, unabashedly. She hated small towns. The girl didn't break her gaze as Daisy expected, and the staring continued long enough to be super awkward. She walked over to confront her, stomping as she had seen models do on the runway. Fierce.

"Problem?" she demanded, circling her neck with attitude, one hand on her hip. She had found that offense was always easier than defense. If you crashed into a confrontation like a wrecking ball, the other person usually assumed you were unhinged and backed off.

The girl said nothing. She just continued to stare, blue eyes drilling into Daisy's. She thought maybe the girl was deaf, and she started to feel bad for taking offense. Still, someone should have taught her that staring was rude. Unless it was a boy doing the staring, in which case she welcomed the looks.

The girl startled Daisy by speaking. "What's your name?"

Immediately defensive again, Daisy narrowed her eyes at her. "None of your business," she said, all hard and ready for a fight. However, her question had thrown Daisy off and she couldn't stop herself from asking, "Why?"

"You must be new," the girl replied. She seemed to have her guard up, but Daisy saw her shoulders soften just a little. "Sorry for staring. I just had a bad vibe or something," she shrugged. Her eyes narrowed and she shook her head like she was attempting to understand her own actions.

"You don't even know me," Daisy scoffed, still defensive. She wasn't sure what else to do. While there was always that one who wanted to start something every new place she moved, this seemed different. She didn't seem like the sort, but one never knows. Daisy had been in her fair share of fights in each of her different schools. She never knew why some people took issue with her or what they thought they saw in her. She squared her shoulders, ready for confrontation.

The girl's face softened and she looked a little ashamed. "You're right." She sighed. "I'm sorry. I'm Aiyanna."

"A who-whatta?" Daisy asked in all seriousness, but the girl laughed in response. Loudly.

"I don't know what came over me. I'm not a bitch, I swear," she smiled.

"I'll never remember whatever you said your name was, so I'll just call you Ai."

"That's cool. I like your hair," she smiled again. And that was the beginning of their friendship.

They were two very different-shaped puzzle pieces that somehow seemed to fit together. Daisy was more outspoken and attention-seeking. She would dye her plain brown hair outrageous colors and augment her thin, shapeless body with all kinds of contraptions. Ai was sort of naturally beautiful, but she did not see it in herself. Most other folks really didn't seem to notice, either, which was fine by Daisy. Don't take her wrong: she loved her friend and she wanted her to shine, but being attractive was sort of Daisy's thing. Ai could be smart and all of that stuff. And Daisy guessed there was a part of her that was pretty jealous that Ai was born beautiful. Daisy ran miles every day and counted calories and worked out and went to salons and Ai just sat at home and read books. It wasn't fair. So it was okay that she blended in to the background and didn't know what she had. Daisy thought that Ai also wanted to be more like Daisy: likable and social, with boyfriends and style. A popular soccer player. She was a trendsetter in their school. Daisy thought Ai knew that Daisy could always hang out with whomever she chose, while Ai really only had her. So really, Daisy was sort of doing Ai a favor by being her friend.

She had to admit, though, she admired the way Ai was a dreamer. Her head was in the clouds (or a book or the future), so she missed a lot of the right now. She didn't put a lot of effort into playing the social game. Despite Daisy's active show of apathy and collected coolness, how she was perceived was all she could think about. While Ai would act like it really bothered her to be nerdy or awkward, she never tried to change herself to accommodate coolness. She was smart enough to work the system if she had wanted to.

It killed Daisy how Ai had finally gotten herself a boyfriend, without even trying! And Daisy hadn't had one in months. And it was a guy she had known first, of course. Ai couldn't have ever met anyone on her own. Daisy thought he was way more her type than Ai's, anyway.

Daisy guessed she always felt a little competitive with Ai. She naturally possessed the traits Daisy wished she had, and while she loved Ai, she also sort of hated her for it. Daisy wondered if Ai noticed. She guessed it didn't matter now.

***

She seriously would not shut up, Daisy thought.

She knew Ai was in love with Ethan, but she didn't have to hear all about it all the time. She could have vomited her guacamole she was so over it.

"Wait, what?" Daisy had been mentally eye-rolling so hard she hadn't heard that last thing Ai said. Did she say she was moving?

"Yeah, I'm so excited!" Her eyes shone with happiness. Daisy was happy she was happy, but also sort of wasn't. Like, at all.

She stated the obvious. "But Ethan lives like two hours away!"

"I'm going to take a few of my things at a time. It won't be that difficult."

Daisy couldn't believe the bitch was thinking of herself. What good was a friend who lived two hours away?! "What the hell?" she asked, feeling her temper rising. "What about your job?"

"I gave them my notice this morning." Ai smiled. Daisy could tell she was genuinely happy. Daisy was totally pissed.

"But what about me?" She knew it sounded petty, and she should have tried to think of other ways of getting her question answered without having to ask it so directly. But damn. Ai was straight up abandoning her. And really, Daisy thought, Ethan should have been her boyfriend to begin with.

"What do you mean? Obviously, we will keep in touch. I'll visit, and we can lunch every time I come to see Jamma." Ai shone like the sun in all her joy, but black clouds of spite embraced Daisy. Noticing her face change, Ai offered, "We can talk every day."

"I don't want to talk on the phone every day. That is not the same thing. I can't believe you wouldn't even tell me you were planning to do this. I thought we were friends!" Daisy pushed her plate forward angrily. She couldn't believe Ai was so selfish.

"Daisy, don't be that way. I'll miss you, too," she smiled, her dimple deep in her right cheek. Daisy could have punched her teeth in at that moment. She was trying to be happy for Ai, but Ai had not even bothered to clue her in that this was coming. She gets herself a boyfriend and everything becomes about that. Typical. Their friendship obviously didn't matter that much to Ai.

"Just go, Ai. You don't have to call. In fact, I'd prefer you didn't." Daisy placed her napkin on the table, grabbed her bag from the back of her chair and sashayed toward her car. Let Ai pick up the check, Daisy thought. Whatever. Easy come, easy go.

She knew she was being dramatic, but she really didn't care. Ai had hurt her, and she does not let people get away with doing that.

When she got to her stylish loft apartment, she pulled out her little black book and started ringing old potentials. Maybe one of them would be deserving of her time. Maybe they would make her feel better.

CHAPTER 10
Amara

Jolted from the recurring dream of rotten wheat and blood-filled boils, Amara found herself on an empty train car headed nowhere. She hated that dream. She could viscerally feel the pain of deep hunger and the desperation of being too poor and too weak to do anything about it.

The train squeaked to a stop. A boy with a stuffed dinosaur sat beside her and smiled as he nestled into the seat. He had dried snot around the rim of his nose. Amara looked away. Kids were disgusting.

Amara moved back to the city as soon as she could escape. They had lived the city life when she was younger, and it suited her so much better. She was sick of trying to be controlled and the small-time values of small towns. Being immoral was much more fun. And when no one knew her name, she was free to do so much more. It opened the world up to new experiences. She enjoyed being carefree and choosing to be whomever struck her mood for that day. Life was meant to be lived, she thought. Who had the right to judge how she chose to live it? *Judge not, that ye be not judged* and all that.

Eve, Amara's mother, spent the entirety of Amara's life trying to influence her to be good. To do good. It just didn't take. Amara would look up at her mother's pious face and ask, in all sincerity, *why*. Why would she open a door for an elderly person? Would they have stopped their snail-like shuffle to open the door for her? She doubted it. Why would she tell the truth about breaking Mrs. Gynitski's window when she knew it would mean getting punished? It wasn't going to repair the window. Why would she only kiss Brian when Michael and Quinten were also cute, and why would she tell Brian if she had? It wasn't his business as far as Amara was concerned. Why not tell Stacey she looked fat in her jeans? She would want to know if that were her in those jeans. None of it made any sense to Amara. And while she was excellent at reading people and playing along to what they wanted, their feelings just didn't matter. She was put on the planet with a will of her own, and she had to learn to rely on herself. Eve was too soft-hearted, too giving. If they only had two nickels to rub together, Eve would still donate one to help the homeless. It was disgusting to Amara.

At the thought of money, Amara pulled the bills she had taken from Eve's purse from her bra and began flipping through them. She had not had time to count it all before her mother would have seen her and blown her plan to Hell. There were not any big bills. Great, she thought. Eve was always so damned self-righteous, trying to get Amara to be "better" and begging her to stay home. Amara might be broke, but hell, so was Eve, and it did not get any better for Amara: the urine smell of the stained train car, people bustling to wherever they were headed, the latest fashions donning their gorgeous frames. Swallowed up in the belly of the beast. Amara was free. No one knew her name or her story. She could be whomever she chose. And Eve was at home, in all likelihood cooking a modest meal or reading her Bible, waiting for her daughter to come home, rocking worriedly beneath the stained glass lamp.

Amara had taken all of the cash in Eve's wallet and one credit card, but it wouldn't be enough to last long. God, didn't she ever bore of being poor, Amara wondered. She would have to figure out how to make some money, quickly. How could she utilize her certain set of skills to make the most of her life? Sales, perhaps? She could be quite convincing.

As she rolled her eyes toward the train's ceiling to consider her options, she caught a balding man staring at her. His pinstriped shirt was tucked into his suit pants, the buttons holding on for dear life as his belly poured over his belt. When he noticed Amara watching his eyes move up and down her body hungrily, he blushed and averted his gaze, his shiny bald head bright pink. Bingo. He would do, she confirmed. Men were morons when it came to beautiful women, and she found she was always provided opportunity when she needed it. She thanked God for her tits.

Amara glided up from her seat on the train, making a show to pull modestly on her skin-tight mini skirt. She pretended to be jostled as she teetered on her stilettos, and she eased herself back down beside him. He acknowledged her presence with a head tilt, so she smiled fully and leaned into him, letting him notice her dimpled smile and the weight of her breast on his arm. He smiled in return, sweating, trying to hold his briefcase in a way to hide the wedding ring on his finger and the fact that his pants were getting even smaller. He was perfect, she thought.

CHAPTER 11
Aiyanna

Daisy had been my best friend since we met in middle school. She was a new student, and I had long been disenchanted with the group of kids with whom I'd been in school since kindergarten. They were not my biggest fans, either. I was an awkward, shy kid in a small town. That's how it goes.

I was engrossed in history and reading when other kids were playing with dolls or making prank calls. I tended to stay inside my own head while other teenagers were immersed in the spirit of community and cliques.

Daisy was my connection to typical adolescence. She had so many friends and was involved in extracurriculars. She actually attended dances and played sports and doodled boys' names on her notebooks. Hanging out with her was what I imagined most normal people were doing: getting makeovers she had dreamed up for me or romanticizing a fairy tale love affair with the most popular boy, despite his vacant eyes and the insane amount of product in his hair.

She supported me in the best ways she knew how, though they could be quite insulting at times. Like the time she bought me a bunch of books on how even the most helpless could learn to socialize and get people to like them. Or how she would give me makeup and hair products for my birthday and Christmas, despite her knowledge that I had no interest in such things. Or how she would plan trips for the two of us, even paying for a lot of it, but without telling me where or when we were going beforehand, so we inevitably ended up in Vegas or at some concert she wanted to see. Or when she excitedly suggested I could go on a weight loss television show and become super famous and get endorsements and everything.

I tried to support her, as well. I would sit on the steel bleachers and watch her soccer games. I attended parties with her, even when she would forget I was there and make out with boys all night while I sat awkwardly on some sofa petting a dog I had found. I would go out with her and her latest beau or listen to her talk about her dreams of becoming an actress or a makeup artist or a vocal performer.

I cared about her and wanted her to have a happy life, and she cared about me, too, in the only ways she knew how. However, I always had to keep her just a little at arm's length, though. A highly sensitive person like myself, having been raised by someone as kind, warm, and tactful as Jamma, could, and often did, get her feelings hurt by someone as bold and outspoken (and even sometimes abrasive) as Daisy.

***

I planted the bouncy halo headband on my skull and slammed the door to my small apartment. Daisy was hosting her yearly Halloween party in her posh apartment downtown, and I was running late. It was her favorite holiday, as she usually included her own birthday celebration, which was the following day. She pulled no punches when it came to her Halloween parties, and it was a personal goal each year to top the previous one. This year had been no different.

I steered my sedan onto the shoulder of her street where all of the other cars had lined up and I smiled at the creepy music emanating from her building. I eased my panty hose-and-wire wings out of the car, avoiding bending my pipe cleaner halo on the door. I stepped around a bony hand reaching out of the ground to climb the steps to her place. I was late, as usual, and I could hear the party had already started by the loud music and shouts of competition.

A tall man with a scraggly beard and painted blue face opened the door. "Hey, I'm Ethan. Sorry, the hostess is engaged in an intense battle of beer pong at the moment," he said with an almost apologetic smile that felt like the sweetest punch in the gut. I was in my mid-twenties, so I had experienced lust before. But this was something else.

"I assumed as much," I laughed and offered a handshake. "I'm Aiyanna, but most folks call me Ai." When my gaze met his emerald-green eyes, it was as if the entire party, the thumping music and the roar of laughter dissipated. He was all I could see. Well, as much of him as I could see beneath his costume of linen and plaid. That smile seemed so familiar. I thought love at first sight was such cliché, but there was some kind of instant attraction there. It was not just an attraction to his appearance, which was fine as hell, but to him as a person. I felt like I knew him already, and I trusted him instantly. If you knew my history with men, you would understand why that was so unlike me.

He cocked his head to the side like a dog does when curious. "Have we met already?" His thumb ran across the back of my hand. The way his forehead creased between his eyebrows was so sexy.

"I was just wondering the same thing. How do you know Daisy?" We must have encountered each other in some way over the years, whether from one of these parties or some other passing of ships in the night.

He smiled again and hooked his thumbs into the waistband of a weathered-looking kilt. "I played the piano for a banquet at her workplace. Daisy was the one who hired me for the gig." (He failed to mention they had consummated that agreement later that night.) He crossed one arm across his chest, his hand tucked into his armpit while he tapped his teeth with the thumbnail on his other hand. A leather bracelet with Celtic inscriptions bound that wrist. Wow, this guy was committed to his costume. His gaze bypassed all of the unspoken rules of averting your eyes and casualness. He stared directly into my soul. It was a welcome intrusion.

"Aiiiiii!" Daisy threw the empty Solo cup to the floor and rushed to hug me. "You have to taste these olive eyeballs I made!" she giggled as she led me toward the kitchen. I glanced over my shoulder, shrugged and smiled at Ethan as I was pulled into the other room. I watched Daisy compete with a group of guys at a game of beer pong, sipping my dyed beer and nibbling the eyeball, wondering how long I had to put in before it was acceptable to leave. I really despised these sorts of social situations. Daisy didn't seem to mind that she had on the shortest naughty nurse outfit and nothing but a thong when she would lean over to fetch the ping pong balls that hit the floor. I both despised and admired her absolute confidence. By contrast, I had to rehearse what I was going to say when ordering at a restaurant.

Ethan sidled up to me in his kilt, and I smiled broadly. He was a handsome man. I only came up to his shoulders, broad as they were. His dark hair was disheveled, and I wasn't sure if that was part of the costume or just his normal look. It stood on end in short spikes that called to be petted. He had a slightly crooked, almost mischievous smile that transformed his rugged face from hard, straight lines into a heart-stopping photo op. Now this was a boy whose name I would totally doodle on a notebook. He looked as bored with everyone's drunken antics as I was, swishing his almost-empty beer bottle and occasionally smiling down at me. I kept sipping at my Solo cup since I couldn't think of anything to say. Just a couple of outsiders coming together.

"So, Aiyanna —" he began. In such close proximity, I could feel the heat from his body through my costume. He smelled like wood fires with a hint of body wash.

Then Daisy was there again, draping herself over me, placing her body between mine and Ethan's, her breasts pressed against me and her bottom grazing the front of his jeans. "You've gotta come play with us," she slurred, then laughed at herself as she slid to the floor, skirt up around her waist. I saw way more of her than I ever wanted. She was sloppy drunk again.

I smiled apologetically at Ethan. "I think I need to get this one some pants." As I leaned over Daisy, my halo getting caught in her hair, I could see her wink at Ethan as if she had won some unspoken contest.

***

"You were an angel. Literally," Ethan would laugh, kissing the top of my head. "My angel, from the beginning."

"And you were a bullheaded Scotsman from the start," I would say, grinning and lifting his arm around my shoulders.

We had met one year ago, to the day. Daisy was livid that I decided to spend Halloween with Ethan that year, instead of attending her party. She never caught on to my hints that I sort of hated those parties, and I didn't have the heart to just say it to her. I didn't want her to feel abandoned, but I reasoned to myself that she most certainly wouldn't be alone. There were sure to be plenty of people who could give her attention and tend to her when she inevitably drank too much. I was actually sort of glad not to have to attend, if I'm being honest. It was also the first time I was bold enough to simply tell her no.

It had been several hours since the last trick-or-treaters had walked away from Ethan's front stoop with handfuls of candy. Some of them had been so cute: pudgy babies dressed as little lions and pumpkins, toddlers on wobbly legs waddling around in their capes and wings, even the teenagers who refused to give up fun in favor of being *grown*. It felt very domestic and grown up to be with Ethan, passing out candy like responsible adults.

It made me wonder what our kids would be like one day. We had discussed potential names already, but would they look like him? Would the poor things inherit my hair? Would Ethan train them musically? Would I be able to teach them cooking, as Jamma had tried to teach me? Would they feel a loss at having no maternal grandparents?

An overacted shrill scream from the television screen jarred me from my thoughts. We were watching awful, budget scary movies from decades ago. I pulled my legs up on the sofa and snuggled into Ethan's chest, pulling his great-grandmother's quilt over us and breathing in his scent. It was a whitework quilt and it had supposedly been a bridal gift some generations back in Ethan's family. I'd watched Jamma work on such things, and I knew the sort of effort it must have taken however long ago to produce such a fine quilt. No telling how old it was, either. It was so exquisite, I had urged Ethan to preserve it, but he liked to be hugged in his ancestry and had argued that its purpose was pointless if it was stuck in a vacuum seal bag somewhere in a closet. I couldn't argue with that logic, and it certainly was stunning. It didn't stop me from worrying about stains and other deterioration, though. Time wears away everything beautiful and priceless.

I wrapped my arms around him, admiring his toned body beneath my hands and his flannel button-up. He was solid, whereas my handfuls of love handles had some squish to them. I ran my fingers along his thigh, which could have been concrete. Mine, on the other hand, was soft and yielding. His eyes shone with the reflection of the television. They were dark green in the dimly-lit room, and the shadows danced across his face like it was a perfect painting. He caught me staring at him and smiled, which was always at the ready. It lit up his face, doubling his appeal. He kissed the top of my head and squeezed me closer to him.

***

My first boyfriend was named Brayden. He was the son of a nurse who left her husband to be with a prestigious (and very wealthy) physician. He was a year younger, so he used me to drive him around. Then there was Mitch, who literally drafted a hard copy of what he called his *girlfriend contract*. It was ten pages long. Then Doug, a twenty-seven-year-old college student and compulsive liar and Justin, who was later convicted of child pornography, so there's that. Every one of them cheated on me. I was dumb enough to support Justin, who wouldn't get a job but still felt welcome to move himself in to my tiny 500-square-foot apartment while I was at work one day. That was the extent of my experience with men before Ethan. They were insignificant. They felt more like obligations than true partnerships.

Ethan and I had fallen immediately into a daily regime of togetherness after we met. Though I still lived a couple of hours away, we would talk on the phone for hours at a time, and we would text throughout the night. I often fell asleep with my phone in hand, smiling at the screen.

We had odd days off and would travel to the others' place on those days. When our schedules or other circumstances forbade our spending the weekends together, we would send each other packages or postcards, just for something tangible to hold, I suppose. On one occasion when he knew I had to work late, he ordered a pizza and had it delivered to me, a heart drawn on the inside of the box. Or the time he mailed me one of his shirts, since I had joked that I needed something that smelled like him to snuggle with at night.

It was on our first date that we both knew. I can't really explain it, even now, but have you ever felt an instant connection with someone? That maybe you weren't sure how they would fit into your life, but you knew they would impact it in some important way?

The first time Ethan found himself on my front stoop, he fidgeted nervously as I watched with amusement through the peephole. He was half an hour early, but I was so nervous, I was already dressed and had been pacing, ready to go, for fifteen minutes. I felt wrong letting him worry and fuss like that, but it was too amusing to halt prematurely. He tucked in the moss-green button-up that was already perfectly tucked and tugged on his belt. I watched him tap his teeth with his thumbnail nervously and pace several circles like a dog before it settles. He ran his hand through his hair and seemed to be practicing some kind of speech. Finally, he breathed deeply, set his shoulders and pushed the doorbell. Of course, I waited several seconds before opening the door. Daisy had advised me not to let him think me too eager. (Though we both knew I was.)

I danced violently but silently when he called me after we met at the Halloween party and asked if he could take me out sometime. He had poached my number from Daisy's phone when she was passed out, and he may have also changed many of her contact names to Disney characters. We had talked for hours on that phone call, my cheeks hurting from smiling so hard. He joked about my having left my halo behind at Daisy's house and the implications of that. He told me more about his family, with whom he was close and to which he was strongly devoted. He was also a history buff, specifically Scottish history, and he was a musician. He played guitar and piano. He was as passionate as he was funny, and the conversation flowed freely until we both realized we would only have a couple hours of sleep before we had to go to work the next morning. We solidified the date and reluctantly said our goodbyes.

The week before the date, I spent hours trying to put together just the right outfit that looked like I hadn't put any thought at all into looking so put-together. I even called Daisy for fashion advice. And then I picked something much, much more modest than her suggestion: a cornflower blue sundress with a lighter blue cardigan. It made my blue eyes pop, and it hid the less flattering features of my body fairly well. Of course, I had to wear sneakers with it because forget heels. Perfect or not, teetering around on some uncomfortable stilts wasn't worth it for any man. Plus, with my coordination, it would have been a date in the E.R. Also, I didn't own any.

I swished open my apartment door dramatically and finally put an end to the rehearsal of one Ethan was performing outside. When he saw me, he let loose one of those perfect smiles, full of pearly whites and happy eyes, and my face immediately matched his. All of the fears and worrying leading up to the date were allayed, and I immediately felt at ease. And excited. All wrapped up into one ball of joy. Like I said, it's hard to explain.

I was surprised and impressed when he led me to the passenger side of his car and actually opened the door for me. He let me choose the music for the drive, though we talked over it the entire time. He hadn't really planned anything, as it turned out, and we drove for blocks taking turns at the whole, *Oh, anything's fine, really. What would you like*? routine. I don't think he had fully realized how small the town was. We ended up driving in circles for almost an hour.

We finally found ourselves in a small coffee house near Daisy's apartment downtown. It was overpriced, of course, but it was whimsical and romantic as far as coffeehouses go. Plus, the pastries there were to die for. We ordered some overly-complicated names for coffee and planted ourselves in an obscure corner at a metal bistro table painted with purple Forget-Me-Nots.

I picked delicately at a scone (if he hadn't been there, I would have ordered three more and eagerly eaten them all – I was starving!) and eyeballed his funnel cake, impressed at his gumption in ordering carnival food for dinner. He was definitely my kind of guy. He sipped his latte and gesticulated dramatically whilst telling me the story of his first concert when his hand knocked his coffee cup and plate of funnel cake, sending both flying wildly across the table. The plastic top shot off and coffee sprayed everywhere. It was like a coffee crime scene. He clumsily rushed to clean it, horrified, and in doing so, spilled my coffee all over the table, his chair, and the front of my dress. His expression was mortified. I don't know if it was the shock of hot coffee or the look on his face, but I couldn't keep myself from giggling. Which erupted into laughter. His thoughtlessly reaching across the table to helpfully pat my chest with a wad of napkins before realizing what he was touching and dropping the wet wad like a hot pan made my laughing uncontrollable. He started laughing, too, and we must have looked like lunatics with a powdered sugar coffee mess all over us, tears streaming down our hysterical faces.

He later told me that was the moment he knew I was the woman for him. He said he fell in love with my *joie de vivre*, or joy for life. The funny thing is that joy came from knowing him.

It was always interesting to me that he loved something he saw inside of me, something he must have thought came from within. But the truth was, I felt it was only ignited after knowing him. He was everything. I thought I had been grateful for the little things in life before him, but I had known nothing about gratitude. It is funny how love opens you up to the world. After knowing him, the cold air slapping numbness into my cheeks as I walked outside was exhilarating instead of irritating. Jokes were funnier. Work was less frustrating. Food tasted sweeter and richer, and dining became an experience instead of a requirement. My lips could feel every kiss, as if the nerves had never really worked before. I became grateful for every working muscle in my body, for the weather, for everything. I tried to be a better friend to the only one I really had, Daisy, and a better person, in general. I got closer to Jamma, her love exacerbated by the supplemental I was now receiving, her kinship and support all the more pronounced. I even socialized more. I was opening up like a sad, hairy little caterpillar coming into her own; from a life spent unconscious in some cocoon, I was emerging as a free animal. Awakening as something beautiful at last, able to fly about and see the world from a totally different perspective. He made me appreciate the good things. He made me a woman. He was the one who breathed life into living. As explained earlier, I had always felt sort of out of place. Like I didn't belong, and I was just floating as freely as if I'd been in outer space. Well, he was the thing that kept me grounded. If I were the kite, he was the string. I finally felt like a part of society. I felt like I wouldn't have to be alone forever. I finally had my plus-one. He made me happy.

Therefore, when my lease was up and Ethan asked if I would be willing to move in with him, it never even warranted a second thought. He had become my home.

***

I watched his bare chest, which he regularly shaved, rise and fall with deep breaths. He was glorious. I would often rest my head in that hollow depression between his shoulder and pectoral muscles, tucked between his body and his arm. I traced the lines of his face lightly with my fingertip. Across his straight forehead and his chipmunk cheek, over the cleft in his chin. I let the stubble of his beard softly scratch my skin. I delicately traced his pouty lips, ran a fingertip along the bridge of his long, straight nose. I was envious of his dark, silky hair. If my hair got a whiff of a hint of moisture, it puffed up like a Chia pet. Water glided off of his, spiking it into a short, black fauxhawk. He had strong features of maleness, like the square jaw, wide shoulders and muscular body, mixed perfectly with boyish charms like his pinchable cheeks and his habit of sitting on his feet. He was perfect.

I whispered, "I want to memorize you. Every square inch."

He smiled and opened his eyes from beneath a curtain of long lashes. He rolled over to face me, grabbing my waist and pulling me closer to him. "You don't have to memorize anything. I'm right here," he whispered, his breath still smelling of his mint toothpaste as he brushed my hair behind my ear. "I'll always be right here." That one crooked tooth in front jutted out just a bit farther than the others when he smiled. His emerald green eyes stared directly into me. My breath would always catch just a little when we made eye contact. Until then, I had never realized the difference between someone looking at me and someone really seeing me.

I ran my fingertips across the back of his hand and played with the leather bracelet he always wore. I traced the outline of a Celtic knot stamped into it. I loved his hands. The hands of a musician soldier. "I love you, Ethan." I kissed his palm. Those three words never felt sufficient in telling him how I felt about him. I had decided early on that he was the man who was meant for me, and I couldn't compliment him enough or explain my affections in a way that resonated. He was everything.

He was beautiful, both as an attractive male and as a decent human being. He was gentle and kind and strong and stubborn. He made me laugh.

Not just the polite laughs that cut silence, but deep belly laughs that left me with watery eyes. He really was my better half.

"I love you, too, Aiyanna. I'm going to marry you so hard one day," he laughed. He rolled on top of me, his full weight pressing down on my body, his hips firmly on mine. He kissed me deeply, pulling the sheets back over us. God, how I loved that man.

***

The buttons were white. Small. There were so many of them, probably twenty or so. They matched the pattern of tiny ivory flowers on her navy dress. The buttons were sewn in a perfect straight line from the back of her neck to her shoulder blades, but the one...she had missed one button. I saw it when she turned to serve some more tea. I tried to admire her furnishings or think about the weather, but I could not stop myself from staring at that one missed button.

It must have taken him several full minutes to unbutton that dress. I could not contain my thoughts. They were daggers in my heart, each one, but they ran through over and over again. The thought of his anticipation as he unbuttoned each white button, his hands cupping her breasts beneath that navy fabric, pressing himself behind her. If she could feel the cold gold band of his wedding ring as he touched her or if she even cared. If he had unbuttoned them where I was sitting now. The scent of her home, her perfume. How he smelled of it when he kissed my cheek as I made his dinner. How I couldn't wash her scent from his shirts, despite my scrubbing, scrubbing, scrubbing until my hands were red and raw and pruned.

I could almost feel him pressing himself behind me from the night before, just as I imagined he did with her, as I stirred the sauce on the stovetop.

He was my husband. He looked at me with love in his eyes, still, even as his mouth spoke only lies. When those very lips kissed another.

I stared at the tiny button.

My friend finally turned to me with a smile, offering a delicate china cup on a matching floral-painted saucer. My hand shook as I accepted it, my heart broken, disappointment spilling into all the cracks as I sipped my tea.

I sat up in bed with a start. Ethan was still asleep beside me. Cooper was curled into a ball at the foot of the bed on top of the thick comforter. He was awakened when I sat up, but he acknowledged me with a couple of blinks and plopped his head back on his paws. The ceiling fan whispered as it spun round and around. I folded the hot blanket back from my body, leaning my head back and exposing my neck, which glistened with a nervous sweat. I looked over at Ethan again, sleeping on his stomach and looking perfectly peaceful.

I was so mad at him. So disappointed. It was he who was cheating in my dream. Rationally, I knew it wasn't reasonable to be angry at him for something that happened in an unconscious state, but I still couldn't contain it. It was my first night officially living with him, and I hated that I had that dream.

I had residual resentment lurking in my brain, and I knew from experience it would prevent me from falling back asleep. Damn nightmares. A part of me had thought they would subside since I was so happy in my life at that point. I slid quietly out of bed and padded into the kitchen. I poured myself a cup of water from the sink and drank it all in one breath. Why did that dream feel so real?

"Babe? You okay?" Ethan stood in the doorway in just his boxers, scratching his head and squinting his sleepy eyes. He looked confused and worried.

I loved him so much in that moment, from his messy, spiky hair to his bare feet. He was glorious in the dark room, the only light that of streetlights outside peeking in through the blinds. He was tall and toned, with bulges and divots in all the right places. I went to him and wrapped my arms around his solid torso. He bent to hug me back, his head resting on top of mine, loving me without question. He tucked my hair behind my ear and asked again if I was okay, concern wrinkling his eyebrows.

"Yeah," I smiled up at him. "Just another dream."

"You have them pretty often, don't you?"

He made us each a cup of hot tea as I sat atop the bar stool at his kitchen island and explained how I had been plagued with poor sleep and vivid dreams for as long as I could remember. He listened intently, asking questions and being supportive.

"It comes and goes, I guess," I said, blowing at my tea and taking another sip. "And it's weird because sometimes things happen exactly as I have dreamed they would. And sometimes it feels like I'm a character in someone else's life entirely."

"I get that," he nodded understandingly.

And so we sat, talking and laughing, until the street lights were replaced by sunlight and Cooper whined to be let outside. I opened the back door, and his round little body went bolting into the yard. Then, Ethan was pressing himself behind me. It felt just like it had in my dream, but I filed away that thought and spun to face him. He kissed my lips and my neck and slid his fingers beneath the thin straps of my camisole. I let him lift me as he cupped my bottom, wrapping my legs around him tightly as he carried me back to the bedroom.

CHAPTER 12
Ronnie

Damn, thought Ronnie, *I need a woman*. He was lonely. He loved females. He saw them as so soft. And helpless.

He liked to feel like he was aiding them, but he also enjoyed the authority that came with it. The breadwinner has all of the power. The person doing the good deed is the one to whom the debt of a favor is owed. It was a delightful arrangement in Ronnie's perspective.

It was never very difficult for Ronnie to get girls. He was in a band, after all. He was tall, slim, and relatively attractive. He could write beautiful poetry. He knew about art history and musical composition. He was in love with the idea of love. A romantic. A dreamer.

The last few lovers Ronnie had were strays, so to speak. Chrissy had run away from her abusive husband and had severe emotional issues. She was afraid all of the time, and she needed someone to keep her safe. She was so sweet.

Tracy was Ronnie's favorite. She was a whore, which is the friendliest and most fun type of woman there is in Ronnie's eyes. They worked together at a fast food joint, and she let him feel her tits behind the deep fryer. She was older, with an eyebrow piercing and thin, dyed-black hair made crispy from too much hairspray. She let Donnie choke her when they fucked, though, so he took her in and looked after her financially for a while. Her, her mother, and her two kids. He always wanted kids. He really loved her. They were best friends. They were married for five years before he caught her running around on him. It's kind of tragic, really. He saw on the news that she and her lover disappeared one night. Last anyone heard, they were on their way to Destin, Florida. Ronnie smoked a joint and calmly watched her mother pack up and take the kids. They never even waved goodbye.

Ronnie met Heather at a seedy bar downtown, and she was eager to hook up. Probably because she was pretty repulsive - sloppy, with pallid skin and pointy dog teeth. He took her home, though, of course. She put no effort into sex, but she let Ronnie do whatever he liked. She told him afterward she had no place to go. They were together a couple of years. She never paid rent or got a job, so she needed him to provide for her. She spent her waking hours wallowing out his only chair and collecting cans and dirty plates in a half circle around it while she watched television. He missed her. He wondered what she was up to.

He was feeling the need again. He loved to be in love. He was lonely.

CHAPTER 13
Amara

Halloween had always been her favorite holiday. Samhain, as the Celts called it, when the veil between the living and the dead is thin, the spirits of the past closer than ever. When you could be anyone or anything you wanted. An excuse for short skirts and crazy makeup and mischief.

Amara would anticipate the day every year.

She gave myself permission to do anything that pleased her on Halloween. Tricks or treats or trouble. All of the above. She could never get enough. Of course, that was every day in her life.

Halloween was not a family holiday – she had always hated those. Awkward dinners with her mother. Pushing food around the plate until it was cold. Giving thanks or talking about the Lord. No thanks. Pass. Halloween was a holiday of imagination, though. You could steal candy from other kids while hidden behind a mask, your identity and culpability camouflaged. It was perfectly acceptable to walk up to a stranger and demand something from them. How great is that? And even as you get older, the parents with their tiny tots must give way to rambunctious teenagers and aggressive adolescents. It was a day for those who dominated and elbowed their ways to what they wanted. It was thrilling for Amara. Her kind of people.

She studied the day. As a child, she even went to the library, with its smell of old people and dust jackets, to check out books on the pagan holiday. It was fascinating. *Maybe I should open my own Halloween store*, she wondered. She loved the holiday that much.

If that weren't enough, Halloween was also special to her because it was the day that she truly discovered herself. Her mother, Eve, had become so frustrated with her that she sent Amara to counseling. Therapist after therapist tried their hands, only to become fearful and afraid. That part amused her. But the incompetency and redundancy bored her. Which angered her.

She finally saw one therapist who took a keen interest in her. After exploring the depths of her teenaged body, he would swim through the hot geysers of her mind. She was not sure it was as much helpful to her as it was exciting to him, but nonetheless, she found herself. The veil was thin that day, the timing right. Samhain shone a light on how to get there, but she guided herself, just as she had always done. She discovered the true power of what Eve had been talking about, and she never looked back. She stole some cash from her mother's purse and took a bus to the city. Once she truly understood the secret Eve had talked about since she was a toddler, she knew the power that came with it. And power in the wrong hands is terrifying indeed. It would change the course of her life, and subsequently, many others'.

CHAPTER 14
Ethan

Aiyanna was still in bed, and Ethan thought she was so beautiful. She was glowing from the twinkle lights she had hung around the bedposts. Her blonde hair was messy, partially covering her face, her soft lips slightly parted with the lightest little snore. She was so supple and velvety. Her cheeks and mouth looked like a doll you would see puckering angelically behind the plastic screen in a pink-colored box at a chain store. Cooper was sprawled out on her feet. Her eyelids fluttered with whatever dream was occurring in that special brain of hers. Ethan hoped it was something enjoyable.

She would wake up soon and instantly be bashful about her unruly hair (*oh my gosh, this frizzy hair hates me,* she would say as she raked her fingers through it) or soft body (*pleasantly plump,* she would call it as she self-consciously crossed her arms over herself). But she was amazing to Ethan. Every inch of her was beautiful. She was the most stunning woman he had ever seen, and he had seen quite a few. He didn't know what, or who, it was that tore her down, but she never gave herself enough credit. She was a goddess.

Ethan had already been awake for an hour, but he was sneaking around the house, trying to be quiet. He knew his girl hated the mornings. He could not blame her. He was that way before the military broke it out of him. And she had not been sleeping well. She would often wake Ethan with her cries or whimpers in the wee hours of the night. It broke his heart.

He knew this girl was different. She was going to be his wife. He loved her with a part of himself he had not known was even there.

He could admit it – he was a player. It had never mattered before. Women were just recreational diversions. They would use each other for a while before they both moved on to the next. She would have the boyfriend label and a good-looking guy (if Ethan did say so himself) to take to parties, and he would have some sex and feel a little less alone for a while. It is a lonesome world, and we are all superficial, our kisses never really connecting and our hugs never reaching our hearts.

But Aiyanna…she had soul. Ethan saw it the first time he met her, and it blew him away. There was something in those blue eyes that sparkled, like stars lighting up a cobalt sky, setting his heart ablaze. She obviously got that from her grandmother, whose eyes had that same fire when he first met her, too. There was so much love emanating from them. It was inspiring. It made him want to be the man she thought he was.

Aiyanna lived her life as if it were a gift, and Ethan had never known anyone like that. She would actually stop and look up at the stars or admire the way the wind whispered through the leaves. She would pull the car over to gawk at a sunset or stop the shopping cart to see if some elderly person needed assistance reaching something on a higher shelf (a lot of help she would be with her short body!). She ordered dessert. Do you know how many girls won't even order dessert at dinner?! It's a travesty!

From that first date, he knew. Like an asshole, he spilled coffee all over her, but she just laughed contagiously. She didn't get mad at him for ruining her outfit or anything – she just laughed, with a smile that could melt any icy heart. She seemed almost relieved not to have to behave so properly. Though to be fair, how can someone pull off acting uptight when they've got a hot beverage down their front? She had a deep dimple in one cheek and happy eyes. She laughed with abandon, loudly and melodically, with no concern whatsoever of how she was perceived. It was a song to Ethan's music-loving ears, and he fell in love with the girl right there.

CHAPTER 15
Aiyanna

This is the part of my story where everything fell apart.

It was four o'clock in the morning, and Ethan still wasn't home.

I had been living with him for about four months, and it was glorious. I had cohabited with a couple of boyfriends in the past, but it was nothing like playing wifey to Ethan. We laughed all the time, and I was relishing becoming domesticated. I experimented with recipes and attempts at baking, having Ethan close his eyes and taste the different dishes. He was kind enough to lie and eat every morsel. He taught me the perfect way to sear a steak. I actually got some kind of pleasure out of washing and folding his laundry for him and packing a lunch for him to take to work. It was sick. He cleaned off his desk and set up special logins on his computer so I could look for work, since I'd left my job to move in with him. My smiling face was his computer home screen. He started to teach me to play guitar and different self-defense maneuvers. We would snuggle into the covers every evening and watch comedy shows on the television while we ate dessert in bed. We even had a great time hauling off garbage and assorted yard junk to the dump one weekend, coming up with our own song for a "dump date." We were that disgusting couple you love to hate.

That simple life was so exciting to me, since I felt like I had spent so long trying to achieve it. For years, I had dated dirt bags and liars. I worked hard to save money and I longed for my own home, but it felt like I wasn't progressing in life. If I were invited to some wedding or party through my friendship with Daisy, I always attended alone. I was the only single at the office Christmas party. Even in relationships, I was lonely. I was constantly apologizing for their behavior or explaining to Jamma how they really did care – they just acted like they didn't.

Now, I can see it more clearly. I don't know by whose standards I was judging myself, but I wanted to be a part of a family of my own so badly because I felt like that was where I was *supposed* to be in life. And Ethan was the man with whom that was going to happen. It felt like my destiny, like all of the pieces finally had fallen into place for me. It was reinforced by the fact that Daisy had essentially introduced us, and they got along so well. She never cared for any of the guys I dated before him. Also, Jamma seemed to approve. She had given her blessing and had him over for dinner on many occasions. Having my best friend and my boyfriend joke and tease and agree to go to the same places at the same time, and watching Ethan and Jamma sit together comfortably, convinced me that I had finally gotten it right. All of the important people in my life fit together.

***

"Hey, babe, should I keep my crock pot, or do you want to use yours?" I leaned over a huge cardboard box labeled *Kitchen* in black marker, unearthing pots and dishes wrapped in newspapers and magazine pages.

"Which one do you like better?" he called from the garage, where he was breaking down boxes and clearing off shelving for more of my things.

Unpacking was a slow process, as Ethan already had a full house upon my move into it. I sort of wish he weren't such a responsible adult and were more of a stereotypical bachelor with a few scant objects in an empty house, since I had so much of my own stuff. Consolidation was a matter of constant compromise and frequent trips to the secondhand store with a truckload of boxes and bags for donation.

"We'll use mine. It's red."

"Rojo," he said, rolling the "r" in his mouth for a moment. "El color de la passion," he said in an overexaggerated accent.

"Exacta mundo," I laughed. I was so happy in that moment, there was a palpable feeling of fullness in my chest. I was finally in a steady, loving relationship, and I was going to make a family with this man.

I had never met a man who loved or had ever even conceived of the kind of love that gripped my heart with feeling while setting my mind at ease. I had always thought that passion came with tumult and comfort came with a cost of sacrificing excitement. Then I met Ethan. He was silly and fun, but also stable. He had income from the military as a veteran, and he booked gigs as a musician. He was the perfect dichotomy of grown man and carefree boy, and he expressed both sides in his love for me.

I grabbed a couple of bottles of beer from the fridge, smiling at a picture magnet of the two of us making funny faces in a photo booth at his friend's wedding. I walked one bottle out to the garage and kissed Ethan on the cheek. I popped the top off of one for myself and carefully lifted another box marked *Important* onto the kitchen countertop. I pulled each layer of newspaper and bubble wrap away as if they were delicate petals of some soft flower. Smiling, I rubbed one fingertip across the glass picture frame. My mother. Amara Astilbe Burns. A hell of a name.

It was the only picture I had of her, found while looking for evidence of my own history in Jamma's room. Her blonde hair shone in the sunlight, creating an aura about her face as if she were an angel in a Renaissance painting. Her smile was wide, with one dimple in her right cheek. She was holding a toddler in her lap, her long, slender fingers cradling my tiny, pudgy hands.

"She was beautiful," Ethan said over my shoulder, walking in from the garage. "You look just like her." He slid his arms around my waist and I leaned back into him. He nuzzled his face in my hair.

"Amara Burns…mystery woman. Jamma would never talk much about her, and I can't help but wonder why. I had that one teacher who had recognized my name like he had known her, and he acted like I was devil spawn." I laughed, touching the photo again. "She must have been mischievous." I sighed, that same old longing in my heart. "I just wish I could have known her."

"I know, babe," he sighed sympathetically. He'd lost his own father to cancer when he was eleven years old. He didn't talk about it much, but I knew he understood that sense of loss.

He brushed my curls from one side of my neck and kissed me lightly in the spot where neck meets shoulder. It never failed to send shivers down my arms. "What would you say to her?"

"What do you mean?" I asked.

"I mean, if your mom were here right now?"

"Well," I stalled, as I searched for words that would never properly disguise that I had absolutely no idea. She had only ever been a concept to me. It was the mystery that surrounded her that made me hold on so strongly. How Jamma had always been so elusive about her and what had happened. I had no clue what kind of person she really was or what I would even say to her if I had ever had the chance. I mean, she did abandon me in infancy. The truth was, I really knew nothing about her at all. "She isn't here, is she? So, I guess I don't have to worry about it," I mumbled, choosing bitchy self-pity over explanation.

He put his hands on my hips and spun me around to face him.

"How do you know she isn't?" His green eyes bore into mine.

I cocked my head and raised one eyebrow. "You've just had the one beer, right?" I laughed nervously.

"No, I'm serious." His eyes were like a postcard of some exotic green sea, and he tapped his tooth with his thumbnail, as he always did when he was in deep thought. His usual smile had disappeared, and a small crease had taken its place between his eyebrows. "We don't know for sure what happens when we go. Maybe she's still around you right now."

"That's a creepy thought!" I laughed again, slightly uncomfortable. The thought of ghosts hovering about was not something I wanted to consider, especially one witnessing what we had just done on the kitchen counter a few minutes prior. It was also unlike Ethan to be so intense. It put me on edge a little for him to be so serious about something.

"I'm just saying," as he smiled and dipped his head to kiss me lightly on the lips, "we don't know for sure. I, for one, don't want to think that something as simple as death could sever every thought and every relationship we had while alive."

"That's kind of the premise of death, babe." I said, awkwardly. I meant it to come out funnier than it did.

Ethan took my mom's picture from my hands. He lifted a framed "Home Sweet Home" cross-stitch from the wall, tossed it on the sofa, and gently hung my mother's picture on the empty nail.

***

It was four o'clock in the morning, and Ethan still wasn't home. His side of the bed had been untouched. I'd only slept fitfully, as had become my habit when he wasn't beside me. Which had become a regular thing, as he had so many evening gigs booked. They would often run late into the night or early into the next morning. However, he always let me know. I understood what it must be like for parents who stay up all night waiting for their teenagers to get home before they can relax enough to surrender to sleep. Worried, I rubbed my eyes to make sure the clock on the night stand was actually reading that late and it wasn't some phantom my anxiety conjured. If only it had been that easy. I checked my cell phone. Blinking at the bright screen painfully shooting light into my retinas, I saw that there were no texts, no calls, nothing. Frowning, I slid out of bed and padded down the hall, checking the bathrooms, kitchen and living room for any sign of Ethan, though I knew I would have heard him had he come home. Nothing.

Tiny points of perspiration popped up on my forehead and my stomach suddenly had a rock of anxiety rolling around inside it. I dialed Ethan's number, but it rang unanswered until it went to voicemail. I sent him a text, tried calling again. Maybe he had crashed on a friend's couch. Had the gig he was playing that night somehow run over this long? Why hadn't he at least called? Oh God, what if he was hurt?

I was frozen, standing in the middle of the living room, unsure of what to do. Should I drive around looking for him in ditches? Should I call the hospital? What was the name of the place he said he was performing tonight?

I sat heavily in his desk chair, phone in hand, staring at the screen. I unlocked it, looked up the number for the hospital, hesitated. I dialed, then hung up before it started ringing. Was I overreacting? *Get it together, Aiyanna.* I took a deep breath and set my phone on the desk. As I did so, I saw the plain white envelope with my name on the front in Ethan's small, messy handwriting.

The oddest sensation creeped over me, like tingling nervousness exploding like fireworks across my nerves. I picked up the envelope. The tab was tucked into the back neatly. I opened it slowly, somehow certain that everything was about to change.

On a blank sheet of printer paper:

Aiyanna,

I love you. I will always love you, and you will have a place in my heart for the rest of my time on earth. So here comes what can't be said:

I can't be with you. I'm more sorry about that than you will ever know. You have given me life and love. You've done NOTHING wrong – this isn't your fault. I have my reasons. I can't tell you now, but it's the best thing for everyone. Even so, it's breaking my heart knowing that this will break yours. You are the most amazing girl I've ever known, and I want only good things for you in your life.

I AM SO SORRY.

I don't know if you have ever had a moment like that in your life, where the bottom falls out and the floor beneath your feet is gone in an instant. No warnings and no explanations. It is that feeling when you reach the peak of a roller coaster, when gravity suspends and your stomach lurches into your throat. When you know a drop is coming, but you still feel unprepared.

My head spun and I could hear my heartbeat in my ears. What in the world had happened? This must be another of my nightmares.

I had to wake up. Now. Please, God…

The whole scenario was completely out of left field, and I had no idea what was going on, but I could actually feel my heart breaking. This could not be really happening. I sunk to the floor and tucked myself tightly into the fetal position, hot tears streaming down my face. If I could just wake up…

Cooper whimpered softly and licked my tears, nudging me frantically with his muzzle. He was apparently as confused and stunned as I was. I grabbed his neck and hugged him close to me. It was as if he had volunteered to take on some of the pain, and I could feel a fraction of it transfer to him. I buried my face into his thick fur.

Surely I would wake from this nightmare, and Ethan would be sleeping beside me. He would throw his arms around me and comfort me. I would return to real life.

I must have wept like that for an hour or two or more, bawling my eyes out, my heart and my spirit and my life plans broken in just seconds. I could not wrap my mind around it, despite how hard I tried. Someone he said he loved, whose lips he had kissed and whose ears into which he had whispered promises, at whom he had just lobbed an emotional grenade, lay scattered in pieces on the floor of his house and he was not even there.

I had no job. I had given away most of my belongings. I had no apartment. And apparently, I had no Ethan.

I replayed the last few days in my head, analyzing every detail and looking for the source of this nightmare. Maybe he had acted a little strange, a little distant, but I had not even noticed at the time. Had he been unhappy all along or had I done something wrong?

Devastated and sensing a hot rage boil up inside of me, I stood on shaky knees and patted Cooper on the head. In that moment, I wanted to destroy him. Set his house on fire. Break all of his dishes and cut up all of his clothes. In that moment, I *hated* him. The anger frightened me. It felt like feeding some monster that I could not keep leashed.

The monster inside rattled its cage, and I almost wanted to see its wrath. That would have been so much easier than giving into the reality of it. I knew it would be some kind of consolation to force Ethan to feel even an iota of what he was doing to me. I wanted to hurt him. Had he been there in front of me, I might have. Instead, I inhaled deeply and thought of Jamma. I thought of what she would do, and she would turn the other cheek. She would wish him happiness and move on to find her own.

I grabbed my cell phone and called my Jamma, my hands shaking violently. How she ever deciphered from my hysteria what had happened and that I needed her, I'll never know. But a few minutes later, before the sun was even rising, she was pulling into the driveway, my rescue car awaiting.

***

While I have figured out a few things since, I know now that I'll never fully understand how he could have done what he did that night, that way. I had loved him with all that I had to give, and I had opened myself to the deepest, rawest parts, exposing all of my weaknesses and flaws. I never thought I was supplying him with an arsenal of ammunition to lob against me one day, but I had showed him exactly where to cut to hurt me the most. And that's exactly what he did. As far as I knew then, he just decided on some Wednesday night that I was no longer what he wanted, no longer worth fighting for. He just disappeared, without discussion or any understanding on my part. Just like my mother. He got to make a decision, and I had no say so in it whatsoever. I wasn't even allowed an opportunity to discuss it. He was just...gone. And then, he was truly gone.

When I chose him, I gave all of myself to him, and he let me believe he was always going to be a part of my life, my partner. It had taken me years of yearning and unhealthy relationships to get to the point where I was actually able to love someone with such purity and selflessness.

We all learn to protect ourselves and guard our hearts as we grow older and survive so many failed relationships, but there is a point where our guarded hearts stop allowing any guests at all. Our hearts become fortresses that shoot down anyone who dares come close enough, even while we wait for the one who will come rescue us.

All I had ever really wanted was to be loved, truly loved, and for Ethan to be able to walk away so easily — well, in that moment, it felt to me like he never really loved me at all. That was all that was left of us. In the blink of an eye, Ethan no longer existed. And that — that — is what broke something deep inside of me. It set my life on a different course entirely.

I hope you understand that I couldn't just switch off the love, and I couldn't understand how he had. That his sudden change in behavior caused me to question everything I thought I knew. That having the rug pulled out from under me caused me to come crashing to the ground in a most destructive manner. That I could not even grieve properly because I never had a chance to process the letter.

I had always felt unlovable. The only unwavering affection I had ever received was from my Jamma. I could not understand what the point to any of it was if this was all life ever had to give you back. Why wake up every morning and why work your life away at some dead-end job, struggling to make money you only spend on bills? Why go on awkward dates with boys who just break your heart in the end, anyway? None of it felt worth it anymore. I had no job, no place to live, no boyfriend, no friends. And things were about to get much worse. I became completely ingrained in the deepest depression of my life.

***

"I am so sorry," was the first thing he said to me when I showed up the next day to move my things out of his house. He was downtrodden, and he looked like he hadn't slept. I put my hand up to stop him from speaking. Truthfully, it was because I was afraid I would lose it. I would say too much or beg for him to take me back. I didn't want him to see me cry. He had taken enough of me already.

It had only been a few days, and I was a shell of a human. He had tried to call, but I never answered. What was left to say? I could not sleep or eat or think, and the weight of the disappointment and destroyed dreams was crushing. He could not take back what he had done. It would never be like it was before. I had done nothing but cry, and ask God why (Why me? Why this? Why now?), for days, but I refused to let Ethan see one tear.

Silently, he and Jamma and I loaded up all of my things. The red crock pot, the picture of my mother, every delusion I had of having a life with what I thought was a magnificent man. Funny how just a bunch of stuff can look like something else. Socks and picture frames and pillow cases each hold their own little sentiments, memories of a life that could have been. Boxed up and taped closed, tossed onto the back of a rented truck.

He helped me load the last box of broken dreams into the back of the moving truck and slung the door closed. Jamma was in my car, idling the engine, and I was to drive the moving truck back to her house since I had no place of my own.

We stood there like that for several seconds, just looking at each other. He didn't see me anymore. It was entirely different than just a few days before. Funny how a moment can separate entire sections of your life. Before and After. I would never be the woman I was once that truck was packed and my life with Ethan was over. He had taken a piece of me, something I would never get back again.

Now, I consider it a gift. It was part of loving someone. I gave that fragment of my heart to him willingly, to do with as he pleased. The gift of love.

I said the only thing I could think of in the awkwardness of exiting someone's life. "I really loved you."

Breaking down, his face twisted in anguish. "I know," he cried, his head bowed, his shoulders shaking.

I fought every instinct in me to comfort him or touch his cheek or say something meaningful. Even in that moment, I did not want him to hurt. I could not believe everything we had experienced culminated in that.

My heart heavy, I walked away from him (before he saw my tears) and lifted myself up into the driver's seat. I turned the ignition and put the truck in drive. As I rounded the corner at the end of the road, I finally had the courage to look in the rearview mirror. Ethan was standing alone in the cul-de-sac, watching me drive away. And that's an image I will never be able to erase from my mind. Just a few short days later, Ethan would be dead.

CHAPTER 16
Ethan

It was four o'clock in the morning, and Ethan was wide awake. He sat cross-legged on the hotel bed, absentmindedly staring at the television screen. His thoughts were on what had happened.

He could not bring himself to do it for several days. It was as if he could hear the ticking of a timebomb in his brain for every minute that he waited, but he could not do it. He loved her. That meant he did not want to hurt her. But it also meant he could not let anyone else hurt her, either. It was going to have to be one or the other. It was tearing him apart for days before he finally pulled the trigger.

It was late afternoon, and he was getting ready for another gig. Ai had made pork chops for him, and she was ready with a cold drink when he got out of the shower. She had even hung up his suit so it wasn't wrinkled for his performance. He knew it would have to be the day, but he could not say it to her. She was all smiles and happiness and smelling like sunshine, and he just…could not. Not that morning over eggs and coffee or at lunchtime when she drew a heart in pen on the back of his hand. When she started running her fingers through his hair and kissing his neck, he still couldn't.

He loved her so much it ached. He was so overcome with her, they made love right there on the sofa. He wanted to be a part of her – he needed her. He held her warm, soft body against his and smelled her hair. He couldn't do it. He wouldn't. He didn't want to have to remember her. He wanted to feel her and smell her and be with her in the present of every day.

He popped on the computer to verify the details of the gig that night. The screen glared at him in the dark room, pressuring him. He kept coming back to it, over and over since the first time. He read it for the hundredth time. The message on the screen was crystal clear, reinforcing what was said earlier. He had to do it. For her sake. And for his own.

Her sleepy voice was suddenly behind him, "Hey baby, you okay? You're going to be late if you don't get a move on."

He quickly closed the tab and swiveled to say goodbye to her before his gig.

"Yep. I'm going-" His voice caught on that word.

He did not know what else to say. There was no way he could explain, nothing he could do. She would not understand. He wanted her to just understand, but she wouldn't. He would not be there. She would be alone and broken and he could not make her understand. He loved her so much.

"Okay. Well, I'm going to walk Cooper. Break a leg tonight," she said as she kissed him on the cheek. "I love you." She leashed up Cooper, said she would see him later, and walked out the front door in her yoga pants and cartoon t-shirt.

His heart was breaking in two. He felt like he was going to throw up. He blinked hard, tears slipping from his eyes as he did so. It was going to destroy her. He knew he was a coward, and he hated myself for it. He would break the parts of her he loved the most, and he knew it. The happiness, the joy, the optimism. He would have to hurt her beyond repair, and it was killing him to do so.

He left the envelope in the middle of his desk for her to see.

His stomach lurched, and his insides melted. He was the worst person he knew, and he despised myself. It was the only thing he knew to do, though. It was the only way he knew to protect her. He squeezed the tears from his eyes and bit his cheeks until they bled. He willed himself to focus on the pain in his cheeks, to forget the pain in his heart.

He grabbed his keys and walked quickly to his car before she came back.

He pulled around the corner, and there she was. She was magnificent in the light of twilight, her wet hair up in a messy bun, soft boots floppy on her feet. Her curls caught the light of the waning sun. She smiled and waved as he pulled by her. That was the end of him right there. He was destroyed. He drove away quickly so she could not see him melt into nothingness.

That night was an eternity, the worst of his entire life. He just wanted it to be over, waiting and wondering if she would see the note or when. He was physically ill at his performance and entirely unable to play, so he left early. He wandered around downtown, helpless and broken, and finally rented a hotel room. He didn't sleep a wink. He stared anxiously and vacantly at the television screen as he sat cross-legged and fully dressed on the hotel bed. He bit his fingernails into the quick, tapping his teeth violently, each agonizing phone call or text message stabbing him right through his heart. She was calling, and he couldn't answer. Was she worried? Was she angry? Had she seen the letter or was she calling from concern at his not being home? He did not know what to say or how to say it. He did not know anything anymore. He wanted to be there with her, to hold her and kiss her hair and make her feel safe.

He had put the proverbial gun to the head of his woman and pulled the word trigger that night, efficiently ending their story together. If he had only known that their story was his last story. He was also in the final pages of his life, the ending to which would be executed by the pull of a trigger.

CHAPTER 17
Emrys

Meanwhile, in another place and time...

The fire crackled and hissed, spitting its discontent at the cold drizzle threatening to extinguish it. Emrys felt exactly the same way. Dense fog had settled around their camp, and the elders spoke of spirits and ethereal things. They were convening in a night cloud. The Scottish Highlands were silent and void of light. A motionless, moonless evening, where the echoes of their voices carried into the unseen horizon. The familiar smell of smoking pipes and peat hung in the chill. Undeniably, the night did have a strange sort of ghoulish feel about, but Emrys would never admit the shiver sent down his spine was not due to the cold mist seeping into their kilts and clothing. A rock of dread had lodged itself in his belly since they set out earlier in the morning sun. As the weather had grayed and darkened, so had his frame of mind.

Emrys was but a wee lad when Death first visited him. The bastard stole his da, then his grandda, sickness stole his best mate, and the English took his brother. Battle was nothing to balk about. He had only had to fight a time or two before, though he did seem to excel at the sport of war. A drapery of rage would settle across his eyes, blinding him to all but aggression in that moment. He did not ken what it was that festered inside of him silently between battles, but it bubbled over when swinging his sword. All of the unfairness of living, the nights gone hungry, the guilt of being alive when so many no longer were, all of it boiled his blood and moved his muscles and his limbs in a frenzy of rage. It was so unlike him, and yet, it was there.

He ran his hand restlessly through his hair and down the back of my neck. He wrapped his belted plaid around his shoulders for warmth. He watched his breath poof out in wee gray clouds, tapping his tooth to the rhythm of the rain. He was anxious, restless.

Edan nudged him with his cold muzzle, and Emrys scratched him behind his ears. Dogs always seem to sense when something weighs heavily on your mind.

Edan had refused to stay home, following the group and bashfully tucking his tail and his ears when he was caught. He continued on, however, rejecting all efforts to send him away. Emrys attempted to sternly berate him for misbehaving, but the dog would not let him leave him behind. He flattened his ears and looked up at Emrys with the most earnest look ever seen in a pup. He could do nothing but laugh and let him follow along.

Edan's tail wagged lazily as he stared at Emrys with his soft brown eyes. He seemed to understand that Emrys did not want the day to break, for he was afeared something terrible would come with it. He just knew it in his gut. One of the horses neighed restlessly.

His clansmen teased him for being a romantic, but his thoughts still, and always, drifted back to his Beatha. For all of the fury felt in fighting, she was the reverse reaction in his world. His seraph. She elicited from Emrys silly smiles and tenderness he would never have shown outwardly toward his clansmen. The Scots were a tough and hardy people; they had to learn to be outwardly stern. The sweetness inside was saved for a certain level of intimacy, a level Beatha had unlocked in him. She was the most beautiful woman he had ever seen, with her wild red hair and playful green eyes. She was both earthy and ethereal. He loved her immediately and immensely, and he knew she was going to be his wife. Emrys indulged himself in the recollection of their first meeting.

It had been frigid, with a wet sort of chill in the air, quite similar to this night, but it was Samhain. The Otherworld was closer than ever to our own, and you could feel it in your bones. Whilst walking the cattle down from the hills to the winter pastures earlier that day, even they seemed to sense some sort of eeriness in the air. Their red fur whipped in the winds, which sounded like *bean shìths*, or banshees, calling to the living in their pitched screeches. His kilt whirled about, and he was certain he showed his bare arse to his brother at least a time or two.

Their mum was hooting on about setting the table and lighting the turnips before the festivities. Emrys jerked his head to motion his brother, Cormag, who sighed and mumbled something about women's work.

"Ye've got to set an extra place for Da and Douglas, ye amadan," Emrys berated as he cut the final touches of an Irish smile into the grotesque turnip face leering back at him. "And set a couple o' decanters by the fire, as weel."

Every year, Cormag focused more on the festival than the meaning behind it. Should the spirits of Emrys's brother and da come to visit, they should have a place for them. Spirits were a tempestuous lot, and Emrys was always encouraged to be quite wary and respectful of the Aos Si. He placed my lit turnip proudly on the sill of the small window. He was certain that ought to scare away any wee ghoulies of the human variety planning an invasion. As for the spirits, they would have to wait and see.

Their mum emerged with her dress inside out. She was nothing if not determined to hinder any impish approaches. Cormag and Emrys were content with their iron crosses to ward off any wickedness. They made their way to the bonfires, their mother between them. The need-fires were taller than a man. They approached at the moment the leftover gray of day slipped into the darkness of night. Samhain had begun.

Naturally, a group of lassies bobbing for apples caught the boys' attention.

That was when Emrys saw her. She was so beautiful, even from afar. Her hair looked like embers as it glistened from the fireside, wet on the ends. Emrys approached her immediately, begging leave of his family. Her green eyes startled him. Though they were striking, as was her natural beauty, that was not what had his breath catching in his throat. There was something familiar about her, and yet, Emrys gulped her in as if she were the freshest water and he a thirsty wanderer. He knew her already, never having met her. Knowing her was all he wanted to do from that point forward. Those eyes, they shimmered with glee and mischief, bright like a jewel. He wished he could crawl into them like a cold, green loch and swim about until the end of eternity. He felt... almost as if... he had. They were both home to Emrys and unfamiliar all at once.

A group of wild lads with guises ran by rambunctiously, whirling the lassie into his arms. She laughed and immediately pulled away, but he could feel her still. She felt like fire, warm and dangerous.

He watched her all night, stealing glances and smiling when he could. She coyly returned his glimpses from under her thick lashes. When she did so while dancing, her body moving beneath all that fabric, snaking and writhing in ways he had only imagined before, he had to step away from everyone else. That girl would be his wife. He had no doubts in his mind. She might be of the Aos Si, but she was certainly a Seelie Court. She was a good faerie if ever there were. To show up on Samhain and seduce his mind and his body alike should have scared him, but he would have gone with her anywhere. She could have lured him to an ancient cairn, and he would have lived there willingly. Never had he felt anything was missing from his life, particularly, until he found her, and she filled a part of him he had not known existed. A part he could never be without again.

Emrys had dreamed of those green eyes. His love, Beatha. She owned his soul, and he adored her. She was his whole world, from the stars in her stormy eyes to the way her hair blew in a breeze like a grassy brae.

"Emrys," his uncle snapped, jarring him from my thoughts. "Ye best be preparin' for tomorrow, lad. We're goin' to test your stones in battle, boy."

He cackled. He could see the fear in his nephew's face, and Emrys let him assume he was afraid to fight. The truth was, he was not afraid of battle. He was afraid of losing. He had a horrible feeling in his belly that the odds were not in their favor on the morrow. Flashbacks of his brother stretched out on a stone slab, his body being washed for burial, slid across his thoughts like a serpent. It was not dying of which Emrys was afraid. It was leaving her.

He scratched Edan behind the ears and covered the leather bracelet tied to his wrist with his other palm. If there were any part of Beatha still remaining on the gift she had surprised him with that morning, he wanted to absorb it into himself. Her fine fingers had touched it, had tied it to him and kissed it with those sweet, soft, loving lips, her red hair falling weightlessly on his arm around it. He felt the tickle of her red mane, the love in her eyes when she bid him goodbye. He carried her with him, as he supposed he always had. She had been with Emrys long before meeting her, even.

CHAPTER 18
Jamma

Swimming back downstream with the fluidity of time...
She stared into the overhead lights until they blinded her, black spots swirling in the periphery of her vision. She tried to chase the wiggly amoebas with her sight, but the floaty specks swam away before she could focus on them. Isn't that the way with most things?

She shifted uncomfortably on the thin mattress, the slim polka-dotted sheet and threadlike gown garroting her thighs in one motion. She pulled the wad of fabric from under her body, absurdly angry at it. She was restless.

She didn't care for hospitals. Intellectually, she knew they were places of healing, lifesaving institutions. But the smells, the confusion, the emotion that filled them was repellant. They were full of hopes that never happened and lives lost and pain and anguish. Memories. As one who has always been very keen on the feelings around her, it was overwhelming in a most negative way.

A contemptuous tone caught her attention. "Another with no husband?" They were speaking right outside of the open door with her name, Evelyn Burns, handwritten by the door number. Couldn't they at least have whispered, for God's sake?

"They are calling it the 'Summer of Love', if you can believe that."

"This baby was conceived out of wedlock. There is no love in that."

Eve kept her eyes closed. Those nurses didn't know her, nor did they know her story. Nonetheless, she decided it was better to avoid the awkward confrontation that might occur if they realized Eve could hear them. Mostly because they held her prisoner in their hospital bed. She was basically at their mercy. Unfortunately.

"Miss Eve, would you like to hold your baby?" Though she was still furious at the nurse, and she did give that nurse quite the cold look-over, she could not help but grin at the sight of her daughter's face. She had her father's chin.

Red was not there to touch the doughy little hands of his daughter or admire the miniscule fingernails, smaller than a pencil eraser. He could not stick his fingertip in the dimple in her cheek or laugh when she yawned and furrowed her brow, like a frustrated little grump. He was not there. But it was not because he didn't want to be. It was because he didn't know.

***

He was the answer Eve had been seeking. She had fantastical dreams that deprived her of sleep for the first quarter-century of her very solitary life, but when her head was nestled in the crook of Red's arm, the moonlight dancing in his auburn hair like a bonfire, she slept the whole night through. He would rub her back with his callused hands, rough with hard labor, smoothing her hair and whispering in her ear on the occasions she had a strange dream that woke her. He helped her understand what she could do, the power she held. The secret that had been passed down to her through the ages. How to live with that special ability. How to use it to benefit her life and grow as a person. And finally, how to accept the responsibility it brought and possibly even help others.

Eve had never known the kind of love she found with Red, having been orphaned at birth and raised in various homes. The only connection she had to anything tangible was her name: Evelyn Burns. Eve. It had been her mother's name.

There was much she could not recall until she learned to control her gift. Then, she watched her own small feet buckled into her Mary Janes climb the wide stone stairs of that first orphanage. She could recall the soft clicking of her shoes' hard soles carrying her into an entirely different life. The steps were so tall, and she was so small, she had to concentrate in order not to fall on her face. She remembered her understanding of what was happening and her utter lack of control to do anything about it. Her first true disappointment and heartbreak in a life riddled with them. She accepted it immediately. She did not want Aunt Rose to be upset. It must have been a difficult decision for her. She hoped she had not disappointed her somehow or had otherwise driven her to her choice.

It was the first time Eve could clearly recall feeling powerless in her own life. She knew then that she would find a way to take back her power. To own this life of hers.

A hardened woman with heavily starched clothing and thick, pointed eyebrows led her into a sitting room. She reminded Eve of Almira Gulch from the Wizard of Oz. She was intimidated by her tall, slim frame, jet black hair with white stripes, and her pointed features. She sat stiffly in an armchair, crossed her ankles and lit a cigarette. She inhaled deeply like a drowning person coming up for air and impatiently motioned for Eve to sit. She did so as she choked back a cough. The room suffocated her in its smoke smell. Gulch asked her a couple of questions and took possession of Eve's suitcase before ushering her into a long room full of beds.

The other children circled Eve as soon as they were alone, teasing and taunting as they ripped at her dress and pulled her hair. They tore Eve down to their level on that first afternoon, an initiation of sorts. She could have nothing of her own. Her doll was taken from her. She never saw it again. Her dress was torn from her body, a potato sack given to her instead. She got the coldest cot, just below a drafty window. She cried herself to sleep that night and many nights following. But she would not let them break her.

There was power greater than them that kept Eve calm and allowed her to recognize how little it all would matter one day. She was aware of it, even then. She was young, so she did not truly understand it, but she was aware of it nonetheless.

On occasion, Eve could still feel the hard cement under her knees as she prayed for their forgiveness every night after they beat and belittled her. She prayed ever night after lights were turned out and everyone's breathing evened out. She kept bruises on her skinny knees all of the years of her childhood.

The headmistress would stand above her as Eve washed the floor with a sponge and a small bucket. She smoked her cigarette and prodded Eve with the toe of her boot, dropping ash on the wet floor. Then she would toss the remainder of the cigarette on the floor and tell Eve to clean it up as she stomped off to torture another child during chores. Some people seem to get pleasure from making others feel small.

There was one girl only a bit bigger than Eve who bullied all of the others. She would pinch and twist the girls' breasts or steal their food or hold their noses and mouths closed while they slept. She caught the mice that scooted through their room and tortured them until they died. Eve never understood such anger in someone so young until a veteran orphan, one of the older girls, whispered that she was actually the illegitimate child of the headmistress herself.

The boys of the orphanage were second in charge. Second to the headmistress, of course. They stole and smoked the headmaster's cigarettes and they explored their sexuality with the willing, and sometimes the unwilling, girls.

Eve befriended a small, freckle-faced boy whom all the children inherently knew was being raped by one of the older boys. He was timid and afraid of everything. He would whisper his truth to Eve – that he wished he had never been born. Eve told him he was beautiful. She told him that he mattered. She would sneak him part of her dinner and tell him jokes she made up so she could see him smile. He was so small. She tucked his skinny body next to hers and draped her arm over his shoulder as she told him to believe that there was a better future for them both than that place. She taught him to have faith. She talked of them as adults. They would dress in fine clothes and eat their fill in expensive restaurants. They would sleep in huge, fluffy beds in houses of their own, with children they loved and would never abandon. They would have all of the material things they wanted. They would be safe. And they would be best friends all of the days until they died. He was killed with a kitchen knife by the angry little girl. He was stealing a biscuit to sneak to Eve. That night was the hardest of all of Eve's life to bend down on her knees and pray for that evil girl's forgiveness. She prayed for escape. She prayed for deliverance.

Eve recalled the warmth of understanding that spread through her stomach and her limbs like a sip of hot water. She understood that it was only temporary, but a blip in the movie of her life. The nightmare she was living was as impermanent as her other nightmares. She would wake one day as an adult and it would feel like not much more than a memory.

Eve could either let the beginning of her story be the thing that ruins the rest of it, or she could use her loneliness and isolation for her betterment. Once she was strong enough and free, she could advocate against such horrible conditions. She could help. Until then, there wasn't much she could do but focus on surviving. However, she began to understand that she had a huge heart, full of love, which would either fester and infect her since there was no one in her life upon which to give it, or she could give it back to her very own self, someone who truly needed every ounce.

She had toyed with the lesson when she prayed for her peers. She felt it in force when she held her friend's fragile body in her arms. It was even woven within the notion that the orphanage was not her home. She may live there, but she needn't move in. What she learned was to love. She had just never before given any of it to her own self.

In the evenings, after lights out, she floated away to other places. Her dreams were vivid, and they felt so real. Escapes. Other lands. Other times.

She could be different people. Live entirely different lives. She did not have any books to read or television to spark her imagination. The only world outside of her prison was the scratchy voices in the radio. The headmistress listened to the radio every evening as she smoked her cigarettes and unwound. Eve's dreams were her release. Her imagination was what saved her. It helped her get through those formative years.

Eve's Aunt Rose would check in on her on rare occasions, presenting Eve with an orange or a book or a pair of new shoes. Of course, Eve never kept those things. They would be stolen the second her aunt stepped out of the front door. Eve adopted the notion that Aunt Rose must have been some sort of fairy godmother, dropping by with her luminescent fairy wings and fluttering off again with just a tickle of where she had landed, a glittery trail of giggles left in her ethereal wake.

It only occurred to Eve later that Aunt Rose could have taken her in, though she eventually realized that Rose never could have raised a child. It was not in her nature.

Aunt Rose was flighty and bombastic, her moods swinging like a violent pendulum. She would travel for weeks at a time and tell Eve of grand adventures, birthing babies, fleeting love affairs and sights she had witnessed, but nothing ever seemed to fill her soul. She wandered, not because she had any particular destination, but because she was lost. She wandered to find answers. To find herself. Eve wondered if Aunt Rose's heart had not been broken when she lost Eve's mother. She spoke as if they were sisters of the same soul. Perhaps when Eve's mother died, Aunt Rose was left to roam the earth, like some ghost death forgot. Eve's mother was the only real thing Rose ever seemed to care about, the only connection that seemed to truly matter to her. Unfortunately, that care did not include Eve.

Eve was asked to leave the orphanage on her sixteenth birthday. She wrote to Rose, but never received a reply. She thought perhaps Rose was on one of her extended trips. Eve slept in the corner on the concrete where the orphanage steps met the sidewalk. Despite all of her talk of freedom, she did not know where to go. The orphanage had been her home for so many years, Eve did not even know her way around the city. She was penniless, with no contacts upon whom she could call. She was like a caged bird that will not fly, even with the door to the cage left wide open. She was eventually chased off when that horrible, murdering girl spotted her and told her mother, the headmistress. Eve had the police called on her and was reported as a loiterer, an unwanted and unwelcome lingerer. She roamed around, lost and scared.

Fortunately, there was a large counterculture movement beginning to churn in the U.S. at that time. It allowed Eve to make friends and eat meals. Folks were more giving than they had been in previous years. Eve was often mistaken as a gypsy or a hippie, but she was really just homeless and hungry. She never integrated into a hippie lifestyle – the orphanage was enough communal living for her – but she did appreciate some of their premises. The notion of love being shared. The giving nature. As an example, one starry-eyed brunette spent weeks on the sidewalks of San Francisco teaching Eve how to read. She was a total stranger, but she showed up every day at the same time with a new book. Eve never even knew her name. She referred to herself as Sunshine. There was a sense of community and brotherhood that Eve had not had in the orphanage. She admired the freedom of the hippies and the way they expressed themselves, whether through art or music or poetry. She had so much stored within her that she had no way to release. She felt alone and adrift. If she had not felt a strong drive pushing her to move eastward, she could have easily found herself living among them forever. Strangers welcomed her and shared their meals. They smiled and hugged her and showed her love for the first time in her life. Eve knew there were those who stole and acted immorally, but she never saw that firsthand.

Eve started moving east. She felt a calling to keep heading in that direction. She picked up odd jobs waitressing and housekeeping and babysitting. She practiced her reading and spent her hours off in libraries across the country, progressing from the colorful picture books in the children's section to young adult frivolity and eventually to the adult sections.

She had a position as a housekeeper for a nice older couple when she met Red. He was the gardener, but Eve did not know that when he knocked on the door. The couple wasn't home and she dared not answer the door. He let himself in! Eve was armed with a kitchen knife, always ready to defend herself, when he spotted her and started laughing. He acted so familiar with her. She liked it. He felt like something which she had never known – he felt like home. She trusted his happy eyes and dropped the knife onto the laminate countertop when he started laughing. He followed Eve around the house as she did her chores the rest of the afternoon. They talked the entire time, from the scrubbing of the bathroom floors to changing the bedsheets and mopping the floors. They never ran out of conversation topics. He stayed at the house late that night to finish his planting, since he had neglected his own work to talk with her. She stayed with him and helped, the feel of the cool soil reassuring somehow. Like the magical man she had just met was actually real, as real as the dirt in her palm. Besides, there was nothing awaiting her at the hostel except a group of hostile travelers. It was worth sleeping at the train station that evening.

Eve and Red spent every day together after that. Eve fell madly in love with him and knew he was her everything, her best thing. He was her past and her present and her future. He felt exactly the same way. He rocked Eve to sleep like a baby the first night they spent together. She had one of her regular nightmares, but it upset him. He was distraught. He worried about Eve. She never had someone care about her before, much less as deeply and genuinely as he did. She loved him so much. She confessed to him her lifelong plague of nightmares. He tried to talk her through it. He loved her, too.

It was about two months later when Eve met her Aunt Rose for tea one day. As usual, Rose regaled her with tales about a train ride she had taken through the mountains, her seatmate's life story and all the scenery that had taken her breath away. When it was polite enough to interject, Eve finally spilled everything. She had not told a soul, besides Red, what was happening to her and how exciting it all was. But she also did not have anyone but Red to tell, except Aunt Rose. She was basically a stranger to Eve, so even if Rose broke her trust, it would not harm Eve's life in any way.

In her own way, Eve was trying to let Rose know that she was okay. She did alright, despite Rose not being around. Eve thought she was reassuring Rose as she recounted her lifelong secret, having met the man of her dreams, their discovery of her secret ability, all of it. Rose's steady expression and apathetic amber eyes remained unengaged throughout, the only betrayal to any emotion the crease in her forehead.

Eve stopped talking, and they just watched each other, silently, for what must have been minutes. An understanding slowly and silently passed between them. It was the look on Rose's face. It had given her away.

Eve listened blankly as Rose confessed everything. She said she was waiting for the right time to tell Eve all about her hereditary secret – the one she had discovered on her own. The secret she thought she had to shoulder all alone until she met Red. Rose at least had the decency to look ashamed as she admitted what she had done with Eve's father's money. Rose continued on until she had confessed everything. She looked as though she had unloaded a lead backpack of burdens. She breathed deeply, her conscience finally clear.

It was the last time Eve ever spoke to her "Aunt." Rose died the very next day. Eve did not know until she read about Rose's suicide in the Sunday paper. It said she had no known family. Eve wept quietly for her and for a life unfulfilled. Eve imagined the weight of Rose's imposing promise lifted from her, her own absolution allowing her to finally fly free from a life of ever chasing, never whole. Only later could Eve see with any clarity how she might not have known how to broach such a subject. She was struggling with the same dilemma with her own Aiyanna, whom she loved more than life. If Eve could wrestle for years over the idea of enlightening someone she loved with all of her heart, she could imagine how it must have never been such a priority for someone for whom Rose apparently cared very little. It was just...easier...not to tell Eve. Rose likely did not understand it herself, so Eve could understand that to some degree. She would have inevitably had questions or wanted some kind of support that Rose was never able to offer.

It was not a year after that encounter with Rose that Eve was kissing Red goodbye. Their entire worlds had changed within that fleeting window of knowing each other. It was not enough time. With him, Eve learned about Love and Life. War raged and society rebelled. Red probed her mind and her body, ever curious and hungry to know more. They grew together. Red had given Eve everything he had – his knowledge, his companionship, and his heart. She had given him all of the best parts of herself, too. But she never wanted to weigh him down with her foibles. She did not want to condemn him to a life for which he had never signed up. That was why, when he boarded that train dressed in his crisp uniform, bound for the other side of the world and some Hell they called Vietnam, Eve let him go. She never told him about the tiny human growing beneath her blue belted dress or how he had changed her life.

***

As expected, everything was different once Eve brought her baby home from the hospital. She was working retail, renting a one-bedroom apartment on the tougher side of town. She was struggling: with bills, with her baby, with her own brain. She was exhausted and lonely. Amara cried constantly and was discontent the majority of the time. How silly Eve felt for mentally complaining of sleep deprivation prior to having an infant around. They managed somehow, though, and as time has a habit of doing, years passed in a flash. If Eve tried, she could remember every detail of her fussy baby girl with the brilliant blue eyes and the endless nights of zero sleep. But thinking back on that time, the period itself went by in a blink. Just like that and Amara was a child, with likes and words and opinions and little feet that carried her into all kinds of naughtiness.

By the time Amara was ready to start school, Eve had landed an office job, with benefits, and had moved them to a safer neighborhood with a small yard and a reasonable rent payment. She sewed Amara new dresses and they played pretend with secondhand tea cups and stuffed animals. But Amara had always been a handful. Restless. Mischievous. She was barely speaking before Eve realized much of what she babbled were outright lies. Not imagination or creativity, but malicious untruths. When she got older, the lies sprouted roots that grew deep into her spirit and developed vines that climbed everything around her. She manipulated and used her gifts to benefit herself. She grew more and more lost, trapped between worlds and seduced by overindulgence.

Eve was managing an entire department by the time Amara was a teenager. For the first time in her life, Eve had an office of her own. She was able to afford some of the things they had to do without for so long – like new shoes or occasional dinners at the fancy Italian restaurant in town with the white tablecloths. Still, it was never enough. The more she was able to provide for Amara, the more Amara wanted. Her eye was always on a goal that was just out of reach. The next big thing. If Eve got her the purse with the designer's initials printed on it that she had been begging her mother for non-stop for months, Amara immediately wanted the shoes to match. No gratitude. Just entitlement. She did not stop for just a second to consider that Eve had to work two weeks' worth of hours to pay for it, saved until her birthday because she could not afford to give her daughter anything else and still keep the lights on.

At that point, Eve finally decided to revamp her attempts to teach Amara that everything that mattered in life was on the inside of herself. Eve could admit it – she had gotten lazy. It required less effort to just give in and give her daughter what she demanded than to fight the beast she became when Eve said no. Amara could not go through life that way; Eve would have to be stronger, for her sake.

Eve tried to foster Amara's creativity and allow her to be the free spirit she was obviously destined to become while trying to encourage honesty and integrity and work ethic. The latter traits just did not take. To date, Eve did not know if it was a flaw in her raising of Amara or if it was something born within her that prompted her to embrace delinquency and wickedness. Over the years, Eve tried to unburden herself of the guilt of it, but she had never been able to do so.

Eve's heart broke every day, but the more her daughter hurt her, the more love Eve ripped from herself to give to her. Amara was God's child, and she had goodness in her – Eve just knew she did. But no matter how much love Eve poured into her, it was never enough. She was thirstier than Eve was ever able to quench. Shamefully, Eve had to admit there was almost a sense of relief when Amara disappeared one day. She had ignored her mother's warnings of delving too deeply into things she did not yet understand. Eve had not had time to teach her daughter the finer points of what they had inherited. And Eve was just so tired. She was tired from loving Amara and watching her run full force down the wrong paths and being disappointed by her choices on a daily basis.

Eve was therefore both surprised, and not, when she opened the door one day to a shoebox stuffed with a baby on her stoop. It had a short, scribbled index note as explanation. It was just like Amara to put such a dramatic presentation to the abandonment of her child.

Aiyanna, Eve named her, that sweet, grinning baby girl who became the light of her life, her little blossom. Eve raised her with all of the love that never took hold with Amara. And as Ai got older and naturally became more curious about her mother, Eve could think of nothing to say.

Eve had no idea how to begin to describe Amara. She was ashamed to admit it, but she always skirted the question with allusions that Aiyanna's mother had died. For all Eve knew, she had. Eve never wanted to lie to Aiyanna, not even by omission, but the truth was she really had no information to give to her. There were so many more options to what might have happened to Amara, much more than Ai could possibly understand at such a young age. Eve waited to properly explain it all one day.

CHAPTER 19
Amara

People tell lighthearted jokes about making deals with devil. Amara was never kidding.

She had dreams from a very young age. Dark dreams of death and plague and starvation. Haunting images of flies crawling over the opened eyes of family members. Charity taking the form of hooded death, eliminating all she loved. Pangs in her stomach from a hunger that never quit. Fire and pain. Betrayal.

Amara's dreams made her aware. She never wanted to be without. Poverty was for the pitiful. Money could afford her the sort of lifestyle she deserved, and money was easy enough to earn in the present day and age. She would not have to be relegated to starvation due to some station or class into which she was born, nor should she have to want for anything.

Okay, so she was unfortunately born to a single mother with an infinitesimal income. Her mother never appreciated the things that money could buy. Eve always said that the best things about living were free. Sure...okay. Amara fervently disagreed.

The first recollection Amara had of that feeling of self-empowerment was when she was but a small child. She was playing in the backyard of their first house. It was a small yard, lined with a shallow forest at the edge and quiet, elderly neighbors on either side. Amara hated it. She missed the noise and paper-thin walls of the old apartment she had shared with her mother. She could listen in on other peoples' lives, and she liked it. Especially the nighttime noises.

"Amara!" she heard Eve shout from the back door in a sing-song voice. "Dinnertime!"

Amara ignored her. A tiny frog had caught her attention, so she plucked it from the grass into her small palm. It was frozen, its big froggy eyes wide, paralyzed with fear. She thumped its fat belly to see what it would do. Naturally, it tried to leap from her grasp. So she tossed it onto an ant bed a foot or so away. She watched with fascination as the ants covered it immediately and claimed their prize. The frog writhed and twitched and fought to free himself. The ants devoured the frog within just a few seconds. For the first time ever, Amara felt like she could breathe. She was aware of the hot blood coursing through her little body, the air filling her lungs. She was grateful for the burden of living, the gift she never asked to receive, the thing she had always hated. She decided in that second that she wanted to be the ants, never the frog.

"Amara! Do you hear me calling you?"

She intentionally took a full minute to stand up, dust off her frilly sundress and look toward her frustrated mother, who was staring at her open-mouthed. "Yes, Eve. I'm coming." Amara knew how angry it made her mother for her to use her first name.

"Amara Astilbe Burns," Eve gritted through her teeth as she stormed into the yard, barefoot, and tucked her hand into the small child's armpit, "You will call me mother! I am tired of telling you!"

Amara just blinked at her because she knew her mother hated that, too. Amara smiled, though, as her mother slapped her ankle at the ant biting her pale flesh.

***

It was the kind of cold that stung your cheeks and sent ice through your veins. She wrapped her knit shawl tighter around her shoulders. For weeks, their rickety wagon bounced them across fields and over creeks. John hunted their dinner with the other men, when he could, but days like this one were harder. They had skipped supper last night and breakfast today. They were running out of supplies, and they were exhausted. The entire wagon train was tired, but they had a while yet before their destination. She wondered if all of the West was this cold.

She thought of her family back home. In truth, she missed Virginia. She wondered if her sister had ended up marrying Mr. Stanley after all or if Mama had recovered from her cough.

She turned toward her husband. She knew when she wed John that he had adventure in his soul. She loved him for it. She loved him completely, and she would have followed him anywhere. She traced his profile against the morning sun with her eyes. His long eyelashes and straight nose. His square jaw hidden by a full beard. His broad shoulders and strong hands holding the horses' rains. Perfection. Rugged and worldly and the most attractive man to her. Despite his skinniness since they had been on this trek or his temper flaring at inopportune times, her heart was full. She had committed her life to John, and she would happily spend the rest of it loving him as much as she did in that moment. She was waiting for the right time to tell him that there would soon be three of them.

***

With a jolt, Amara awoke from another vivid dream. Fuck it all. John in her dream was Ronnie in the bed with her. One and the same. What she felt in her sleep and upon waking was what must have been love. Ronnie mumbled something sleepily and pulled Amara closer to him, wrapping his arm around her waist. She was the little spoon, protected by his body, his warm exhales on her neck. It was all she wanted for the rest of her life – to wake up with that man. God damn it all to Hell, she thought she loved him. That just would not do.

***

Amara stared at the plastic pregnancy test, mocking her with its readout. It was the second one she had taken, certain that the first was some sort of mistake. A glitch. A lie. As sexual as she was, she was always careful not to get herself knocked up. She could not afford to ruin her body for some slobbering, snot-nosed curtain climber, only to be tied to some man for the rest of her life. One man would never be enough. That would be her own, personal Hell. She had not had her period for a while, but they never were regular, and she had not thought much about it with all the drugs and sex and loss of time.

Though there had been many men before and since, she knew it was Ronnie's. She had gotten comfortable with him, forgetting her pill some mornings, too high to care. She broke her own rule of no routines. If she were being honest with herself, a part of her had liked it. She liked being with him.

She saw it in his face one Halloween morning, and she knew she had to go. He had looked at her like she was his future or something. He had fallen in love. Not just the normal infatuation, where they wonder if they can keep her as their sexy little secret for however long it takes for their wives to catch on. No, it was actual love that sparkled in his hazel eyes. Truth be told, Amara had felt it, too. That just would not do. She was going places, and she could not be held back by some regular Joe Schmoe with no regular job or any real future. She did not want to get stuck.

So she let his best friend fuck her. He had wanted to since they were first introduced, and it was the easiest way to get out. It was not a memorable experience, but Amara did recall the look on Donnie's face. Utter destruction.

And now, pregnancy. She was always being punished.

***

It was too late for an abortion. Amara was too close to term or something, the doctor said.

She told her current beau, a wealthy stockbroker with a boring marriage and an unfulfilled fetish, that it was a consultation for plastic surgery. Thus, the need for all that cash. The truth was, Amara wanted the best OBGYN in the city. She needed to get rid of the thing inside of her.

But doc said he could not. That was a hard pill to swallow. In too short a time to prepare for it, she had begun to show. The alien inside of her was ruining her life. The stockbroker got rid of her as soon as her bump began to grow, so she lost the apartment that was funded by him. Men were repulsed by her for the first time ever, though it did seem they harbored some sort of paternal guilt because they paid double the usual for blowjobs. There were some freaks who were into the whole pregnant mommy thing, but she could not keep dealing with those losers.

She could feel the parasite move around inside of her. It was disturbing. She attempted to miscarry a couple of times, but to no avail. The beast in her belly was forcing her to stand outside of grocery stores and shopping malls, hours on her swollen feet, begging for money. She actually had to beg. She had even more anger than usual boiling beneath her stretched skin. The thing was controlling her, stealing her nutrition and her looks and her opportunities. She hated it.

Amara had the baby in a motel bathroom. She paid for the room with a fistful of small bills from a panhandling stint a day earlier. She was enjoying a good night's rest on a real bed, sprawled out as best she could with her round belly and achy back. The pain woke her in the middle of the night. She could not afford a hospital, or a taxi to the hospital, or the questions and records that came with it all. So, she had her baby there in the dirty, square shower that was missing some of its pea green tiles.

She held the tiny human close to her, rocking and shushing it, just to get it to stop screaming. If they were kicked out of the room, she had no idea what they would do. They fell asleep together like that, bloody, naked and exhausted.

CHAPTER 20
Ronnie

Amara, his gorgeous blonde vixen with the perfect dimple in her devious smile, emerged from the silk sheets elegantly. She was almost serpentine in the way she moved, but she was like the Garden of Eden, and Ronnie could not resist tasting the fruit. Women had always made him stupid, but this one blew his mind. He pushed himself to a sitting position against the headboard. He crossed his arms behind his head and admired the curve of her naked back, her long blonde hair tousled from sex, the swell of her perfectly round ass as she immodestly moved around the room. She writhed when she walked, and he loved the way her hips moved in a figure eight motion, her full breasts slightly bouncing. The tattoo on her ankle of a flame seemed to dance and move as she padded into the bathroom.

Knowing her the last six months meant everything for his career and his creativity. He wrote more songs for the band than ever before. Lyrics rushed from his brain, his hands barely swift enough to scratch them onto paper. Poetry and emotion and ideas churned in a sea of inspired thought. He felt more physical and alive than ever before. His highs were higher than they had ever been. He was a god onstage, his movements and his mannerisms and voice in perfect synchronization. Memorable. The band booked more gigs than they ever had and reveled in their first wads of cash income. Ronnie could actually afford hotel rooms and meals that did not come from paper sacks and sheets with decent thread counts. His creativity flowed forth as often as his seed. It was all because of his Amara. She lit his fire. The woman was his muse, his goddess, and he had never been higher in his life.

Ronnie had a bit of a hero complex – he could admit it. He had a history of bringing home strays. The unemployed. The tortured. They would inevitably stay too long, until they had fallen completely out of love and out of money. It would become awkward, each of them aloof but not knowing how to end it. The sex would stop, with what felt like a sea of sheets between them in Ronnie's full-sized bed. He became revolted at the sight of them. He would have to make excuses not to touch them. Eventually, probably much later than is reasonable, he would make some kind of excuse and recuse myself from his apartment if they had not already. He would disappear for a while or give them the rest of the money he had to find their own paths. He was extremely generous, if not a little fickle.

Women were just so beautiful and soft and sweet. He loved how they needed men. How they needed him. He understood that every woman wanted a man to tell her she was beautiful and special. To save her from the harshness of the world. To save her from herself.

The first time Ronnie saw her was outside of a convenience store one night when he was running in for some smokes before a gig. She was definitely a stray, with greasy hair and a beer koozie as a coin collector for the donations she solicited out of customers. He watched her for a few minutes. She did not beg for money so much as just accept it. Guys would use the process of pulling out some cash as an extended excuse to stay near her and engage her in small talk. She would smile – *oh my god*, he thought, *a dimple!* – and giggle and touch their arms and they would eagerly keep giving her dollar bills. Ronnie had to admit it – the girl was a knockout, even then. Big titties about to bust out of her undersized t-shirt, cut to reveal her amazing cleavage. A tiny waist he could wrap his hands around. Long, slender legs stretching endlessly out of her high-waisted mini skirt.

In keeping with his ways, Ronnie took her home. She smiled when he approached her. She told him she liked his long hair. She played with his one earring, gently caressing the lobe of his ear. He got hard immediately. She saw it and smiled. His tight, acid washed jeans were not roomy enough to conceal what he was packing. She liked what she saw. He had her within the hour in the back of the band's van while the other members waited outside. He had not even had to give her any money. Following that, she bounced enthusiastically in the front row of the concert, smiling at him and biting her lip throughout the show. It was hard for him to focus on the show. She blew him as soon as he exited the stage. She did not even care that the crew and his bandmates were milling about backstage. A small crowd gathered in the couple of minutes it took her to finish and swallow. They cheered and clapped when she pulled away. Laughing, she wiped her mouth, stood, adjusted her bra and took a bow. Oh, she was Ronnie's kind of girl. He could not wait to get her home.

In the early light of dawn, Ronnie woke to the most beautiful woman he had ever seen. The grease in her hair or the bruises on her arms did not mar her at all. She was naked, and the curvature in her hips and spine was so beautiful. Quietly, he pulled out his pencil and pad and sketched her perfect body. Her beauty was inspiring. Her sex blew his mind. When she woke, they shared a blunt and a shower. She starting saying she had no place to go over her bagel and cup of coffee. He offered up his apartment without hesitation. She could stay if she would just clean the cat's litter box. That would be her only job, and she did it perfectly for three days before the cat disappeared mysteriously. But after three days, Ronnie was already completely in love.

He shook his head, clearing his thoughts of his reminiscing. He loved her then, and he loved her now. He heard the shower start up. He snorted another line before he followed her into the bathroom to have his way with her once more against the white tile wall. Even that rhythm sparked another song idea. She was so beautiful.

Dried off and spritzed with perfume, Ronnie watched Amara roll the black fishnet thigh-highs he bought her up the length of her long legs. She adjusted her sequined devil horn headband and turned to him, her legs open just enough to glimpse her shiny red panties. "Are you seriously going as that?"

"What? Lethal Weapon was the best movie of this year! This costume is bitchin'!"

Amara rolled her eyes and poked him with her pitchfork. "Let's go. You know Halloween is my favorite holiday, and I'm done wasting my time arguing with you."

He loved her cold indifference. He loved everything about her. She was one of those women you could chase forever but never quite capture. He adored it. That was different from the sad, needy women he had always brought home. He was always hungry for more of her. It was like giving a starving man enough food to survive, but not quite enough to satiate his appetite.

But when he caught her at that Halloween party with her black mini dress bunched up around her waist, palms pressed against the wall and panties around her ankles, the drummer in his band wildly and roughly having his way with her, everything Ronnie knew came crashing down. The Halloween music changed to one of his songs. It played on as she watched him watching her, no concern at all on her perfect face, the two of them still and staring at each other for what seemed like an eternity as his bandmate pumped rhythmically to the song he had written for her.

She ruined him, his *leanan sidh*. He never played music again. He could not write another lyric. Her apathetic face haunted him every time he picked up a pen or his guitar. His sheets were the ones they had used to make a pillow fort when it was storming outside, so he had to burn them in the dumpster behind his building. That shower was where they sang his song lyrics as they washed each other's hair. He tore out every tile her breasts had touched when he bent her over or where her she rested her foot when she shaved her legs. He had to pick different places to purchase his cigarettes, since the convenience store was where they met and the bodega was where he bought her a candy ring and dramatically proposed to her on the sidewalk out front. His friends did not understand and got tired of hearing about her, so they ended up avoiding each other until there was no more friendship to maintain. His old bandmates were disappointed, then disgusted, that he could not produce any more songs, and he damn sure could not work with the Judas drummer. They moved on without him. He became isolated, alone with his soured memories.

His days were filled with thoughts of her, his nights restless with growing anger and remorse. Ceaselessly, he ruminated on her going on about her life, with no concern at all for how she had ruined his. He lay awake at night, wondering if she was fucking another man in that exact moment, or if she were having more of those crazy dreams. His hatred grew with each day, rage germinating inside his soul until it swallowed everything.

He would find her. He had to find her. And when he did, he would destroy her. Like she destroyed him.

CHAPTER 21
Aiyanna

Lightning flashes dot my dreams. Vignettes that seem familiar but make no sense to me. Murky waves of black ink crash and break upon me, forcing me down, down, down. Lost in the darkness, not knowing which way is up. My body tossed and bent like a plastic bag in the breeze. My lungs about to burst.

Warfare and wounded men. Blood soaking the muddy ground, as if it rained down from heaven itself in crimson drops of death. Weapons lying as still and useless as the lifeless hands from which they fell.

Kisses, deep and long, heartbeat pounding in my ears, eyes like emerald swimming pools.

Cooper's wet kisses licking away my tears welcomed me back to consciousness. I opened my eyes to a face full of red fur, wet black nose, happy, amber eyes and a wagging curly tail. He kissed my cheeks with puppy licks. I smiled, despite myself, and scratched behind his ears. I pulled him to me and hugged his hot little dog body, my face buried in his furry, fat neck.

"More nightmares, Ai?" my Jamma inquired tenderly, already knowing the answer. She was propped up in the rocking chair at the foot of the bed. She had stopped rocking. There was a wad of teal yarn in her lap and purple knitting needles lying on top. She cleared her throat, clasped her hands over her knitting and waited patiently.

I sat up in bed. The surrounding air hit my moist back and neck and made me aware of the tacky sweat veiled over my skin. I felt clammy. I mopped the oily sweat from my face with the neck of my soggy t-shirt. I felt dirty and alive and confiscated in a greasy prison.

I couldn't keep in my sea of thoughts any longer. They spilled forth.

"It's so messed up, Jamma. It's like how they say that when you remember something, you're really just remembering the last time you remembered it. I feel like that all the time. Like these dreams are real. Even the nightmares. All of it. Like maybe I've played them so many times in my mind they feel real. But they do. They feel *real*."

Jamma nodded her understanding.

"I'm just...miserable. There are no other words. I'm broken. I somehow landed in this wrong life, and...somewhere...on some parallel plane of existence, everything went my way."

I couldn't believe I was crying again. Wasn't there some kind of physiological limit to tear production? When would it stop being so excruciating?

Jamma cleared her throat.

"Aiyanna, there is something very important I must tell you."

Jamma had a look on her face I had never seen before. A wrinkle of consternation planted itself between her brows, and a sadness and uncertainty shimmered in her eyes. The uncertainty was startling, as I had never seen that in her face before. If anyone blazed through life with confidence, it was Jamma.

I blinked at her, my sandpaper eyes swollen with exhaustion and grief, my body too tired to assemble any words.

"I would like for you to see a counselor."

Boom. There it was. I wondered when she would get tired of my depressed state. Even someone like Jamma was sure to have her limits. I was holed up in her house, contributing nothing. She kept trying. She left plates for me for every meal, faithfully collecting the untouched plate from the meal before and replacing it with a warm one. She opened the window shades every morning, though I could not care less for the sunlight. She replaced my sheets with clean ones on the rare occasion I broke away from my bed for bathroom breaks. She smiled at my ill and unpleasant sighs and grumbles. I knew I must have been miserable company. I just could not see the light anymore.

I couldn't remember the last time I had showered. I could smell myself. I couldn't sleep, despite that being the only thing I wanted to do. I couldn't eat. Nothing tasted as it did before. Every morsel that hit my stomach made me feel ill and the ungrateful recipient of another day alive.

I could think of nothing but him. It was driving me mad — I could feel it. But I obsessed nonetheless. I had always felt a pull toward madness, anyway, but the thought that some version of myself was happy and in love, with a life worth living, wouldn't vacate my thoughts. Some doppelganger of mine stole my story. Her happiness and her future were supposed to be my own, in this version of reality. I hated her. I embraced that hatred.

No one understood that something wrong had happened. More than just losing the love of my life, something unnatural had occurred. There was no other explanation for it. My life, mapped out and on course like a high-speed train, refracting sunlight from its gleaming body, bound for a destination unknown, nothing to stop it from racing down the tracks set out before it, had hopped off course. The tracks had changed, something terrible had unfolded, and it was a fiery wreck of mangled metal and dead bodies, screaming survivors forever devastated from what had just happened.

I knew Ethan and I were still together in some other life. I felt it with full confidence. We had to be. Why else would we ever have found each other? Why did we know each other before we even knew each other? Why would God have presented me with someone so perfectly matched with my imperfections, just to turn him and tear him from me? To take everything I had only just learned about loving a man and grind it into the dirt like it was nothing more than dead leaves? I just knew that that wasn't the ending to our story. I just knew that in some other universe, we were in love, and there was some parallel world where everything had worked out and he was, at that moment, mowing the lawn or making dinner or laughing with his contagious chuckle. That was where I was supposed to be. Yet here I was, stuck in the wrong story. Who could understand that? Who could understand the deep torment of that thought?

What if I ended it? What if I just offed myself? Religion ruled that I shouldn't. Would I go to Hell? Would I see Ethan again? Or would I just be worm food? I recalled Ethan's optimism that something as simple as death would not end everything between two people who loved each other. But what is more finite, and infinite, than death? And what if just one of the two people felt love anymore? What if that love had already ended? Could I find it again in the afterlife? I no longer wanted this life. I loved my Jamma, but it just wasn't enough. I was so tired. Tired of trying and even more tired of failing. Everything required effort, and for what? What did I have to show for trying to be a good person?

"It's not like that," Jamma said softly, interrupting my thoughts. "I know what you're thinking, and I want you to know you can take all of the time you need to heal. I will always be here, and I will always look after you."

Always was a promise I now knew could never be made. That was a lie.

"I have someone in particular I want you to see." I had never seen this side of Jamma before. She nervously rolled the fabric of the quilt between her fingers. She looked like a shy child giving a report to the entire classroom.

I was angry and hurt. It felt like betrayal somehow, her asking me to farm out my emotions to some hack, instead of wrapping them around me like a depressing blanket of gloom, heavy and familiar. No one understood. No one could possibly comprehend. How could she think it would help to have to get dressed and sit on some sofa and expose all of my turmoil for some stranger to sift through as they write out the invoice for their all-important and exorbitant time? For the first time ever, it felt like Jamma didn't really know me at all.

"Aiyanna, my beautiful blossom, I know how you feel."

"You don't understand —"

"Yes, I do," she said sharply, cutting me off. "More than you could possibly know."

She sighed and softened her voice. "Now, you know me. I would never recommend something I didn't think would be good for you. I have thought about this long and hard, and I want you to do it. Please. For me."

I was going to protest, but something in her eyes made me stop.

"I know where you are right now. I've been there before," she spoke softly, almost a whisper. "There is an entire universe for you to discover within yourself, and I don't want you to be trapped on this one planet. Going to this therapist is like building the rocket you will need to shoot across the sky. Please, blossom."

She was so earnest. And she looked so... human. Jamma had always been more than that. She glowed with an indescribable effervescence. She was a constant anchor, always steady, always sure. But now she sat in front of me, nervous and small. Her eyes looked tired, her body fragile and bent over the bed. The skin on her arms was like a suit two sizes too big, and it draped over her slight bones like crepe paper. My heart may have been broken, but I still felt a wave of love for her rush over the shattered pieces. I couldn't say no.

***

I laid in the bathtub, soaking, drifting in and out of consciousness as I gazed at the trees through the large pane window in the bathroom. I squinted to blur my eyes, the foliage a smeared painting of reds and oranges and yellows. Fall had always been my favorite time of year, but I was afraid it would forever after represent a sort of falling apart. All of the color and fullness of life lay brown and crisp upon the ground, stripped down to the barest parts. To brave the cold winter alone.

Jamma, in her precious, passive way, had drawn me a bath. It was a kind gesture with a purpose. I guess I had gotten pretty ripe since I'd stopped caring about basically anything anymore. My hygiene had become an issue.

I skimmed my hand along the surface of water, my fingers pruned. That feeling always fascinated me, transitioning from the air into the weightlessness of the water. How it pulled and felt heavy until the water wrapped itself around my hand, then the feeling of weightless floating in outer space. When the bubbles parted, I could not see through the water. It was a dark blue from the bubble bath used, almost black, and for a moment, fear seized my heart. I despised being anywhere near water where you couldn't see the bottom – even if it were only a few inches deep. I wouldn't get into a pool unless I could see straight through it, and lakes and the ocean...forget about it. Even as I acknowledged the weight of my bottom heavily seated on the porcelain bottom of the tub, only inches deep, the trill of terror twittered through the small nerves in my spine.

I used my feet to find the drain, then popped it with my toes and rose out of the water. I rinsed off with the shower and plodded back toward my bed, where Jamma had faithfully changed the sheets while I was in the tub. That was enough doing for the day. At least I wouldn't smell when I went to the psychiatrist the next day.

CHAPTER 22
Evelyn, the First

Sliding left somewhere on the chronological "line" of time…
The pain was unbearable. Evelyn realized she had had no real idea that it would be like this. No one warned her. It was only ever mentioned as a miracle, a beautiful experience.

Evelyn was congratulated as an expecting lady. The wise older women in the grocery store told her, the sad widow she was, how her baby would be a blessing. They placed their jeweled and polished hands on her belly and smiled as though she were presented with a gift. Not one of them warned her of the unbearable pain or the mess or the risk. Not even Rose, her midwife and her best friend. Evelyn's parents were both departed, so she received no advice from that avenue, either.

Evelyn loved her little one already. She laughed at the way she could tickle its tiny foot from outside her swollen belly, receiving a kick in response. She loved how it wiggled reassuringly when she felt alone. The little butterbean ate with Evelyn and dreamed with Evelyn. It was the only part of Randall still living. It was her. Them. A tiny little soul. She loved it so much, but it needed to be born already. She could not hold on much longer.

Sweat and excrement and blood and other repulsive bodily materials covered what had once been clean white bedding. *Deathbed* was such an innocuous and poetic way of describing a scene more horrible than she could have imagined. She could see the blood pooling out from her body. She could feel her life draining.

The ladies in the room were covered in blood. Rose was the color of her namesake. Her assistant held a handkerchief to her face, but it didn't disguise the terror in her eyes. And yet, Evelyn's only thought was for her child. The tiny, foreign creature that had formed inside of her. An actual human being that she had helped to create and germinate. The small seedling that would push back when she poked it and would wiggle her awake in the night. It was dying, and so was Evelyn.

Her midwife and dear friend placed her hands on Evelyn's knees and set her jaw like she did when she was being excessively stubborn. "I need another push."

Evelyn would have given anything to have Randall with her. She clenched her fist as if his hand held hers. The War had taken him, but not before he had blessed their marriage with a little one. He loved her. Despite his transgressions, she knew he loved her.

"Rose…" she whispered, tears tipping over the edge of her eyes. It was such an odd sensation to reach the exact limitation of what she could command of her own body. She had always been so capable. "I can't do this, Rose."

"You will. You must," she said confidently in return. Her watery amber eyes and the fine line that appeared on her forehead betrayed her. There would be no grand outcome to this.

A warmth ran over Evelyn then. There was no better description for it but the Hand of God. A vision of her weathered tombstone: Evelyn Adelaide Burns, wife of Randall and mother of Eve, 1920 – 1944. The warmth and rational understanding of the situation calmed every nerve in Evelyn's body and put her mind at peace. It embraced her and whispered the truth. She knew she would not survive. It was up to her, in that very moment's actions, whether her child would.

She shrieked as she had never done before as her creation ripped her to pieces.

"It's a girl," Rose said, her voice breaking as she pulled Evelyn's baby girl from her body. She handed the small bundle to her assistant and could no longer choke back a sob. She allowed herself, at last, to acknowledge the overwhelming emotion filling the room. She had saved the child, but she was witnessing the death of her closest friend.

As the gray haze gripped her, someone placed Evelyn's baby girl into her arms. She could barely hold her, her body weak and dying, but that baby was the most beautiful thing she had ever witnessed. She was everything in the world, all of Evelyn and everything she had ever known or done, in one tiny body. Hundreds and thousands of people, each with their own stories and loves and regrets and mistakes, had led to the birth of that baby. Her baby. Generations upon generations culminating in the life of her child. She was everything, and Evelyn loved her with all of the life left in her.

Her baby's blue eyes bore into Evelyn's as if she understood. She did not have that lost look of newborns. It was as if she knew exactly what was going on. She was still young enough to know. Someone picked her up, wrapping her in a bundle of blankets, as Rose leaned close to her friend. She gripped Evelyn's hand.

"Please take care of her," Evelyn whispered, too weak to wipe the hot tears from her face. "Rose, she has to know. Tell her. Please...she must know who she is."

And then the room was filled with white. Light and love so brilliant, it was blinding. Evelyn was warmed by it, like holding her hands over the fireplace on a mid-winter night. She could see the faces of her father and her mother, an indescribable and all-encompassing love filling her heart to the brim. Randall was there, waiting for her with arms outstretched. The light was so beautiful. It was the most magnificent thing she had ever seen.

"Do you see it, Rosie?" she whispered, uncertain whether her friend could hear her. A deep peace, one which words will never properly explain, overcame her.

"I will name her for you," Rose cried. The last thing Evelyn ever heard was, "I will name her Eve."

CHAPTER 23
Amara

The fire bit at her ankles like a pack of dogs, ripping and tearing her flesh. She refused to cry out, though the pain was excruciating. Her flesh split and sizzled. The smell of it consumed her. The bloodthirsty crowd of townsfolk staring at her with wildness and anger in their eyes would not get the show for which they had waited.

They called her witch and sorceress, spitting at her with hatred and disdain. They cheered – *they cheered* – at her slow and agonizing death. Those Christians who preached of forgiveness and neighborly love, the most religious and moral among us, clutched their crosses and smiled at her execution. Forgive them for they know not what they do. They were certain of their righteousness. They despised her wicked way, her wayward morals, but what truly bothered them were her dealings with their preacher.

His wife had caught him in her skirts, in the very church from whence he spoke his sermon every Sunday, so now she was paying the price. He was there, too, their fearless leader, piously gripping his Bible beyond the flames and all the more respected for having beaten his battle with temptation.

She knew not why she was hated by the women in the parish and avoided by the men. She was young, five years more than a decade alive, beautiful and unmarried. Her father had recently fallen ill and left her to be with the Lord. She was alone in the world, and she was so lonely.

She was expected to be a woman, but she still felt like a lost child. That was how her purity was sacrificed when she allowed her neighbor into her house alone. It was improper for them to be alone together, but he was the only one to pay her a visit after her father left for Heaven. He stopped by to offer his condolences and leave her a loaf of bread and cheese. She had not left her home since her father had gone. She was lightheaded from hunger and mad with sorrow.

Her neighbor's salt and pepper beard and the wrinkle at the corners of his eyes reminded her of her father. She was lost and brokenhearted, and she just wanted to feel protected again. Her neighbor was at a loss on how to comfort her in her grief, his eyes shifting nervously as he wrung his hands. She sat him down and carefully crawled into his lap. He sat motionless, stunned, but for her, it felt so lovely. She asked him to hold her the way her father had done. He acquiesced and rocked her like a newborn babe.

He was a gentle soul. She was wrong. She had sinned. He was kindhearted and she had tempted him. He attempted to excuse himself and get back to his family. She asked him to stay. He was a good man in God's eyes. He had a wife and seven children. She was like a starving person, though, desperate for company. She simply could not tolerate being left alone again. He attempted to excuse himself again, despite her tears. She kissed him to make him stay. She gave in to the Devil. She placed his hands on her body, silently begging him for his time. She wanted him with her. She wanted him all around her and inside her. She did not want to be alone. She was led by the Devil when she rubbed the front of his breeches and kissed his lips and his ears and his scruffy cheeks. His nervous protests gave in to his human needs. He kissed her greedily, hungrily. He, too, was desperate, it seemed. She liked the way his beard felt against her face and the thick muscles beneath his clothes. Her blood rushed through her limbs. She felt alive. She needed him to stay with her. She was enveloped in sin when she lifted her black linen mourning clothes and straddled his shaking legs, joining him to her in flesh and soul.

She would soon be destitute and displaced, for she had no other family or kin. Despite what dark future was in store for her, she was not alone in those minutes. The man cared about her. That was what she thought. He moaned, gripping and pulling her down further so he was deeply a part of herself. He shuddered. Then with a stricken look, he lifted her from him. Panic took the place of sadness in his eyes, and he apologized. He wiped himself off and pulled up his breeches. He apologized again, tears streaming into his beard. His wide eyes darted around as he hasted out of her house with more apologies. There, alone on the wooden floor, bleeding into her dress, she felt more alone than ever. She had sinned enormously. She pushed herself into a prayer position and begged the Father not to forsake her.

That had been weeks before. The Lord had not been enough to fill her heart, and He had not seen fit to forgive her sins or provide for her. She was starving, and no more neighbors stopped by with Christian gifts. When she ventured out to seek some sustenance, none of the townsfolk looked at her. No one spoke to her or acknowledged her. She was alone in the church, praying for a friend, praying for deliverance. She was lost and lonesome. She would soon have no place to live. She needed someone to pity her or help her in a Christian way. She was hungry. She was at fault. She was a sinner. It was her penance.

In desperation, she told her truth to the preacher that day. He hugged her as she cried, and she let him. She permitted the preacher push her hair away from her crying eyes. It felt good to be touched and not treated like a pariah. She allowed him to lean in close enough to smell the tobacco on his breath as he prayed with her. She was surprised when he softly kissed her neck, but she still let him. She permitted his holy hands to roam her body lightly, then harder. She longed for human touch. She was afraid, but she did halt him when his breathing got heavy and he pressed his body against hers in a firm hug. For those things, she was wrong and she deserved her punishment.

She was a sinner and he was a man of God. It felt good to be embraced, like she had been forgiven. For those embraces could not be sinful if the preacher felt compelled to perform them. She did, however, tell him to stop when he lifted her skirts and ran his hands along her thighs. She knew that was not right. It had hurt when she let her neighbor hold her, and she did not care for the afterward. It felt against God's will. Her God had greater things in mind for her. She was a sinner, but she was not lost.

The preacher, though! She slapped his hands away when he grabbed her waist. She pleaded for him to stop. He did not. She fought him as he ripped at her dress like an animal. She clawed his face and strained to shove him away. She begged him to stop as he bent her over the altar and plunged himself inside of her. She yelped in pain and shrieked for help. Hot tears rolled down her cheeks. She cried to the Lord and in answer to her prayer, the preacher's wife walked in, flooding the dark church with brilliant sunshine. Deliverance. The Lord had not forsaken her.

She stood speechless and still as the preacher rushed to pull up his breeches, excuses fumbling out of his mouth like a serpent's spittle. The girl was shaking so much it was difficult to wipe the tears from her face with the torn sleeve of her dress. Her savior, the wife, strode angrily across the church floor toward her husband. Then she proceeded to slap the girl firmly across her face. She called her horrible names and accused her of tempting her husband, a righteous and God-fearing man.

The girl's arms were tied behind her to the wooden stake. The villagers who called for her burning were those who averted their eyes when she was starving and pulling weeds from the earth to eat, to save herself and the child growing within her. The villagers were the same who sat stiffly and righteous in the church. Those who said their prayers every day. Her neighbors. People who had known her for the entirety of her life. They cheered for her death. The preacher watched her burn without emotion, his Bible clutched to his chest, his eyes unrepentant.

Flames used her skirts to crawl up her legs like serpents, eating the poisoned flesh from her bones. She had never felt such pain in any life. Every nerve was a heightened agony. Her hair was burning off in clumps. The smell of flesh frying engulfed her, and she finally cried out. She screamed with all of the life left in her, for all of the wrongs she had committed, for all of the pain she had caused and for her the loss of what could have been for her child. She screamed for forgiveness and for mercy. Her throat was raw and seared with smoke as she rolled her eyes toward the clear azure sky. The black smoke mingled with a wisp of white clouds as she begged the Lord to accept her soul in Heaven and forgive her of her mortal sins.

***

She awoke as Amara, terrified, in a four-square-foot shower stall, the tiles covered in thick blood and placenta, a tiny baby in her arms. Her thin, bruised legs stretched out before her, as best they could in the stall. The red and orange flame tattoo on her ankle looked as if it were on fire. She could not let go of the vision of those eyes staring at her through the blaze – Ronnie's eyes.

Her baby was awake, staring at her with her own gentle, innocent blue eyes, a dimple in one cheek. It was like looking at a blank-slate infant version of herself. If this poor child had any part of her mother in her, she was cursed already. The thought of that filled her eyes with actual tears. God had forsaken her, as she had forsaken him. Her body racked with silent sobbing, for her baby's soul and for own. She was shocked – she had not felt anything real in as long as she could remember. Face to face with that tiny person in that dingy motel room, Amara decided to do the only decent thing she had ever accomplished in her entire life. It was her baby's only chance. She would give her over to the only person she knew who could teach her to be good.

CHAPTER 24
Rose

*You can see by now we are jumping around in time...it is not always so
linear, you know...it is weebly wobbly...*

"It's a girl," Rose said, her voice breaking through the swelling lump of raw
emotion in her throat. The beauty and the tragedy of the moment was too
real for her.

She had been a midwife for years, having learned the craft from her
mother, who had learned from hers. She liked the medical procedure of it,
the literal holding of life in her hands. She was well enough acquainted with
the proper steps of it. The smells. The sounds. This was not like those. She
knew it was not going to be a happy ending. Eve's face was an ashen color,
and blood was everywhere. Much more blood than there should have
been.

She squeezed her friend's hand, wishing she could do something to
keep Evelyn alive. Rose knew the female body. She understood its nooks
and processes. She had spared many women and many infants during
complications. She saved them. Why could she not save Evelyn? She was
impotent.

Evelyn was Rose's closest friend, and she loved her. She was a light in
Rose's world. Evelyn was one of those people who gave warmth and

comfort when she had only ever known shades of gray, like a firefly in the darkness or a soft blanket on a cold night. Have you any idea what it's like to see the sun when you have been blind your whole life?

Evelyn whispered to her, "Please take care of her," and begged Rose to tell little Eve their family secret. Then she was gone. Just like that, the light was snuffed out. With nothing but a whisper of smoke to know that it was ever there.

Rose really had tried. She washed the rest of her mother from the child with a basin of bloody-pink water and a clean cloth. She gingerly wrapped the tiny infant in a soft, crotched blanket with tatted lace on the edges. Evelyn had knitted and stitched it with her fine fingers.

Rose took the child home, in spite of her broken heart, and she woke up with it in the night when it screamed in a pitch that shredded her eardrums. She fed it bottles of warm milk, rocked it, sang to it. She did this for too many nights to count. Time strode on, but her feelings did not change. Rose had gambled that they would – that the little girl would grow on her – but they never did.

Rose had thought she could keep it as her own. It would be her penance for her betrayal. And the little thing would be forced to love her for its very survival. That is all Rose ever wanted – to be loved. She would love that child, and the child would love her. That was what was supposed to happen.

Rose actively befriended Evelyn early on in her affair with Evelyn's husband. It was so much easier to maintain control of Randall when his wife was just a few houses away and Rose's very best friend in the world. Of course, as bosom buddies, Evelyn and Rose would never keep secrets from each other. Evelyn trusted her enough to tell her all about her own secrets, and she had a huge one. Evelyn was tediously noble and wholesome, but oh, she had her secrets. Suffering through her stories was nothing compared to what Rose learned from them. Even Randall had no idea what Evelyn had been hiding. And she, of course, had no idea that Rose was her husband's secret, even when he would steal kisses when his wife was not looking or return home to her after being with Rose, sweat-soaked and smelling of her perfume.

Nonetheless, Evelyn had genuinely become dear to Rose. Over the months, Rose had grown to love her. She really was her best friend in the world. Her only friend. Evelyn truly listened to Rose drone on about her dreams and desire to travel the world. She listened to actually hear her and not just wait to respond politely. For Rose's birthday, she presented her with a handmade travel journal. Full of empty pages. Full of hope. No one had taken Rose seriously before. She was but a small-town midwife, creeping onto a life as an old maid. Evelyn made her feel like she mattered. She had a way of loving even the most unlovable creatures, like the mangy kitten she saw while shopping at the grocer. Rose kicked it to the side with the toe of her shoe, but Evelyn took it home and named it and fed it warm milk at nights. She kept that cat and loved it back to life. She did the same with Rose.

It made Rose furious at Randall for lying to Evelyn, and she almost ended the affair on several occasions. However, she decided that she deserved happiness, too. And the angry love-making for the few months after that was even better than before she had met his wife. Rose supposed she had her to thank for that, as well.

It had always been a battle between right and wrong with Rose. Sometimes, she could make herself stick to the straight and narrow, as they say, but sometimes, she just could not resist. She wanted to be good; she really did. It seemed to be so much more difficult for her than it did for most people. The other side was just too tempting, and if morals had poles, Rose was magnetized for the negative side. All it required was for her to stop trying, and naturally, she would sway toward wickedness. It was exhausting to fight her tendencies all the time. It got her heart racing in the way we like to scare ourselves sometimes, like haunted hay rides and ghost stories. Like the tickle of temptation when Rose met Randall and decided she had to have him.

Then he went and got himself killed in the War. It made Rose so mad at him. How could he leave Eve and her like that?! However, her anger blossomed into hatred when she learned he had obviously maintained relations with his wife. Evelyn whispered shortly thereafter that she was expecting, a glow of happiness on her face. She had called Rose over for tea to announce it. As close friends do. Rose was sick to her stomach. That bastard. Had Rose not been enough for him?

Randall had not been like most men. He was intriguing. Tantalizing. A challenge. She needed a lot of attention, and Randall only ever gave her enough to get by. Like an intravenous drip.

He never chose Rose. Then he went and died before she had a chance to totally win him. She reasoned that perhaps the void left by him could be fulfilled by having the child, his child, love her more than its own mother. She would be an adoring auntie type who showered the child with gifts and attention when she would visit. The child would adore her, as Randall should have done.

Then Evelyn had to go on and die, as well. Rose was certain that meant she had finally won until she actually had to remove her first cloth diaper and coo some kid to sleep. How was it that Evelyn wound up the victor, but Rose was stuck with the burden of her winnings? After all, Randall had cheated on her with his wife or the baby would not even exist. It was a symbol of betrayal, and Rose had grown to hate her.

Rose, in her restlessness, moved them to a different town. She thought removing the memories of Randall and Evelyn from her everyday view would be the cleansing she needed. A fresh start. Where no one knew them or the whole tragic story. She refused to live the remainder of her life in Evelyn's shadow. She had lived there long enough.

Rose was just a widow with a small child. It worked for her for a while. When Eve Number Two was an infant, Rose would at least receive some female attention and praise for such a beautiful child, and others were in awe of her slim physique after the assumed childbirth. She would beam and shyly thank them for the compliment while explaining it was in the genes.

However, the demands were constant. They kept on even when no one was watching or giving out accolades. If she was not washing or changing Eve's cloth diapers, she was having to feed her or stop her crying or some other immediate and urgent need. If Rose were too tired or not in the mood, she would be subjected to that awful crying. There was no one else to pick up the slack. Men looked the other way, like she had some kind of plague. It had turned into a life she had not asked for, and she had grown unhappy. She deserved more than that. The child was not even her own mistake.

She had been working under the premise that she could direct her accumulated affections toward the child, having lost both her friend and her lover and therefore without immediate companions upon whom she could show love, anyway. She would not be able to have any children of her own, so it was a sort of solution. Her being barren was something that had never been of any concern for her, since she never wanted children. She thought it was amusing, really, the irony of the sterile midwife.

She had made plans for the way she intended to direct her life. She saved every dollar she could stash away for her great escape. She had the travel journal Eve had made for her packed away in a leather suitcase, ready to leave at any moment. She wanted to travel and have adventures and live a life enviable of all of the women in town who were stuck in their parlors, nursing infants and hanging laundry and tending to the needs of their families. She would see the world and order room service and have many lovers and never bother at all about her reproductive organs. That was her plan.

That was not what unfolded, though. Instead of being so busy with life that she never thought twice about her infertility, Rose was reminded by it every day in the face of the child she was now burdened with raising. She finally had a windfall of income from Randall's death, finally enough money to see some amazing places, but she was imprisoned with a child instead of experiencing the exciting escapades of which she had always dreamt. Little Eve was a constant reminder of the death of Rose's friend and her affair and her failure to have her own, and she wound up hating her more every day. Eve's big eyes would watch Rose, sparkling with curiosity and inquisition, and it would feel like a visual interrogation. As the years passed, she looked more and more like her mother, until Rose could no longer stare at her demons on a daily basis.

Little Evie had not asked any questions when Rose dropped her off at the orphanage. She just stared at Rose with those cold blue eyes, as she always did. She did not even act puzzled by it. Rose had nothing to say. She could not explain to a small child that she had only ever wanted the excitement of her skirts lifted in rushed secret encounters by a man who wasn't hers. That she had grown to love Eve's mother and had grieved with her when her husband died. That her heart was broken when Evelyn left her, and her child's blue eyes reminded Rose of her and her own mistakes every time she looked at her. Rose walked Eve to the front stoop of the orphanage and urged her to knock on the door. As she ascended the stairs to the thick wooden door, Rose hurriedly walked away, leather suitcase in hand, her head hung in shame and defeat. She headed directly to the train station.

She used Randall's survivor's pension to travel the world. She thought she deserved it. She should be happy. She was the only person left in their little love triangle who was still alive. And she had earned it. After all, she had taken care of the child for a while, and Eve had everything she needed at the orphanage. Rose even dropped in on occasion to make sure.

The money would have just gone to waste being given to a child, anyway. Eve would wind up spending it on sweets and dolls. As far as Rose was concerned, she had fulfilled her promise to Evelyn to take care of her child. As for the promise to tell her what Rose knew about their family secret...well, the timing never seemed right. Her visits with Eve were always so awkward, with her staring at Rose with those eyes like she knew things. Each visit renewed Rose's need to get away, to find something that filled her up, as she always left feeling hollower than she ever had. She never lingered long. She always swore to herself that she would tell Eve the secret...one day.

Then, as the fates would have it, on the very day Rose finally decided to tell her, Eve had news of her own. She was old enough to finally understand. She was on her own now, living in the world, and Rose felt she would finally be able to understand everything.

Rose had eased in with the usual talk, mostly about her travels. She did not know where to begin, so she just kept talking. It was in a pause she had taken to sip her tea that Eve blurted it all out. She had already figured out the family secret, and Rose would not have to tell her after all. Eve told her that she was happy.

The way Eve's blue eyes sparkled were like shards of glass ripping Rose's heart to pieces. Eve looked so much like her mother in those moments, Rose was practically paralyzed. She could not look away, but she could not think of anything to say. She was realizing something. With everything Rose had seen, her travels around the globe, her many affairs, all of her experiences – they all meant nothing. She was a perpetual empty bucket, but with a hole in the bottom, forever unable to be filled. Then there was this child, helpless and homeless, whom she had abandoned, who dug herself out of that ditch in which Rose had tried to bury her and found her happiness, anyway. Eve was beautiful and interesting and had so much more to say than Rose ever would. And god, she resembled the ghost of Rose's friend, her mother, who had haunted Rose for many years. It was just too much to bear. Evie's eyes, as blue as the sky, twinkling with contentment was the last thing Rose thought of as she kicked the chair from below her boots. The rope snapped her neck instantly.

CHAPTER 25
Ronnie

Those blue eyes of hers were still all Ronnie could think about. How they were as cold as an iceberg as she just stared at him, Lloyd's hips thrusting hard behind her, her head jerking with every thrust but her face, expressionless...

Ronnie felt himself break within that moment. His mind split open, garbage and pain spilling from it like a tipped-over trash can. He spent his life on the edge. That was where he liked to live. He woke up every morning with a cup of black coffee with a shot of whiskey and stared directly into that onyx abyss. He appreciated that there was a monster within him. He enjoyed having the power to keep it suppressed. He imagined that was why women liked to wear sexy underwear – that knowledge of naughtiness unseen. He dabbled in darkness, but it didn't feed him. He starved living on it alone. The combination was what kept him alive. And she had taken that from him. Amara pushed him forcefully straight into the fire.

She was going to pay. He would wrench some feeling from those eyeballs, one way or another. She could not just use people and move on like nothing and no one ever mattered. She could not just destroy people without any compassion. Had she felt nothing with Ronnie? Oh, she was going to feel something now. She was going to feel so much.

Once he had decided, Amara was not hard to find. Her name wasn't exactly a common one, even for the city. He never could figure why she had not changed it. She only ever had terrible things to say about her mother and her heritage, her stupid name, the town she was from, and, well, pretty much everything.

She was mesmerized with morphing into whomever she wanted to be that day. She could wear a cardigan and flats on Friday and leather and chains on Friday night. It was part of what made Ronnie fall madly in love with her. She was a chameleon, always adapting. He could take her to meet the parents over a lovely home-cooked meal, then fuck her from behind in the car while it's still parked in their driveway. It was that inability to pin her down or predict her next move that kept Ronnie wanting more. He was never fed enough of her to feel fully satisfied. She was like one of those slivers of cheesecake that is somehow ever expected to be enough. Even if you gorge yourself, you just wind up ill.

Ronnie had decided what needed to be done. He had a plan. Once he mapped out every route and planned every minute of his timeline, it was fairly easy to find her. She was living with some old fucker in a penthouse apartment in the city. He followed her, night after night, pleased at the thought that he could be just feet from her and she never even knew.

It felt powerful to be able to watch her and smell her and sit on the very uncomfortable lipstick red modern sofa in the apartment that was rented for her as a secret sex hideaway while she was out. To touch her things and be such a part of her life without her knowledge. It was thrilling, like hunting some doe-eyed elk on the Serengeti. The night Ronnie was motionless under her bed while he made music out of her rhythmic breathing was probably the closest thing to the exhilaration he had felt when he was with her. He partook in every type of drug imaginable since to try to achieve that same high, and nothing ever worked. The feeling of her velvety lips on his skin was unattainable in this life by any other means. He needed his fix.

He watched from the corner, shielding himself behind the brick wall, as some dude in a chauffeur's cap opened the back door and she slid out of the shiny black Lincoln. It was like the movies, a slow pan up the perfect leg of a flawless actress as she gracefully emerged from the expensive vehicle in stiletto heels. She was trussed up in some complicated-looking cocktail dress, her blonde hair cascading down her back, adorned with what looked like expensive jewelry. Slut. She slithered into the towering apartment building, every eye following her every move. It was show time.

* * *

He had not planned for this. This wasn't the plan, god damn it!

As soon as Ronnie had gotten her to his apartment, she started crying. I mean, really making a show of it. Ronnie believed, until that point, she actually thought she could get herself out of the situation on her looks and charm, as she usually did. She knew Ronnie had always loved her, that he always would. She believed she could manipulate and control him like she had from the second they met. But Ronnie was in charge now.

When she walked in his apartment, however, and saw the drawings of her face, her body, her lips littering his walls, the hundreds of pages of loose paper where he had made his plans and sketched out his ideas, pictures he had taken of her as she slept all those months ago and pictures he had taken of her since, she lost it. He could see the fear wash over her, her face lost color. Her eyes darted to the murals on the walls, the drawings, his face. She was no longer in control, and she knew it. He could think of nothing that would torture her more.

But he would certainly try.

He commanded her to strip off her clothes. She shed each article of clothing slowly, weeping softly, shaking with fear. She still could not shed her sensuality. It was as if she were trying to delay the inevitable by taking her time, but she did not realize it only heightened Ronnie's senses. He had every intention of feeling the high of what it was like to be inside her again, even if she made him sick. He craved her. She was his drug, his addiction. He got rock hard every time he daydreamed about taking her, and he would not have to be gentle this time. He would have her every way he wanted. He would have her for every time he had wanted her over the months and she was not there. For every time he couldn't sleep because he would remember the noises she would make when they made love or the way she would bite her lip or roll her hips. For every detail he couldn't let go of until he had drawn it, from her eyelashes to her ankle tattoo.

But now that she was naked in front of him, the contemptuous goddess, Ronnie could not get hard at all. Angrily, he rubbed himself and growled in frustration when it still refused to stiffen. Then she laughed.

She fucking laughed. With that, she was in charge again. She was not afraid, her hands on her naked hips, her dimple deep with amusement. She laughed at his limp nakedness. His weakness. His emasculation. Again. He had brought her home to show her he had the power, to dominate her and finally put her in a position of submission. But she was fucking laughing at him with those icy blue eyes, the same unfeeling look as when she broke him the first time.

His hands were around her throat before he even thought it through. He was on top her, skin to skin, his knees digging into the concrete floor of his apartment, scraping with every jerk and thrash from her body as she bucked beneath him. He pressed all of his weight onto her. She scratched and pulled at his arms, fighting him, but he was much stronger.

Her eyes were bulging, tears streaming down her face. He could just kill her right there. He had her life in his hands, literally. He wanted to end her, to rid the world of her evil presence. All she did was destroy. Like some plague that sweeps in and leaves nothing but death and destruction in its wake. He wanted revenge. But this was not the plan. He argued with himself for several long seconds, but he finally let go. She gasped in deep, raspy breaths, desperate for air. None of this was part of the plan.

He spent months perfecting every single move he wanted to make, planning every detail of each agonizing idea to make Amara suffer. Like she had made him suffer. And nothing had gone to plan, other than getting her to his apartment.

Frustrated, and not quite sure of his next move, Ronnie zip-tied her wrists and ankles and lashed a rope around the ties to the metal bed frame. He set a beer can alarm, in case she somehow managed to get free. She was crying now, pleading. He was elated. He was back in charge.

He wanted her to see the error of her ways. That was justice. And they were only getting started. He ignored her pleas and her promises as he wrapped one of his headbands around her mouth.

He climbed onto the bed, her naked body warm and smooth and as perfect as ever in the dimly lit room. He put his head on her flawless round breast and was out in seconds, the rocking of her crying body beneath him lulling him to sleep.

*****

The morning sun crept into the tiny loft apartment through the one dirty window, streaks of light breaking through the gaps in his blackout curtains, waking Ronnie from the first deep sleep he had in ages. He stretched lazily, a small smile on his face. He felt rested and something close to content. Amara whimpered, and he remembered. Why they were there. How successful the day before had been. How he got his girl back. Relishing in her scent, he ran his hand over her shiny blond locks, down her bruised neck, across her breast, nipple, belly button. He stopped short. The way the light shone through the small window lit up the shiny slashes across her belly. The ragged scars looked as though a tiger had clawed her belly from either side. Stretch marks. What the fuck. Those had not been there before.

A tear rolled from Amara's swollen eyes, down her cheek, and disappeared into the threads of his dingy pillow. She had managed to wriggle the headband off of her mouth during the night. Her lip trembled and her eyes were desperate, obviously seeking some kind of escape, as she whispered, "She was your baby."

The world spun. Hatred and anger and shock poisoned his blood and it bubbled up, hot and heavy, spitting like a volcano. He could feel his heart thumping against his chest, his pulse in his neck. *What? I'm a father?!*, he wondered in shock. What did she mean, she *was* his? He wondered if she were just fucking with him again, toying with his mind.

He ripped the headband from where it had slipped from her mouth and demanded answers. She gave them willingly, but she knew very little. The more she spoke, that deep well of rage took over him. She was not giving him the information he needed, *GOD DAMN IT ALL*! He sprung to his feet on the mattress and kicked her naked body, his bare toes bending and straining against her ribcage. He stomped her instead. Like the useless bug he knew her to be. Then slowly, deliberately, he straddled the woman who had borne his child. He choked her soft, thin throat until he could see clearly again. His hands wrapped easily around the tender flesh. He squeezed and leaned his body into her neck until he felt just a smidge better about things. His knees pressed into her ribcage. Until her breath sounded close to death. Then, just as slowly, he padded into the bathroom to take a piss and rinse his face. He had a child to find.

CHAPTER 26
Robert

There was something compelling in the voice on the other end of the phone. Compassion or tenacity… something. Robert Haney pressed the receiver of his old home phone into his shoulder.

"Ma'am, I admire your persistence, but I have been retired for years. I no longer see any patients. Even if I wanted, I'm not licensed to do so."

Robert crossed his thin legs, ankle over knee, and sipped his coffee. He was uncertain how this woman had found his number. He supposed you could find anyone online these days. She sounded older, however, so maybe she was a patient of his before. She was a little too familiar with Robert for his comfort, and she was not accepting no as answer. It was both flattering and a little off-putting at the same time. He was almost ready to hang up on her, but there was something in her voice that sought help, and Robert had never been one to walk away from someone in need.

He placed the oversized mug of coffee on the arm of the patio chair and sighed, allowing her the time to tell him more about the patient she wanted him to see before he was going to have to let her down. His gaze fell across his yard, admiring the azalea bushes his wife had planted years before. It was actually nice to have a phone call.

"My granddaughter's heart has been broken," the lady rattled on. "She is not sleeping, is not eating. There is no light in her eyes and no will to live each day. She is in a very dark place, and I need someone able to pull her out of that descent. I'm afraid she will do something about it herself." Her voice cracked on the last few words.

He let the silence sit on the other end of the line. He had learned that trick in his working days: remain silent when someone is pushing you for something. It stayed that way for several long seconds, and he was tempted to hang up. He started to suggest a young colleague of his who was still practicing psychotherapy, someone who was actually licensed. He could not understand why the woman was so adamant that it be him.

What she said next made the hair on his arms stand up. A trickle of adrenaline raced its way across the nerves in his neck and spine.

He agreed to meet her granddaughter the following morning, first thing.

CHAPTER 27
Aiyanna

His name was Dr. Robert Haney. He was retired, and his license to practice had expired years before. Total hack. What in the world was Jamma thinking? I could have found someone more reputable online. He actually wore a blazer with the leather ovals over the elbows. If ever there were a shrink cliché, it was this fake Freud.

If you can't tell, I was quite resistant to the notion of therapy. No words were going to heal my heart or restore my faith in love or people.

I had been hurt too many times. Disappointed, used, lied to and abandoned. I could not take any more, and I no longer gave a damn. Everyone has a limit, and I had reached mine. I spent my entire life giving of myself and believing in the best of people. They, without fail, inevitably let me down or just left. People were selfish and vain and shallow. I did not want to be a part of the human race anymore. I wanted to stop the planet and be let off. I wanted to end it all.

"Aiyanna. What an unusual name."

I just blinked at him. I wasn't necessarily trying to be rude on purpose - I just didn't have the energy, or the inclination, for small talk.

"Is it okay if I call you Ai? Your grandmother said that is what you generally go by...?"

"That's fine. Listen, sir, I —"

"You don't really want to be here. You are here because your grandmother thinks you need someone to talk to. Is that right?"

I paused, slightly caught off guard by his blunt admonishment. Or acknowledgement. I couldn't determine which from his calm, expressionless-but-for-a-faint-smile face. He was bald but for a ring of closely cropped snow-white hair around the back of his head.

"That's right. I mean no disrespect. I just don't see how you can help me. Talking isn't going to help anything. Words aren't going to help me." I pretended to fidget with the clasp on my bag so he could not see the despair and tears in my eyes.

"I understand, Ai. I wonder, however, if you'd allow me to *try* to help you?"

I took what felt like a full minute to examine his brown eyes. I saw no malice in them. In fact, quite the opposite. I could picture him playing a slim Santa in the Christmas season. He had joyful cheeks and happy eyes.

"I guess I can't get much worse," I shrugged, resigned to the psychological experiment. I was just so tired. Whatever I had to do to be done with it was all I wanted. If this old guy thought he had some answer that would draw me from the pit of darkness and despair in which I was drowning, then let him have at it.

"Well, Ai, I usually spend some time becoming acquainted with my patients. We have several sessions of chit chat, getting to know each other and building trust. Then I would have you explain what's going on in your world. We would take it session by session, figuring out together the best path for you.

"However, your grandmother has described your situation to me, and I believe time is of the essence. I would not feel right just sending you home after a few hellos and empty get-to-know-yous. I can see the light has left you. I feel it's important to try to get that back as soon as we can.

"There's something specific I would like to try. It has worked before in helping my patients find the answers they are looking for, especially patients prone to vivid dreams. It is an extreme form of therapy, but it is my understanding that something drastic is needed here. Would you like to try it? Would that be okay?"

Again, there was something in his soft eyes and genuine manner that encouraged me to trust his methods. I didn't have much to lose, anyway, truth be told. I did not want to wake up anymore. Every afternoon, when I finally woke from a fitful sleep, I would sigh, wishing that I never opened my eyes. I could not comprehend the point of any of it.

Why do we wake up every day and jump on our little hamster wheels, going nowhere? Why do we invest ourselves in people and hobbies and careers, to just have them mean nothing in the end? Why were there sick and starving children who fought to stay alive, while I did not even want such a privilege?

If it were not for Jamma, I would not still be living. All I could see was darkness. It was turning me into something I did not recognize, but Jamma was a candle in the night. I knew she needed me, she loved me, and it would break her completely if I took my own life. So, whatever the hack therapist wanted to do in that mess of a mind of mine, I was willing to let him. He could douse it in kerosene and light it on fire and it wouldn't destroy a damned thing.

"Sure," I committed with a shrug.

"If you become uncomfortable or if there is anything that makes you feel unsafe, we will stop immediately, okay?"

My eyes shifted back and forth. "Um, okay." What did he mean by that?!

"Shall we begin?" The eagerness in his eyes was almost unsettling, like he was about to embark on some grand adventure. It set me on edge how hurried he seemed to be to get started. But, like I said, I really did not care at that point what happened to me.

***

It was that feeling when you have completed all of your nighttime tasks and you climb into bed, turn out the light, and relish those first few seconds of black silence. And the minutes following that, when you can consciously feel your muscles start to relax, the burdens of the day lifting from your body, your mind shifting its to-do list to tomorrow - that is what it felt like as I lay on Dr. Haney's couch. He had me lie on the soft, worn brown leather sofa, putting a pillow beneath my head. It was a very comfortable couch, squishy enough in certain places and firm enough in others. I had watched enough movies, but I did not realize lying on a couch was an actual thing. I ran my fingers across a crack in the leather.

Dr. Haney told me he would like to try a different approach. Something called regression therapy. Apparently, he was going to hypnotize me and ask me about my childhood. Oh, joy. Fun.

His silky voice sung on and on, lulling me further into relaxation. It somehow made me hyper-aware of every ticking second, but in that awareness, time was all at once suspended. Each click of the second hand on the clock was a full minute in my mind. I was weightless, awash with emotions; but instead of my thoughts and worries and dreams and heartbreak drowning me as I felt they had been, I rode the tide – I surfed on its waves – until it took me to a sort of sleepy awareness. I landed ashore a place of my mind I had never before been, Dr. Haney's monotonous voice the gentle oars guiding me there. It was neither dream nor reality.

Back, back we swum together, Dr. Haney and I. The watery recollections lapped the land and shifted the sands of memories further, then further with every wave, with every infinite second of the clock ticking.

Then there was Daisy. She was so young! But it was definitely her. Freckles scattered across her cheeks and the shiny metal and brightly-colored rubber bands of braces filled her smile. And there was I! I was watching a younger version of myself chewing a pencil already scored with tooth marks up and down its stem, releasing some sort of anxiety in crushing the wood beneath my teeth. I sneaked wary glances at young, unaware Daisy. But here was the surprise: I hated her. I never remembered hating my friend, but there I was, glaring at her beneath my long lashes, resentment festering in my eighth-grade gut. Before I could figure it out, I was falling further down the rabbit hole.

I was studying a much younger Jamma's delicate facial features. In a slow, exaggerated manner, she repeated the word, *Grandma*. I blinked as she bounced me in her lap and made pony sounds, occasionally dropping me through her knees, which elicited a squeal of joy from me as she effortlessly scooped me back up.

"Jamma!" I giggled, proud of myself for making that sound. Evelyn Burns laughed with glee, her cobalt eyes crinkled at the edges. My chubby hands wrapped around her body and squeezed with all of the love in my little heart.

A whisper crawled into my chronological adventure, pushing me further. I could sense Dr. Haney wanting more, his voice like velvet in the far reaches of my mind, goading me to keep going. But I was hesitant. There was something there that had forever lurked outside my cognizance. I had always been afraid to gaze into the abyss, for I understood that it had always lived inside of me already, a dark pool ready to seize me should I ever dip a toe in.

Then there she was. It was her. My mother. I shouldn't have known who she was, but I did. A scent of incense wafted around her as her long blonde hair tickled my face. It was a beautiful sunny day, with a hint of a breeze. She was holding my tiny infant hands. Jamma was there. She snapped a picture of the two of us, but she was not happy. Her mouth had turned into a straight line across, as it did when she was displeased.

My mother was rattling on about something, as if I could understand her. Or perhaps it was for Jamma's benefit. She was jittery, her blue eyes bleary and unfocused. Something was wrong. I did not like it. I began to cry.

With a curse word, she shoved my soft body into Jamma's arms and stormed off. "Shhh. It's okay, my beautiful blossom," my Jamma cooed softly. Safely. I hushed and drifted into sleepiness.

And then…I was not here anymore. I mean, I was distantly aware that I was still stretched out on a sofa somewhere, but I had traveled somewhere else. I had gone too far. I was not Aiyanna anymore. *I* was someone else. My body felt different. My burdens and recollections had been replaced with a whole new set of memories and worries that this Aiyanna had never known. I was in a different a moment, in a different time, in a different body. I was in a different life.

CHAPTER 28
Anastasia

I had regressed into an entirely different time and an entirely different life. It was as if I were watching a period movie, except the setting was real and this character was actually me, not an actor. It wasn't a script, though. It was physical and material and authentic.

I was distantly aware of myself in another place, on a sofa and under hypnosis, but that was but a whisper as I was very much alive in this life I had discovered within the confines of my very own mind. I could barely remember to recall every iota of detail, for this was but a moment on a scale of time and experience I was only beginning to understand. My mind felt stretched further than it should grow. I struggled to mentally hold both ends of a spectrum of which we are only naturally privy to a piece. I was straining - I was distantly aware that it would be over soon enough, and I must recall every bit of somatic sensory from the present-past.

The salt air almost slapped my face, a moist coolness rushing through my curls. The ship's wooden planks rocking beneath my boots, lurching my stomach with every upheaval. Where the black sky and the black sea met was indistinguishable, with no horizon whatsoever. The stars could have well been the crests of the waves crashing and wrestling against each other.

As I turned from the mesmerizing match of nature's brawling, the crisp sea air on my face, a warm hand clutched my elbow. I looked up to see whose hand held me steady, and I knew him instantly. His eyes smiled straight into my soul. I knew him and I loved him - both versions of myself: Anastasia, a curly-headed Victorian, and the wisp of myself witnessing from lifetimes yet to occur. We each knew this man from the very depths of our hearts. He was home.

Adelbert, as he was called in this time, was stocky and stern-looking, but with an indescribable softness in his face. He had a broad, rectangular-shaped body with a cleft chin, thick mustache and eyes like a hawk. I, as Anastasia, loved him as my father. But this man, not the body but the soul within it, called to me across oceans and time as I lay on the couch in Robert Haney's office. I had loved him in that life as my Ethan, and I loved him in this life as Adelbert.

In that life, I could barely breathe as my mind raced, caught in the spell of recollection. My chest constricted with love and emotion and surprise, like that feeling you get when something, be it a smell or a certain song, triggers a memory long forgotten like a punch to your heart. I had been trapped in that feeling before, within my nightmares, for as long as I could recall. But I was also still under hypnosis. It was an eerie and unclear feeling to be exploring my present brain in a semi-cognizant way, while fully aware as an animate being in an entirely different time.

It was *real*, though. It was him. Not a dream, but something similar. As Anastasia, I loved the man who had raised me, who had coaxed me to sleep after terrible nightmares, the man who had surprised me with a puppy on my eighth birthday. I clasped his hand in mine, acutely aware of the warmth and life in his thick, blunt fingers. They were so unlike Ethan's, and yet love coursed through it just as it did with him. It was a different kind of love, but none the lesser for it.

An arm slid into mine on the other side, and my gaze met a dark-headed beauty packed into a small, lithe frame. My new stepmother. Violet smiled broadly and beautifully, revealing a row of perfect white teeth. There was not an ounce of authenticity behind her beam, however. Her eyes were as wild and volatile as the sea. It was just a momentary slip on her part, but it startled me into dropping father's hand. I was taken back to what was both moments ago and years ahead, to my other self as a schoolgirl, hating the new girl from a distance. This woman was Daisy in this life. But how could this sly-eyed vixen be some version of my best friend?

My father's dinner coat-clad back disappeared into a crowd of stargazers on deck as he continued his brisk pace, tapping his thumbnail to his teeth. I panicked for a moment, unsure of why I felt so suddenly terrified. Some animal instinct arose within me, and an urge to flee bolted through me. It was the distant me, Aiyanna of the present, elusively aware of some bad feeling for Anastasia, for myself. A shiver of fear sent goose pimples over my flesh, but Violet's hand remained on my arm. The looming storm and the shadowy night sent a chill down my spine.

A crack of thunder boomed above us. The churning sea below spat its agitated surf into the side of the wooden ship. The wind whipped at my face, stinging cold. Black water. There was nothing visible below the surface or above it but for the indigo crests of the ocean waves. The sea and sky and the salty air all dissolved into a shadowy struggle of water versus ship. Terror seized my heart. It was that same fear from my life as Aiyanna, that indescribable reluctance toward dark water. I stepped back from the railing and the black water below – staggering right into Violet.

"Oh," I smiled nervously at my stepmother, "Do excuse me." I bowed my head politely, but kept my eyes on hers. I didn't trust her. There was something in the wild loss of composure a moment before that had left me feeling uneasy. I turned to catch up to Papa.

"Of course, dear," she cooed, as she linked her arm in mine, halting my movements. Her voice was refined and articulate. There was something in it, though. I couldn't pinpoint what it was. "I have wanted some time with you," she kept on in a measured voice as she guided me away from the group gathered on the deck ahead of us.

Her champagne-colored evening gown was elegant against her limber frame. Her black hair matched the sky that night as she walked away from me and leaned her back against the railing. "Oh, come join me," she encouraged as she patted the railing, her charming smile again ingenuine. I nervously glided beside her obligingly. As Aiyanna, I could not decipher what it was about her that was so unsettling. As Anastasia, I did not want to discover it. Be it the corset stays were too tight or the strange sense I got from Violet, but I felt it difficult to breathe. But to insult her by being impolite would have been unforgivable to Papa. I would have done anything for Papa.

Violet had entered my father's life unexpectedly soon after my mother died, and she had somehow managed to win my father's affections in a very brief courtship. After the death of my brother in the Great War, my father retreated into himself. I was the only one who was allowed inside – until Violet. But he would never love anyone more than he loved his daughter, and that never did sit right with her. I was the light of his life and his singular priority. I had known all along that that notion upset my stepmother, so I tried to disappear. I attempted to make myself smaller and quieter, trying everything in my power not to be a bother. After all, I was almost a grown woman and my father deserved to be loved. It would have hurt me immensely to think that he missed a second chance at love for my sake. He made sure I never wanted for anything, and I felt it was my chance to do something selfless for him. Thus, I kept my opinion unspoken that there was something deeply untrustworthy, and even terrifying, about Violet.

"You know, you could have been so lovely," Violet smiled, as she smoothed my wild, windblown curls. She smiled as she petted me. "I am so sorry."

Startled and confused, I began to question why, but before I could do so, a jolt sent my tall frame over the ship's railing. There wasn't even a second of black sky and Violet's grinning face from the railing before the frozen punches. The waves reached out and swallowed me up before I could cry for help. Inky depths wrapped my heavy skirt about my legs and filled my boots, pressing me down, farther and farther into its belly. I thrashed wildly, but there was nothing to grasp, no air to breathe, no ground and no help. The water rolled me and tossed me like a crocodile until my lungs burst and there was nothing left of me except brown curls and sinuous lace billowing in the black sea.

CHAPTER 29
Aiyanna

With a glaze of cold sweat covering my body and residual panic gripping my chest, I was back in Dr. Haney's office. His tweed sports coat was less ridiculous now; it was almost comforting. His gentle brown eyes were reassuring. If what had just happened to me was a tempest of time and emotion, he was the captain of the ship and I was actually grateful for him. What *had* just happened?

"I ... don't know what...what the hell that was," I stuttered. "I can barely remember it now."

"Well, how do you feel?" He leaned back into his chair, one ankle resting on the other knee. Perfectly calm. His face was blank. He was a pro. If I were him, I would be pretty weirded out.

"It was him. It seems there were other things, too, but I saw him."

Dr. Haney smiled gently and remained silent, graciously giving me time to sort it all out. His face remained unbiased.

"I don't know how to explain it, Doc, but Ethan was there. In my mind somewhere. In my memories. Like a dream. But more than that... he was real. But it wasn't *him*." I shook my head, fully aware of how ridiculous I sounded. Had I been describing it out loud as it happened? Did it *happen,* or was I just asleep? Did he take the journey with me, or was it all in my own mind?

I could not make sense of what just happened. I shook my head, hoping somehow to have my thoughts fall back into proper place. As it was, they were like a box of building blocks scattered across a carpeted floor. I did not know the man, and I therefore wanted to blame Dr. Haney for the strange thing I experienced, but I knew somehow it came from within me. I did not understand what had just occurred, but it was dawning on me that whatever it was would change everything. Life as I knew it would be different from that point forward.

"We've just had a big day, Ai. Why don't you take the time before your next appointment to think about everything we've discovered today?"

"Think about it how? I want to try again. I feel like I could remember more this time."

"Take a beat to ponder on what you felt today and how that translates to your life."

"That's completely unhelpful." I know it was rude, but come on. "You can't guide me to this... whatever this is, and then just leave me."

"I'm not leaving you. I'm right here if you want to call me or discuss anything. But you have to make the breakthrough on your own. If I were to interject myself at this point, it would be to your detriment," he said, that same warm half-smile on his face. It was infuriating. "I will see you Thursday." I hated the way he spoke while saying nothing. Words, words, words, without any meaning. Could he not just tell me what the hell was going on?!

"You don't understand. I saw Ethan! I saw him, but he was different. He was alive. He still loved me," I choked out. The last couple of words stove up inside my throat like a brick, salty tears brimming my eyelids.

"I'm not leaving. You need to take me back right now," my voice rising with each word. What was his problem? I had just felt the love of my life again, the way he loved me before. The man I thought I would never touch again. I had his hand in mine, and it was alive. I felt him. It was real. In some place I didn't know how to get to on my own, he was alive. And I needed more. "Please."

"You got there on your own, Ai. It wasn't my doing, so I can't take you back. If, after some consideration, you would like to try again, we can do so. In your next session."

"No, God damn it!" I shrieked and threw my bag on the floor. I ran my fingers through my messy hair, hot tears falling effortlessly down my cheeks. "I need to see him again. I can't leave him. I won't let him go again."

"I understand your frustration. That's why I need you to really consider what happened here. Think it through this evening. You must understand that there are serious repercussions for exploring depths like those we did today. It can certainly help you, but it could also hurt you." He stood up and patted my shoulder. "Let me walk you out."

I felt betrayed. Confused. This man, this stranger, had been inside my head and had guided me somewhere I could never find on my own. Somewhere where there was still love with Ethan and me, where we could be together. It was a version of life that actually worked out for me. And then he just kicks me out, unmoved, without hearing me out. I would have told him what a disappointment he was, but I needed him to get me there again. So, I bit my lip, yanked my messenger bag from the floor and slung it over my shoulder, wiping the tears from my face on my sleeve as I exited his office.

***

That night, Ethan visited me in my dreams. I want to say my mind created it to cope with my heartbreak, but it was so real. It was as if I had stepped into my own life in some other dimension where everything hadn't gone to hell. It didn't feel like a fabrication of my psyche. It felt like a trek I had taken to someone else's life, but that someone was me, magazine in lap and feet tucked beneath me, ignorant of any other reality.

He was real. Gloriously handsome. Perched beside me on his sofa. So real I could see the faint pulse of his heartbeat in his neck. He smelled like ashes and hot chocolate. Like winter and warmth. I could feel his presence beside me, hot life emanating from his taut skin.

"Picking colors is a thing, right?" he asked, that one slightly crooked tooth in the front of his heart-stopping half-smile. He draped his arm around me casually. The weight of it rested across my shoulders. It felt like home.

"Is that really the extent of your wedding knowledge?" I laughed, poking him in the ribs as he sat next to me, the whitework quilt spread out over us.

"Well, I want to help. I want to be an involved fiancé," he laughed, pronouncing the last word in a strong French accent.

I examined his face – I mean, I *really* looked at him. His long, dark lashes, his cleft chin sprinkled with a five o'clock shadow, the hint of wrinkles just starting to form at the edges of his eyes. Even in my dream, I remembered to analyze every detail. It would be something to hold onto when I awoke.

"I love you, Ethan," I said softly and seriously into his green eyes, the color of moss in the low lighting. I needed this fantasy version of him to understand that before I lost him again.

His smile dropped, and a small line of concern creased his brow. "I know, baby." He cupped my cheek in his musician's hand, the leather bracelet brushing my skin. "And I love you," he spoke, staring straight into my soul. "You are my future and my life. Where you go, I will go. My home will always be wherever you are. Your love is everything to me. Your love is life."

I dropped the wedding-themed magazine and wrapped my arms around his body. I buried my face in his chest, breathing him in, and I swear I could feel him in my bed back home. His body heat and the way he held the back of my head to him, hugging me even tighter. I could feel his love.

It was like a live thing that crawled through time and sleep and woke me with stinging tears.

I sat up in bed, my dream interrupted, and silently sobbed at the blackened bedroom with but a sliver of light leaking in through the parted blinds. I was back at Jamma's. Alone. And Ethan was gone. Back to the reality where he no longer loved me. Where he no longer lived. He was gone...all the way gone.

But I swear I could still smell him on me when I finally felt exhausted enough to cry myself asleep again.

CHAPTER 30
Emrys

Back in the Highlands...

Edan sniffed his master's cold fingers and gently nosed his hand until he was able to slide his wooly head beneath the stiffened digits. The weight of his master's arm against his shaggy skull was a superficial comfort. Edan knew it wasn't real. He could smell the lack of life, the scent of it overwhelming. It was over. Everything was over. He knew it instinctively, but it was too much to endure.

Master Emrys lay stiff and unmoving amidst dozens of kilted-clad corpses in various stages of decomposition. The scene was gruesome. A slaughter. His eyes, the color milky and diluted, stared disturbingly at the gray sky. The clouds themselves cried soft tears of regret, the gentle rain dotting down upon the dead. The world licking its wounds.

Edan had disappeared during the intensity of warfare. The battle cries and screams of pain stung his sensitive ears as his paws propelled him away from the racket. He hid amongst the trees until the noise died down. Then he found his way back, sniffing out his master from a sea of bodies and broken dreams. He knew then that nothing would ever be the same.

He whimpered slightly and licked his master's hand. The leather bracelet he had worn slid slightly down his wrist. The love of his life had given it to him. Crudely inscribed upon it was a truth and a promise more poignant than the smell of rotting flesh and families without fathers: *Ne Obliviscaris*. Never forget.

Edan would remain beside the body of his master and his friend through the night and the next day, guarding the body from scavengers, human and animal alike.

CHAPTER 31
Amara

She was not sure what time it was when she finally awoke. Or what day, for that matter. Following Ronnie's assault, she was out for God knows how long. When she finally came to, her eyes were almost sealed shut from old tears. The effort it took to purposefully open her eyes and force herself to take stock of her surroundings was incredible. Every muscle ached. Her body was in agony, having been abused and tied in the same position for so long. She had urinated on herself at some point, and the scent was sharp with dehydration.

She rolled her eyes around the room, but even that was painful. Ronnie was gone. It was just her, alone in his deplorable apartment. There was just the one mattress on the floor where she was and a camping chair on its side in the middle of the studio-style room. Loose papers were strewn all over the place. Some looked like sketches; some had writing inked on them. Plaster peeled away from the wall. A steady drip emanated from somewhere.

She had no idea how to get out of this mess. She never, in a million years, assumed Ronnie would be the sort to do something like this. I guess you never know someone...

She learned to control her mind when she was just a teenager. Eve took her to enough therapists, counselors, psychoanalysts and shrinks to make her head spin. But they never could figure her out. More so, they never could *fix* her. She never wanted to be fixed. Just because she was different from Eve did not mean she was wrong. There must be darkness to be light, after all. Through all of their techniques and tricks, though, she was able to discover her ability to travel within many different lives. She learned to go back on her own, without some psychotherapist practicing his hypnosis on her.

Life always felt too small for Amara, so it was exhilarating to find that she was not limited to just the one. She could cross the boundaries of linear time and singular dimensions, and she felt more freedom than she ever had before. If she did not particularly care for a certain situation in which she found myself, she could travel to another plane, another place, another time, where things may have worked out. Or maybe they didn't. Maybe there were not supposed to. Wherever she landed seemed to inevitably provide her with some sort of answer to whatever burning question she had at the time. From there, she gained clarity on how to better direct her aims, so to speak.

With that kind of control over her own mind, paired with her ability to manipulate people, she had since felt unstoppable. She was magnetic, in the same way you cannot look away from car wrecks or gruesome injuries. She was no good. But being a bad girl was a good time, and anyone who spent any time with her tasted that temptation.

She was never imprisoned pursuing some dream within this lifetime of fame or love or everlasting life – she had had those things already at some point in some life or another. She could have those things whenever she wanted by closing her eyes and going back. This life was but a fleeting moment, a blink in time, and all of the loud people proclaiming this and that with all of their self-importance were ridiculous. Amara knew they were nothing. They would always be nothing. In the tick of a second, they would be worm food. Not remembered, nothing to show for their time here but a slab of granite with some words written on it. Even those etched letters would wither to something indecipherable. Doomed to a nameless history, their bones browned and dusty beneath a rock. They would be reborn without her skill set and have to start all over in learning the same shit they had just spent a lifetime never grasping before. It was tragic.

Amara just wanted to enjoy herself. We would all end up in a grave at some point. She wanted to get there by means of the most exciting paths. She did not care about the consequences. If she were hungry, she would eat. If she wanted a man, she would get herself one. There were lots of lonely people, and many of them had money enough to spare. She did not need their attention or empty, romantic gestures, and they could keep her a secret and separate from the presentation of their lives. It was a business deal, as far as Amara was concerned. They could have the use of her body and the pleasure of her company for an allotted amount of time if they gave her food, clothing and shelter. And since her end of the bargain was high-end merchandise, she preferred the same from them, to keep things fair.

But Ronnie had been different. That was why she had to leave him when she did. He was poor. Unambitious. He placed value on intangible things. Like his love for her. He asked of her the sort of feelings she did not have to give. At least, she thought she didn't.

She was attracted to his smile. She found herself really listening to the lyrics he wrote, a rivulet of pride trickling through her when she watched him perform with his band. Girls would lose their minds, flashing their chests and making advances, but he always kept his eyes and his hands on Amara. She got comfortable with him, wearing t-shirts from his closet because of how they smelled in lieu of her leather tank top and push-up bra. She liked the way he looked at her as if she were magic. He made her feel like more than just a pile of flesh – future worm food. She felt loved. Special. Alive. She could not let herself indulge in those things. She dove face first into a life that looked just like that ages and lives ago, and it ruined her. She lost her family, the one into which she was born and the one she created. She had tried, and she had failed. She would not fail again. She could not. She had to go.

***

After Ronnie, after Amara gave her baby away, she embraced all of the worst parts of herself. She was a sinner, and redemption was never going to be an option. She spent her entire life doing whatever she wanted, and she always wanted the worst of everything. She broke her own heart, and a proverbial mirror had been held up to her repulsive face. She could not even remember where she went wrong – she just always *was*.

A hollow feeling consumed her like a thundercloud from under which she could never step out. There was no sunshine and no light. Regret and depression pulled her deeply into an abyss ever since she walked away from her baby after placing her tiny innocence on a doorstep. Amara just left her there for someone else to raise and to care for. For someone else to love. She would never hear her baby's first words or watch her take her first steps in this shithole world. She would never advise her on boyfriend drama or help her pick out a prom dress. Amara made a choice, and even in the knowledge that it was right for her child, it felt wrong.

She needed to lie in the bed she made, the bare mattress on the floor of Ronnie's dreary apartment.

Everything her mother wanted for her, everything she warned Amara against…it all made sense. It took so many years and her completely ruining everyone and everything she touched to learn it, but she did. It was just too late by then. What was she to make of her life after all of that? Therefore, she decided to harness the wickedness within and use it to better her own circumstances. It was only from that vantage point that she would have the power to make any real change in her life. She vowed to never again get herself in the sort of position where she was penniless in a crappy hotel room. If she were doomed to an eternity of darkness, she may as well reap the rewards of it while her flesh and bones still wandered the earth. She learned to embrace her doomed destiny many lifetimes ago. Her body shivered with the haunting, ancient memory of deep hunger and illness inside of it, coursing through her blood and spreading its crimson ruin over everything that mattered or meant anything at all.

It was such a beautiful time in history to be fluid in any idea of what makes you you, with the technology and tools to sculpt yourself into anything you wanted. With a plan in mind to direct her own outcome for her disaster of a life, Amara purchased herself a very nice laptop by giving the pock-marked adolescent salesman the best blow job of his life. He tasted like overly salted seafood, and his nervous sweat almost gagged her, but she finished the job and got her merchandise at a deep discount. She had decided. The internet was the highway on which she would ride to luxury. With it, she could be whomever she chose.

She had always been clever. She was sure her mother thought that was an unfortunate trait for someone so mischievous – poor woman – but she could utilize it to get more of what she wanted. She relied entirely on her looks for so long, she had quite frankly forgotten how smart she could be. She had not needed to be, and beauty expedited outcomes, while wit took forever to cultivate and convey. But she really needed to approach the rest of her life in a businesslike manner.

Her body was not the same after childbirth. She was slender again, having not gained much weight during pregnancy since she was poor and starving most of the time. But she was not as perky as she was before. She was softer, hung a little looser, and her skin showed the stripes of stretchmarks. Her deep unhappiness colored wisps of hair white at her temples, and tiny wrinkles at the corners of her eyes began to emerge. Still attractive, but not perfect. She would need to use it in combination with her wits if she were to continue living the lifestyle to which she had become accustomed. If she used all of those resources, she could be unstoppable. She could still live a life she had always dreamed.

She walked to a nearby fast food restaurant with her laptop held protectively against her chest. It had just become her most prized possession. She ordered something from the dollar menu with the few bucks in the wallet she took from the teen at the electronics store. She opened her new laptop and logged into the free Wi-Fi. She proceeded to search for the wealthiest men in the city.

She developed a system and a story to insert herself into the right circles. She learned to research and dig and she used her well-honed ability at crafting believable lies on the spot. There were women who were eager to befriend someone beautiful on the chance that their sex appeal score went up by proxy. Others were looking for a wild outlet, which she was more than ready to provide with crazy, crowded clubs and piles of drugs. Eventually, she was invited to all of the right parties with the right people. She could afford to don herself in expensive fashions and sparkly jewels. Those connections led to more, and eventually, she was part of a rather elite circle in the city. And so many of the people with whom she mingled were as frivolous and shallow as she ever dreamed of being. The thing was, it no longer held the luster it once had. The thrill of the game held no thrill at all anymore, and Amara often found herself wondering about her baby and missing the stability and acceptance of Ronnie's love.

***

She did love him, you know. Ronnie. He would pop into her mind as she was smiling brightly at some politician or gossiping with his wife about so-and-so's dress and how inappropriate it was for such an esteemed function, despite having held her hair out of her own alcohol-induced vomit the night before. She missed Ronnie's arms around her and his genuine, sweet whispers in her ear as he tucked her hair behind it. He was so passionate, so full of life, but she did not realize much of what she loved so much about him was that thrill of madness just below the surface. The instability of it all, like climbing a beautiful mountain harboring a raging volcano within it. Up top was a thriving city of a soul, bustling with creativity and life and love and a well-lit skyline. But below, gushing beneath all of that, was a sewer of rottenness. A streaming black river of anger and betrayal and all of the rage and frustration from the unfairness of life. She supposed she had seen a glimmer of it, and she supposed she understood it all too well herself. At the time, it made her feel connected to the man. As if he comprehended something about life so many others want to wish away. It was the thing that compelled him to write poetry in his lyrics and to love her with just a look. And if Amara were honest with herself, she knew how easy it was to transform that into hatred. It is but an imperceptibly thin line separating love from hate, light from dark, life from death. It is a delicate balance, indeed, and investing in a man who was capable of truly feeling the one would always come with the risk of the other.

***

Exhausted, Amara tried to force her eyes open enough to survey the room in which the man she loved – the only man she had ever loved – was holding her captive. Her prison cell. The walls were covered with hand-drawn portraits and prints of her. It was like a broken mirror, with a thousand shards showing different versions and sizes staring back at her. Words like "Slut" and "Bitch" were scribbled in an angry hand in black marker in the spaces between the photos. The guy was completely loco. She thought she knew him. She thought she understood him on a basic level. But he hated her. She had to get out of there.

Then the fog cleared and she remembered. It felt like another punch in the gut. She had told him.

She thought he was the kind of man who would let her go if he knew they had a child together. She thought that would buy her way out of the situation and silence his rage, but she may have poured gasoline on a fire. An urgency rose within her – she had to warn her mother.

There was nothing left to lose. She worked and wriggled the headband around her mouth again until it opened up a gap. She took a deep breath, her belly expanding and her ribs screaming in pain, and she screamed as loudly as she could. She shouted and shrieked as much and as loudly as she could muster for what must have been a few minutes. Then the walls closed in and the world went black.

CHAPTER 32
Aiyanna

I was on my way to my fifth session with Dr. Haney. I was addicted.

After the second session, I paid close attention to the steps Dr. Haney took in hypnotizing me. I wanted to remember how to try to regress on my own later that afternoon. Then I would not have to rely on his help or wait for appointments. I would have the luxury to do it as often as I liked. Step one: put myself at ease. Make myself comfortable. Then come the deep breaths. Back, back... but I couldn't get there. Almost, it felt like. It was like that place between wake and dream, when you are both here and not. I couldn't quite get there, though. I made other attempts after my third and fourth sessions, but it was more of the same. So close. Almost. I was so frustrated not to be able to fully go back alone. It was so effortless for Dr. Haney. He just talked, really. Why could I not get there on my own? I wanted to be the captain of my own ship. But I was just a dinghy on an exploding sea, without sails or a strong arm to row, my flimsy rubber tossed and thrown by the raging waves.

I was therefore waiting on Dr. Haney again, my leg bouncing nervously. I hoped he wouldn't notice I was a complete regression junkie.

With every successful regression, I was introduced to another ending, another outcome, a different story. It was delicious. Infinite possibilities and endless lives from which to choose, and they were all mine at some point in time. I could visit another story and stay for just awhile, without being cornered into a life I no longer wanted with no way out but death. It was so much better than reality, and I wanted to spend all of my waking hours not actually awake, but in that state.

Even the scary regressions - the tragedies, the fears - were no worse than the ongoing nightmares strung throughout my life. I would wake from them with a glaze of sweat on my brow just as I had done countless times from my nightmares. I know now that my dreams and my memories were always basically one and the same. Of course, I couldn't piece them into a coherent picture in my dreams, but they were nonetheless glimpses of my pasts. Sometimes just a piece of a picture. Seconds of a story that spoke to me in ways that were more than fantasy. They were each a cut of clay that was massaged and molded into the form that I am today. And every day, I am being remade. Every new experience, every new fear, is another chisel, another pixel of my portrait. It all adds up to who I am and who I am going to be.

It was a crystal ball, of sorts, this ability of mine. Of course, I could not predict the future, but I was experiencing things that I may never experience in my lifetime. Not this one, anyway. I was seeing things, touching them, real and tangible, that I should not be seeing or touching. It was stronger than reality and science and physics as we understand them now. And yet, it was entirely irrational. Illogical. Impossible. But it was true. As anyone with any intellect articulates, knowledge of history is the greatest tool for our future.

The knowledge developed facets of my personality I might never have had in an organic progression. I could live out moments behind a sort of screen, moments that would otherwise have established disorders or damage within my soul. I could openly love the man who broke me. I could mourn his death and had every right to do so. I could murder. I could commit adultery or any number of sins. I could ride aboard the Titanic or have shellshock in the trenches of a war.

No one would believe me if I told them. I'm not sure you believe me now, but we are too far in to stop telling you my story. So we soldier on.

Dr. Haney and I went through the motions. We said our hellos, I got myself prone on his comfortable couch, his velvety voice towed me through time, further and further back. And then...

CHAPTER 33
Adsila

It is the sensation of sliding into a canoe. You can feel yourself floating, balancing on a solid sheath beneath you, but knowing that it is supported by something slippery and intangible. That was regression therapy. Dr. Haney was my canoe, my something solid to hold on to as I made my journey, but my memory was the water and the real guide. I went where it took me.

This time, it took me to a grove of trees that created a cool canopy over a verdant ground. Spots of sunlight beamed through the leaves. It was a warm day. It must have been Spring because white clover bloomed all around, mixed in with the grass. It smelled like honeysuckle and fresh air. Sky blue Forget-Me-Not flowers dotted the shaded grove. Vines hung from the trees like drunk ballerinas, lithe and twisted throughout the branches. The grass was lush between my bare toes, but there were bald spots where other couples had apparently stood before. It was a special spot in this part of the world.

And there she was.

In this life, she was my fiancée, and this was our wedding day. Walter was my name in this world. I was lanky, with wide shoulders and narrow hips. I had a shock of red hair upon my head. I wore suspenders and brown tweed britches with a cuff several inches above my bare feet. I could not help but smile at my woman as my heart squeezed with love and memory and a tinge of sadness for the person lying on a sofa all that space away who longed for the feeling I was experiencing. It was real, true romantic love. There were no walls between us – only honesty and respect. And hope.

Adsila, descendant of the Hopituh Shi-nu-mu (or Hopi) people, took a deep breath, inhaling the scent of sunshine, honeysuckle and wildflowers. My love. I admired the way the rays shone through the tangle of trees like shafts of light through a church window's stained glass – the art of the glass itself begetting more beauty and art as it enhances all it shines upon in a mosaic of color. There were people who were like that, too. Adsila was one of them.

She was raised to appreciate the majesty of nature. To live as one with the land. Her people believed Maasaw created the world to fulfill every need we could possibly conjure. Whether the gods with which she was raised or the one for whom I was taught blessed us in this life, I only knew we needed all the help we could get. I was relying on that, as we were sure to be penniless. While it was not uncommon, an eligible white bachelor of breeding age in the West marrying himself to a Hopi girl was not looked upon favorably. It was more accepted than it would have been only a few years earlier, but it would be a struggle for us nonetheless. Love has a way of having the final word, though. Adsila and I were connected, and we knew it from the very first second. Our love only grew with every day we shared until we were sure we wanted to share every day henceforth.

She was a modern girl, for the most part. I met her trading furs at the market. She dressed in regular clothes, though, not hides or anything especially Indian. Her skin was the color of an acorn, while mine was more of an aspen tree. She smiled at me, and I was hers. Her high cheekbones outlined her deep brown, happy eyes. They were warm and genuine and sweet-spirited. Looking at her was soothing. The butterflies that stirred at my first sight of her settled cozily in the pit of my stomach. She was interesting in a comfortable way. It felt like home.

I studied each of the few faces surrounding us on this, our wedding day. I recognized them all, in this life as well as the distant one – that life I could barely keep as an undertone in my mind to remember everything. The faintest of whispers to never forget. It was difficult to keep hold of, though. That murmur of memory yet to come wasn't my life right now – this was. This moment was all there was, and keeping a grasp of that distant self was so difficult. I wanted to stay forever in this sunshiney moment of absolute joy. I could deal with whatever was to come if I could just keep the memory of this day. I wanted, I needed, to remember every detail.

My gaze landed on Adsila's older sister, her shiny amber eyes showing strength and love in equal parts. Raven-headed with sharp cheekbones and an aura of love much like Adsila. Who did those eyes remind me of? So devoted and so honest. It was...Cooper? How could it be that my dog, who bites at imaginary fleas and chews holes in my socks in a world that seems a million miles away is the woman who was raised with my wife? But it was. I don't know how I knew, but I just knew. Like when you are in a dream and you do not look like you or behave as you would, but you know in the dream that it is supposed to be you.

My Jamma in my distant future. She was my mother in this world of sunshine and tree groves. She was fair and freckled, with the same uncombable red hair I had. She smiled, and a crinkle of joy occurred at the edges of her narrow eyes, her long blond eyelashes brushing her freckled cheeks. She was willing to love and accept Adsila, despite societal norms or pressure from the townsfolk to marry off one of their white women. I was overcome with love in that moment, between knowing her now and loving her as my Jamma many moons from now. I rushed to her, gathering up this stranger of sorts into my arms. But she wasn't really a stranger at all. I loved her in this life, and I loved her in all others.

"If you are ready, Walter, we will begin," smiled an abrupt, but pleasant, white man standing at the edge of the worn circle in this beautiful grove of trees. He must have been the pastor, but I swear I recognized him distantly as Dr. Haney. My canoe. It was vaguely odd, like we were in Wonderland, each caricature some version of someone else, but I didn't care. I never wanted to leave this moment. Everyone and everything I ever loved was there.

Adsila's soft eyes glistened, the brown blending in with the woods around us. I smiled, a tiny gap between my front teeth. Her hair hung loose, past her shoulders. She was not full Hopi, but she was not a white woman. She had lived a nondescript life as just another person in the village. To the rest of the world, she was perfectly average. But to me, she was the whole entire world. And I loved her as immensely as my heart could hold.

As I slipped a delicate, thin gold ring upon her finger, I was the happiest I had ever felt. In any life I could recall. Her sister hugged me tightly. As a wedding gift, my mother presented Adsila with a pristine whitework quilt. It had been wrapped in packing paper, and it was perfect. It must have taken her months to complete such an intricate design. My wife hugged it to her heart as our first family heirloom.

The sense of love and joy of the day seized me and I felt myself starting to pull away, back through time and space and parallel planes to a life I did not recognize anymore. I didn't want to leave. That moment was everything for me – it was the moment I would never have but here, and I willed myself to stay. I begged my brain and my body and whatever gods controlled this process to let me live the rest of the days this life in this memory. I wanted Adsila and this grove of trees and this version of the people I loved.

But I suppose I was needed elsewhere because I awoke in Dr. Haney's office, angry at myself for doing so.

I was not aware of what parts of my occurrences Dr. Haney was able to experience with me, but he must have understood somehow. He patted my shoulder and walked me to my car without a word.

I understood from this regression that those who are brave enough to love you, despite all odds, are the ones who matter most in life. I also knew that I needed nature. It helped to calm me and re-center myself to be surrounded by it. Perhaps Jamma and I could pack up Cooper and head out of town for a few days. Somewhere isolated, with just the whisper of the wind through the trees and each other's company.

I wanted to keep that memory of the grove and my marriage for as long as I lived. It had not even made me think of Ethan – Adsila didn't remind me of him at all, strangely. And for the first time I could recall, I did not dream at all that night.

CHAPTER 34
Jamma

Eve could not wait to hear what had happened in Aiyanna's latest therapy session. It was amazing to watch her girl work through things and discover more and more about herself and the unique history that created her. Eve loved hearing Aiyanna's descriptions of Dr. Haney and her analyses of different lives. It was her honor that her granddaughter shared such things with her and her pleasure to do her part in helping her understand what it all meant.

It was time she told Ai all she knew, now that she could understand. She needed to know the rest. She was entitled to know the drawbacks and the repercussions of glimpsing into scenes you should never technically see. You cannot be a spectator of your own life without there being penalties. Eve had to sit her down and tell her. She had put it off for so long already because her little blossom had been so spirited after her discovery. It was like turning a key to her old Aiyanna. She was alive again, and to see the twinkle in that baby girl's eyes was everything to Eve. Her happiness was the ultimate goal, and as such, she should understand the whole picture. It is easy to appreciate the art that is life when you have a magnifying glass on the individual paint strokes, but nothing compares to taking a step back and examining the entire framed canvas. That's what takes your breath away.

Eve's knitting needles clicked away as she mused on about the implications of their secret familial gift. She was in the process of knitting Aiyanna a scarf. It was a sort of tradition of hers to make Ai a new scarf of a different color for Christmas every year. This year, Eve selected a teal color yarn with tiny sequins woven through it. She hoped it would make Aiyanna's eyes sparkle. They needed to sparkle again. She smiled to herself, thinking that Ai was never the typical child. She never took those gifts for granted or rolled her eyes at something homemade. She appreciated the effort and the love that went into it. (Especially since Eve's attempt to teach her how to knit and crochet years before. She kept the 10-inch section of crocheted tan yard in case Ai ever wanted to pick up where she left off.) If Eve could not wrap her own arms around her granddaughter and keep her safe in her coldest seasons, a scarf would have to do. She could no longer swaddle her tightly and rock her in her arms until the hurt went away. She was grown now. It was harder than ever to shelter her from the painful parts of life, as illustrated by her breakup with, and sudden death of, Ethan.

That young woman would never know how very much Eve loved her. How she had always loved her. If she could have taken on all of the heartaches and anguish Ai had ever experienced and any hardship that was yet to come, she would do it in a heartbeat. Aiyanna was good. She was a decent, kind human being who shone bright with love if ever you met her. She was joyful and she laughed her way through life. Eve did not want the trials and tribulations of living to take that away from her. It was a rare enough thing already.

Cooper sighed lazily, rearranging himself in his bed on the floor beside Eve's chair. His bed was as old and worn out as she was. He was exhausted from his rawhide mastication, as evidenced by the chewy, wet, mangled wad still beside him.

As the news reporter droned on about something depressing, Eve felt the itchy urge for another coughing spell. She grabbed a tissue from the box she kept beside her chair. She was exhausted from it. The constant shortness of breath and gurgle in her lungs had drained her of late. She supposed it just took longer to recover from colds when you are old. She woke throughout the night, coughing. She stayed so tired. But Burns do not quit, so she shouldered on, rising early every morning and continuing in her routines as best she could. Idle hands and all that. Besides, Ai needed the stability after all she had been through.

And then it came. The racking cough, pulling from deep in her chest and yet, never satisfying the urge. Her body shook with each hack. She could not get enough air in. Minutes later, what seemed like an eternity, she pulled the tissue from her face. She inhaled in a measured rhythm so as not to spur on another coughing episode. She tossed the tissue in the small trash can she kept for bits of thread and other throwaways. That was when she noticed dark crimson specks staining the white surface. It looked like a Jackson Pollock painting. Oh, God.

Worried, Eve popped up from her armchair, but her legs were unsteady. Her knees wobbled and gave way. Her papery weak frame hit the floor. It was as if it were happening in slow motion. She noted how different everything looked from the angle of falling. A dust bunny she must have missed when she swept last. The wood floor and its plush area rug rushing toward her face. The last thing she remembered was Cooper frantically licking her face and the rhythmic twinkle of Christmas lights in the background, fading from her sight as the news droned on.

CHAPTER 35
Aiyanna

I was anxious to tell Jamma everything that had happened that day in therapy, to get her insight and opinions, as I did after every session. She always knew the right words to say, what to do, how to do it. If I needed answers or intuition, she would have them.

I looked forward to evenings this time of year. We would sip hot cocoa and decorate the old Christmas tree with our sentimental assortment of ornaments, classic carols playing in the background. We would hang the old, decaying decorations I made in pre-school, with glue and macaroni noodles. The plastic needles of the fake tree would shed, as they did every year, onto the handmade tree skirt, its once bright crimson color faded to a watery red. We would hang the hand-stitched stockings on the mantel: one old knitted green sock for Jamma, my red cross-stitched stocking, and a small red number form the dollar store for old Cooper dog.

I unlocked the front door and walked into the house, tossing my keys on the entryway table. It smelled like cinnamon. Cooper's toenails clicked on the floor as he came rushing at me, panting, the whites of his eyes showing. I pet him, reassuring him it was just me, but he spun in nervous circles and whimpered. Something was wrong.

When I found Jamma, skinny limbs were all over the place like a game of Pick Up Sticks. I pushed panic aside, mentally directing the Plinko Ball of Mental Collapse into the slot designated *to deal with later*. I checked to see if she was breathing. Called 911. Ran my hand through her thin hair and whispered reassuringly while I sat with her on the floor. Ambulance, waiting, worrying, pacing the waiting room, still waiting, seen to her room, waiting, waiting while they run tests on her, waiting, and then.

A doctor with gray temples and an expressionless face moving his mouth, lips wrapping around his teeth, tongue flicking, indecipherable noise blending with the buzzers and phone calls and televisions blaring from other hospital rooms. An engulfing clamor to the point where it merges into a single sound that might as well have been above my register. I could not comprehend everything he was saying, but a few words stuck out and struck me across the face. I stopping breathing.

Lung cancer. Metastatic to the brain.

There was no way this was actually happening. It was not real. It couldn't be.

Cancer was a bitch. Would there never be a cure?! Lung cancer? Jamma didn't even smoke! My thoughts raced around my mind like a horde of angry wasps, chaotic and terrifying.

I'm ashamed to admit it, but I went straight into pity party mode.

Why was everything being ruined? What was the point in destroying every single thing that was beautiful in the world? And Jamma? She was the most beautiful one. How could someone as good and kind and selfless and strong as Jamma have such a horrendous affliction? And at Christmas? It was all so unfair, and I was automatically angry at God. Truth be told, I had been for a while. Why was he testing us? We were good and decent people, even when it was inconvenient. Jamma treated others with kindness and always gave the benefit of the doubt before passing judgment on anyone. We spent Thanksgiving ladling chicken soup for the homeless. Why can't the unscrupulous and cruel be tested? Why did life appear so easy for those people who deserved it the least, and so hard for someone like my Jamma? I thought I had been experiencing heartbreak in the months before, but they were nothing compared to the mauling that doctor's words gave me.

Walking stilted like a zombie, I watched in slow motion as machines and people whirred past. My thoughts were zipping and flying in every direction, screaming in my head. I felt like I was going to vomit. Or pass out.

I made my way in a rush toward Jamma's room, but it seemed an eternity had passed in the time it took. My legs just would not move. They felt like concrete bricks. As did my heart. I didn't think it could break any more than it already had. I was never more wrong in my life.

"I want to know everything," were Jamma's first words when I approached her hospital bed, eyes shiny with anticipation. Her bony knees jutted out under the standard-issue powder blue blanket. She pointed to a straight-backed chair on her side of the curtained room.

I began, uncertain of how to proceed. Uncertain of anything. I thought I was going to be sick. "Well, the doctor was saying—"

"Oh, pish posh. Not that! I want to know how it went with Dr. Haney." Her smile was warm and showed little indication of the illness Dr. Gray Temples was running on about. Her eyes were bright with anticipation.

"Jamma, you're sick."

"I know that, child. I am not worried about that. Now tell me."

"It's not just a cold, Jamma. This is really bad," I started, but a rock formed in my chest and my throat closed shut. I willed the tears pricking my eyes to go away. Jamma did not need to see that right now. How could I explain to her that she was dying? How could I ever accept that myself?

"Aiyanna, I know. They already told me." Her eyes were like a calm Mediterranean Sea, cobalt and bright. They conveyed absolute understanding of the situation. "Everything is going to be okay."

At that, I broke down completely. Jamma had always been the stronger one.

CHAPTER 36
Robert

It was a surreal experience, witnessing it again. Robert Haney had only successfully helped one other client regress to such a remarkable understanding of themselves. It was an incredible feeling.

Each time Aiyanna was able to make her way back, his palms got sweaty and his breathing got faster. He had to force himself to remain calm or he would break his concentration. If that occurred, there would be no telling the repercussions for Aiyanna. She depended on him to guide her through the process. Truth be told, in all of his years of research and study, there were still aspects of it that he did not understand since he could not witness what was happening firsthand.

He wished, more than anything, to be able to see what Ai was seeing. He wanted the ability for himself. How extraordinary that would be! Can you imagine? To be able to see and comprehend occurrences that formed who you are as a human being?

He was alive again with the memories of his youth, just starting out in the field, hungry for knowledge, completely in love, truly alive. There was so much more life yet to be lived. The unknown. Possibility and hope. He was the author of his own story, with many blank pages yet to be filled. Unlike now, when he was definitely closer to the end than the beginning.

He found the similarities between his regression patients fascinating. Intellectual stimulation had him feeling so alive, and he wanted more. He had more research to do. He pulled a heavy book from the top shelf in his home library. It had been the first textbook he found, back in his days of searching, that mentioned regression therapy. He cracked open the dusty tome, a shiver of thrill going through him. He was excited to be a part of something so special once more.

CHAPTER 37
Jamma

It was a sense of déjà vu listening to the whirring of hospital machines and the soft scuffle of shoes down the hallway. Eve was taken back to the same smells and sterile sensations of when she had her first and only child, Amara. Granted, those were very different circumstances.

She wondered what Amara was doing right that moment. She wondered if she was happy. She hoped her daughter knew she thought about her all the time, every day. She hoped her daughter knew she loved her, and she would always love her. She believed in Amara. If not in this lifetime, she would eventually see things the way they were. While the world does not work in just black and whites, one can still live her life in the Light.

A familiar feeling washed over Eve from all of those years before: everything from this point forward would be different. These separate trips to the hospital were pivotal points in her life, each for different reasons, and that tradition would continue for her Aiyanna. This surprise visit to the hospital would be a day she would never forget.

Eve smiled softly at the sight of her granddaughter, curled up in the hospital chair beside her bed. She refused to leave, to go home and get some rest. She had called their neighbor to take care of Cooper. She had not left Eve's side. She knew Eve loved her, and she was strong. So much stronger than Eve realized. She was at a point in her life where she could manage without her old grandmother if she had to.

Those thoughts zipped and swirled about Eve's brain until sleep wrapped its fuzzy arms around her and embraced her. She drifted back through the mental equivalent of a worn box of frayed photographs and closets of clothes that no longer fit. Old heeled shoes and uniforms for jobs she no longer held. Her thoughts were flipped through and pushed aside like old yearbooks and magazine clippings for ideas she never followed through. It was her life, this life. The photos were of Eve, in various stages of her lifetime. Photos that did not exist in reality. The costumes were symbols of the significant events in her life. It was like a life-sized scrapbook of everything that had mattered or had made her within the confines of her life as Elizabeth Burns.

On the other side of that dusty closet of her mind was a door. She watched her own wrinkled and age-spotted hand slowly and dramatically turn the brass doorknob. Like some Narnia fairytale, it opened into the brightest light. It was unspeakably bright – the most brilliant, glowing star any mortal soul could have never seen, for it would have blinded them. Beyond was a field of flowers, with the souls of those gone before with smiles on their faces. They welcomed Eve with warmth and love.

She implicitly understood what it all meant. She was almost out of time. But there were things that needed to be said, and certain items to tend to before she could go gently into that good night.

CHAPTER 38
Aiyanna

Everything in life is a calculated risk. Every single day. At a minimum, we pay a toll of our time on everything we do, or everything we don't do. We are taxed, regardless. Most consider the maximum risk that of their lives. I no longer think that way. Time is everything. And even as currency, it is malleable and unexplored, not like silver or nickel, the solid weight of which you can feel in your palm. The value is both underappreciated and infinite. Some of us waste our entire lives away while others are cherishing the very last of theirs (as far as they know). There is no way to store it away for a rainy day. We spend time even as we sleep... or dream.

Travelling through time – wow, that phrase still sounds so sci-fi and absurd – within my own mind requires a toll, too. I have lived these lives already, and my spending precious moments of the one I should be enjoying (instead of passed out on a couch or in my own dreams) reliving ones I already have is a waste.

Jamma confessed to me that she, too, had the ability to see her past within her own mind. She doesn't know much about what she calls this "gift," but it is apparently passed down through our maternal genes. Perhaps it is something inside of everyone, or maybe it's some sort of mutation that allows us to see memories we shouldn't have anymore.

Nonetheless, it was comforting to know that Jamma understood what I was going through: from the shock and discovery of this "gift" to the absolute immersion in it.

She told me of the years of her life spent reliving years of past lives. How dreams plagued most nights of her youth. How she met the man who would help her harness those thoughts through regression and how to better control them. How she was fascinated by the many lives she had lived, her failures and flaws always trickling into the next time around. She told me about her lost love in this life, Red, and how she spent almost the entirety of her pregnancy with my mother seeking him in other lives. She had no idea what kind of affect that had on her baby. At the time, she thought it was worth the payoff (as I thought about my own travels), but she would give anything to have more time with me now. To take it all back. To go back and do better by the daughter growing inside her belly.

Jamma learned in her research and experiences that time was the most valuable currency we could spend, and she tried to tell me that every journey past the consciousness of this life takes time away from it. For every memory I live again from a time gone by, I lose that time from the life I'm living now.

It didn't seem like such a high price to pay to be happy again, to see Ethan alive again, in any form. What life was this, anyway, without love? Jamma was sick, and without her, I had no one in the world who gave a damn that I existed.

Jamma, however, disagreed. She urged me to stop looking for answers in the past and to point my actions and intentions toward the future of *this* life. She said I was meant to change the world, if even just my small space within it, and it would be an injustice not to do so. But for her dreams, she had stopped regressing years and years ago. She realized she was consumed with the other lives she has already lived so much so that she was neglecting her life in this time. The people in her life now, this life, were her priority, and she felt it would have been unfair to give them anything less than her full attention. That included her own self. She was certain the cancer in her lungs and brain was a poisonous gift from her own adventures of *travel*.

She explained to me that regression confirmed the belief that was lurking just beyond her comprehension for all of the years of her life. It was an itch that could not be reached or a whisper that could not quite be heard: reincarnation does exist. For many, it is just a passing thought to wonder as to whether it could be. For others, it is a principle of their faith. For Jamma, it was an answer.

She threw herself into study of the idea of reincarnation. It can't be proven or confirmed, but it also cannot be discredited. Though the scientific community may try, there are stories and examples of people popping up over the years, stepping forward to tell their truths. There are others in the world who have the same abilities as the Burns. They are able to regress through hypnosis and catch glimpses of their pasts. Some believe that each one of us, even as you read this now, have that ability. It is simply a matter of capturing it, like catching an elusive monster on film. As Jamma explained to me, it is the belief of many throughout history and various cultures that reincarnation is our chance to do better, to be better, the next time around. With each life, we learn more. We are given another precious chance to be good to each other, to help one another. To evolve into a higher human being.

Jamma tried so hard to tell me, to have it really sink in. The importance of what she was saying to me then continues to grow as I get older. While we have an ability to travel through our pasts and pick through memories and time, we cannot foresee the future. We do not know what waits for us in the time yet to come. Those moments are still ours to create. The time yet to happen is our chance to be that better human being.

"Every day is a choice, baby girl. You can decide how you want to spend it. That's the magnificent beauty of it. You can make up your mind to be a better version of yourself today, and even better tomorrow. You can choose to pull yourself from the darkness and rise into the light, or you can choose to embrace whatever wickedness you may feel. You can learn something new or fall in love or adopt a pet or volunteer. You can run away or quit your job or start your own charity or have an affair. It is never too late to make those choices. Every day is a brand new blank page for you to fill with whatever you choose, to write your own story. There is no more magical gift than that. I just hope you choose to write yourself as the good guy and not the villain, for we all have the capacity to be either at any given moment. We are just people. We are not all *just* good or bad – we are broken or we are sad or we are lonely... or we are joyful. The story is yours to create. And now, this story of mine, I can feel it coming to a close."

At that, my eyes welled up with fat, hot tears.

Jamma patted my arm reassuringly. "I like my story, and I'm proud of my creations," she smiled, as she touched my cheek. "Now, I can rest in peace." Jamma smiled again, a content, serene smile.

"I hate this talk, Jamma," I confessed, a tear sliding down my cheek and falling into the cotton of my t-shirt, dissolving into the fabric, the only sign it was ever there being the shirt was a shade darker on the tiny spot where it fell. Wasn't that just like each of us, too? We are gone in a blink, the only sign we were ever here drying out shortly after?

I could think of nothing to say in response to Jamma's beautiful, stabbing words. It was obvious she wanted me to heed what she was saying, that she thought it was important. But truth be told, I could not pay attention to her words. What I heard were the raspy cracks in her voice as she talked or the wheezing when she inhaled. I could not hear her telling me to live on as she was dying before me.

"Please don't leave me," I choked out, a sob of loneliness and desperation slicing its way through my windpipe. I knew it was a ridiculous and inappropriate thing to say, but she was my Jamma. She was my best friend and my person. She was the thing that made the world alright to live in. I had been mourning Ethan for so long, I had forgotten whom I had truly loved – the sort of love that would never fade. True soul mates. I was so stupid. The hours I spent under my covers with a broken heart as Jamma rocked softly beside me... I had taken them for granted. I should have been playing cards with her or cooking with her or telling her how very much she meant to me. I had complained of a life without love when, all along, I had been awash in it. It had been in the air with every breath I took in her presence, in the food she had cooked for me for so many years, in the scarf around my neck that she had crocheted for me with her own hands.

"Shhh, come here, my girl," Jamma whispered and patted the bed beside her. I curled up next to her like I used to do when I was a child. I would have crawled into her lap in that moment if I had thought it wouldn't hurt her fragile, bony legs. "My love for you is eternal, Aiyanna Burns. That is something that time and space...and even death... will never take. Memories and even history can fade, but your soul and mine will forever be entwined. In this life or the next one or a thousand years from now. The love never dies, Ai. That is what I want you to learn. Our flesh is but a pile of meat with an expiration date stamped on us the moment we are conceived. But our souls, our choices, our love... that is what makes life. And that will always be life. It is the only thing you get more of by giving away. It feeds us all. Love *is* life. And there is so much love to live."

A chill ran up my spine. It was something I knew I wanted to remember. I tried to hold on to her every word, knowing what she spoke was the most important thing I would ever learn. I was not sure then that I was fully comprehending, though I understand it all so much better now.

"It's okay, though, my precious blossom. We still have some time," Jamma smiled. "I just needed to tell you these things before it's too late. Some will not make sense until later on, and that's okay. Just don't give up on the life you've been given this time around, my love. It is a beautiful, precious thing." She kissed the top of my head.

I couldn't comprehend it all in one stab. It was all too much. All of the drama and the shocks to the system and the heartbreaks washed over me, and I fell sound asleep in the safety of my Jamma's small arms.

CHAPTER 39
Beatha

We visit the Highlands once again...

Edan would not leave Emrys's side. Emrys's body was stiff and cold. He had left them. Edan curled his shaggy body in a tight little knot on the dirt floor, tears staining the soft fur beneath his eyes. He, too, was suffering from heartbreak. The somber-faced women washed the corpses of those departed, the men they loved. Each had a story both similar and entirely dissimilar to Beatha's. Mothers, daughters, sisters and wives. They all had loved and lost, and yet, each of their stories were uniquely heartrending.

Beatha wept over Emrys throughout the night, her tears making their jagged journey over the wounds and dried blood on his body. Edan lie by her feet, beside his master, unmoving. Beatha wondered if he could understand that Emrys was gone. Forever. She, for one, could not understand it.

As commonplace a thing such as death was to them all, Beatha never expected it to come calling on her or hers. She had only just met Emrys but a few months earlier. They were just married. They still had a lifetime to live and a family to make, but he left her there alone. Well, almost alone. She pressed her palm against the tiny swell of her belly.

She was angry in a way she could not explain. What was she to do, just forget his consuming love and live on without it? Was she expected to disregard that he and he alone owned every piece of her heart? No. She squeezed the leather bracelet still in her hot palm. Ne Obliviscaris. Never Forget. And she would not.

It had been a crushing defeat for their men, only a few bloody stragglers limping their way home. It was a sight she wished she could cleanse from her own eyeballs, the sadness for every family in the village almost too much to bear. The guilt of living bearing down on the shoulders of those who watched their comrades die. The Battle of Culloden would change everything. Every aspect of their lives before were about to be undone and dismissed. Their culture and their history would be challenged. They would be oppressed. She dreamed it all, waking with cold sweats and fear. For herself, for her family, and for each generation to follow. It would never be the same again.

When his uncle dropped Emrys's leather bracelet into Beatha's palm, her heart broke into a million blackened pieces, like charred ashes from a once roaring fire. Emrys had not wanted to go to battle to begin with. He had had a notion that it would end poorly, and so it had. However, Emrys was not a man to disappoint his clan nor run away from responsibility. Honor was everything. Thus, he would ride with his clan bravely into battle, despite his certainty that they would all be lost.

She could not let go as easily. She threatened to club his kneecaps to keep him at home. He smiled his crooked, charming smile and he kissed her red hair and her cheeks and her hands, vowing to find her again in the next life if he were lost to her in this one.

"I will love you forever, Beatha. Through time and death, should it come to that."

"Beatha," her mother said, soft and stern at the same time. She interrupted Beatha's memories, which were more like dreams in her exhausted and miserable state. "It's time to go now, lassie. You must say goodbye."

Goodbye. She said it as if Beatha were waving to a fellow villager on her way to the market. She wanted her to say goodbye as if that were something she were capable of doing. It was something she would never be able to do. It was something she never *wanted* to do.

CHAPTER 40
Amara

And so we go, back and forth through time, like mixing two cups of
differing liquids by pouring into one, then the other...

When Amara came to, or at least what she remembered next, were the fluorescent lights of a hospital room. It is as if they think the light and sterile smell of sanitation will drive out the dark cloud of death that always hovers about hospitals. At least she was alive. Maybe. Perhaps it was purgatory, with the wheezing of machines and soft hush of funeral pallor and sickness, the almost imperceptible shuffling of nursing shoes down the squeaky-clean hallway.

"Oh, you're awake," came a surprisingly high-pitched voice for a man of his size. The nurse was tall and dark-skinned, with a well-trimmed goatee. He flitted about, checking the saline bag and documenting this and that from the various machines monitoring her. He threw the standard-issue blanket and sheets from Amara to check some wheezing machinery that randomly squeezed her legs. It gave her a chance to objectively analyze her body.

Ronnie's attack had come out of the blue, as far as Amara was concerned. She had committed herself to never seeing his face again once she walked away that Halloween night. She had no notion that he was plotting for so long to hurt her.

She allowed her eyes to scan the length of her body as if it were not her own. As if she had not just endured a trauma that she did not even know how to begin to explain. As if all of the unprocessed feelings were not lurking just below the surface in a pressing way that made her feel like she wanted to scream and cry and retaliate. Her body was bruised. Badly. But not mangled. Still shapely and supple beneath the injured exterior. She was not in any excruciating pain. She was numb, in a way. Not in that she did not feel the achy bruises covering her body, but in a way where she was not certain if any of it was real. She wondered how she could obtain some of whatever medication they were giving her for later. At any rate, she was alive.

Then she remembered what had happened. Her mind was floating from thought to incoherent thought, but she forced herself to go back. Ronnie. He had done this. Who had found her? Oh, yes. A neighbor must have heard her screams because she recalled a flash of a handsome policeman, then the wail of the ambulance and the crisp white shirt of a paramedic. She wondered how long she had been at the hospital, but her monstrous nurse had already left her again. So much for asking him. How much of a head start did Ronnie have? The window, bordered by mint green mini curtains, was blackened, so it must have been evening.

She had to get to Eve. There was no way in Hell Amara was ever going to be able to pay some hospital bill, anyway, so she gingerly pulled the tape attaching a needle to the outside of her hand and withdrew the IV. A machine began to beep. Slowly, painfully, she slid herself out of the hospital bed, peeping every couple of seconds at the half-open door to make sure no one was coming. She shuffled in the non-skid hospital socks to see if she had any clothes in the closet. None. She guessed the paramedics had taken her there as naked as they must have found her. Damn. She grabbed the toe of each sock and yanked it off, her ribs screaming in pain. Gliding out of the door and scanning the hallway, she was pleased to find it empty. There was no one at the nurses' station across from the elevators, but she took no chances. She found the stairwell and made her escape. There was no time to waste by getting stopped or being asked questions. She had to get to her daughter before Ronnie found her.

CHAPTER 41
Daisy

That made twice now. Two separate phone calls that went unanswered. Two times Daisy tried to make peace with Ai after their fallout, to show her that she was a good and caring friend, and two times she was ignored. Dismissed. Daisy had, of course, heard about the breakup between Ai and Ethan a couple of days before. She wanted to make sure her friend was okay. And get all of the details on the matter, too, of course. Ethan's friend had not been very helpful in providing clarity when he told Daisy what went down.

The gall of that girl to just ignore Daisy, though. All *after* Aiyanna, the bitch, was going to abandon Daisy for some boy, anyway. They were supposed to be friends, but Ai was such a shitty one. Daisy was done. She was tired of being the friend who made all the effort. She knew she deserved so much better. After all, she made Aiyanna. Ai, who would not even have a boyfriend if Daisy had not introduced her. Since, you know, Ai never left the house and had no friends of her own.

Well, thought Daisy, *I guess if we aren't friends, I no longer need to side with her*. She had drawn a line, and it seemed the rest of the world, including Daisy, was on the other side of it. Daisy never could quite crack that girl, and she always felt like some kind of outsider. She was sick of it.

Maybe Ethan needed some comforting, too, she considered. Daisy had been the one to introduce them, after all. It should have been her, not Ai. He should have chosen her.

After all, Daisy and Ethan made a better pair. He was tall and fit and personable, like her. He could use some help in the menswear department, but Daisy could also help with that. Aiyanna would *never* be able to advise anyone on fashion. And Daisy was sexy. She could be great arm candy for the right man. Ethan also seemed to be doing well enough for himself, which was the next prerequisite to date Daisy. He owned a house, at least. Yes, Daisy realized, perhaps she should reach out to her friend to see if he needed anything.

She made the two-hour drive and rang his doorbell in her highest stilettos and tightest bodycon minidress, with the slit up to her hip. It hugged all the right places on her body, and she intended to present her best assets. She wore the sparkly choker necklace that hid the birthmark on her neck. When Ethan opened the door, bedraggled and looking like he had aged ten years since she saw him last, she knew she was in.

He was clearly shocked to see her. She hugged him tightly, pressing her cleavage into him and wiggling ever so slightly to make sure he felt all of her. His grip tightened on her back. Without letting go and looking up at him from under her false lashes, Daisy whispered, "I know it's hard," and bit her bottom lip seductively. "It's so cold out here. Can I come in?" She shivered dramatically, rubbing her body hard enough to jiggle the important parts.

Hours later, it was pitch black outside. Daisy's hair was tangled, her lipstick completely gone, and her mascara had made black smudges under her eyes. Her false lashes were still somewhere in Ethan's house. With her shoes in her hand, feeling successful, she let herself out of Ethan's house. And screamed as she ran right into a warm body who had been hiding outside.

CHAPTER 42
Red

The train station back home. The screaming of the train as it slid to a stop. The station, crowded and full of fearful young men trying to appear brave. Hugging their loved ones. The blue dress she wore: straight, sleeveless, cut off right above her knees. How it perfectly matched her blue eyes, dark with their goodbye. A belt around her waist. Her calves and buckled leather shoes. Her blonde hair, parted in the middle. The tears in her eyes. The scent of nervous sweat and machinery. Her face as the train pulled away, her beauty undeniable. She had to stay. He had to go. He returned to that last glimpse of her over and over again. He lived for the day he could do it all in rewind and watch the station grow larger and larger as the train pulls closer. Watch her face emerge from the crowd and wrap his arms around her body. When he could finally return home and live a normal life again. It would never happen, though.

Red spent a year of his life in the jungles of Viet Nam. It was only a year. Though he was young, it was only a year. But it would change everything. It was completely different from everything he thought he knew. He was completely different from the man he thought he was.

When they landed at Bien Hoa, he was unprepared. He had already been through basic, but how much can they truly prepare someone for war? They were taught how to handle a rifle and to obey orders without question, but being there was so unlike anything else in life. War is Hell. The heat was oppressive. The humidity soaked through Red's uniform and his pack. He got used to the tickle of sweat on his face and the sting of bug bites on any exposed skin. The sounds and scenery were completely unfamiliar. It was not the roar of crickets and the distant whistle of the midnight train. It was silence or it was chaos. Tranquility was suspicious. They had to be ready to die at any second, without warning. One would think that would be an impetus to get right with God, so to speak, but how can you reconcile that with murder and violence and chaos and fear? There was no order to any of it. Good men lost their lives every day. The enemy would win one day, Red and his group would slaughter them the next. Whose side was God on? They were alone in that distant land, left to fend for themselves.

Red thought he knew it all. He was young and strong. Unlike most of the drafted, he was an intellect. He had a degree. He was clever. He was certain that would come in handy. It did not.

He did patrols and broke jungle with his machete right along with the other guys. There was no use for his mind or his schooling in the jungle. He did as he was told and kept his rifle and his marching boots in top order. That was his entire purpose. Men - boys, really – from inner cities and small towns who had known nothing of life but chasing skirts and smoking doobies were his equals. They were high school dropouts and fast food cooks, and they were all in that Hell together. Red had to admit, he resented it at first. He was a snob. Until his first firefight. The same men he underestimated, the same ones over which he felt superior, saved his life. The VC snuck up on them in the jungle, as they were so prone to do. Red was fussing with his rucksack when a bullet whizzed by his face, close enough to deafen him momentarily. Those boys, those uneducated and impolite boys, immediately pulled him to safety and mowed down the enemy. They had Red's back, and from that moment on, he had theirs. They were brothers.

The family Red made over there did not stop him from praying (so to speak) every single day for the end of his rotation. Each day, every single stretch of those twenty-four hours was harrowing. They could be completely bored for days, even a week or two. Then, without warning, they would be bombarded with gunfire. They had to be on guard every single second. They couldn't shit without watching over their shoulders. He witnessed so many of those new brothers of his lose their lives. Bodies torn apart, caught on fire. Skin fried like chicken. Eyeballs and organs scattering the jungle. Their pleas for help and screams of pain. The light leaving their eyes as Death wrapped its arms around them. They could be joking around or sharing stories of their women one second and Red could be holding their hands as they died the next. He wanted to go home and live a normal life again. He had to get out of that godforsaken land. He had to get back to Eve.

Then the day came, seemingly like so many others in the jungle, that ended everything.

Eve was all he thought about. Quick images would click through his mind like a Polaroid flash. Snapshots of her smile or the curl in her hair right above her ears. The skin of her hands or the dip of her throat. He dreamed of her, of times they had together and the life they would make.

Then that day came. He was daydreaming of her when the bullet pierced him like a blazing hot fire poker. Instant pain from the sting of some bullet serpent. His brothers were screaming, crawling to help him amid gunfire and Hell. He wondered how Eve would take the news. Then his vision narrowed and disappeared. The world went as black as lights out. His time was up.

CHAPTER 43
Amara

Amara had not seen her daughter since she left her on Eve's front stoop in the wee hours one morning. Her daughter was beautiful. She was a miniature version of Amara, with one dimple in her cheek and bright blue eyes. But she was washed of all the anger Amara had always harbored. There were no dark shadows in her eyes, no wickedness in her smile. She was pure and happy and healthy. Amara had obviously made the right decision several years before.

Eve had named her Aiyanna. Amara would have chosen Ann or Amy or something simpler. She knew what it was like to have an uncommon name, the kind you never could find on a magnet in some boutique shop.

It was obvious from the onset that Eve had given her the Light she had always attempted to impart to Amara. The only thing Amara ever had to offer was Darkness. It had been within her for as far back as she could remember, centuries and lifetimes before. She thought it had given her everything she always wanted because all she ever wanted was to feel nothing. But she didn't feel nothing. She was full of anger and hatred and bitterness. She was a black wave, washing all around her of everything good and leaving nothing but misery in her wake. She was exhausted.

She was one of those souls who never sheds her hardships. She carries a pack of them on her back, heavier and heavier with each lifetime. Granted, it would seem that she created and fed many of the struggles she endured, and perhaps that was true, but they plagued her. Tiny whispers of malice and self-destruction, some incoherent even, but always constant. Her dreams were filled with the hopelessness of plague and the hollowness of hunger. Her attempts at change had never mattered. Disappointment and dread and darkness washed her and became her black velvet security blanket, of sorts. Rather than death and taxes, the only certainties in life, in any life, were despondency and disillusionment. She wanted better for her daughter. And so it would seem she was: better.

Amara knew it would be hard, showing up unexpected after all that time. She knew it the moment she first tried to knock on the front door weeks before. She simply could not do it. Even knowing they were in danger, knowing that timing was so important, she could not bring herself to do it. She could not face everything she had done. She had failed. She failed her mother and herself. She could not fail her child. But she could not face it, either. Her selfish embarrassment won in the end.

She found herself walking over to Steve's house instead. She knew him from her school days. He lived in his parents' old house just a block over from Amara's old residence. They got high. Of course, she had to sleep with him to pay him back. But even that just was not fun anymore.

She kept seeing Ronnie straddling her with hatred in his eyes, and she would subsequently lose all pleasurable sensation. She stared at Steve's ceiling until he finished without ceremony. She no longer felt powerful from any of it. Before, she would get a rush from being in control of men. Since Ronnie, she did not feel in control of anything at all, even herself. She created a life from which she could no longer run.

She got high again before she went back to her mother's doorstep. She needed to dull the pain in her body, as well as her mind. She still ached from Ronnie's assault. It had not been that long before, and while the sharp pains of his assault had dimmed, the dull aches of past injury remained. She had Steve burn strawberry incense to try to soften the undeniable odor of marijuana that permeated her hair and clothes.

Amara took a deep breath while she nervously checked her appearance in the tall, slender pane of glass next to the front door. She tried to last-minute talk herself out of it, but she knew she had to proceed. She had to at least try to warn her mother about what she had gotten her involved in. She sighed again and knocked on the door.

Eve was shocked when she opened the door to Amara's face. It must have been several minutes that they both just stood there, looking at each other. Amara's palms were sweaty. It felt like her mother was reading her like a book. Finally, her face softened.

"Come in," Eve said and took her daughter in her arms. She hugged her, a real solid hug. "Welcome home."

Amara blinked, confused. She was welcomed in without question.

A toddler, just a nugget of a human, waddled into the room. She was just learning to walk, her gait still stiff and awkward, laughing gleefully every time she fell. She smiled up at Amara, blonde curls in every direction. For the first time in her entire life, Amara truly loved someone else. At least she acknowledged the feeling. The truth was, she had loved Ronnie. She loved her mother, too. She knew it the moment Eve answered the door. The weight of guilt from disappointing her was almost unbearable for Amara.

The child, Amara's child, smiled and proudly showed her a stuffed dinosaur. Aiyanna was so unlike Amara. She offered immediate love in her gentle blue eyes to a perfect stranger. She was shy and kind and good, and more like Eve than anything like Amara.

Amara looked, really looked, at her child. Her eyes were like white fireworks over a blue sea. They drew you in with her childhood curiosity. She was pure and joyful, and her little fat cheeks were round with smiles. That baby was the only selfless thing Amara had ever accomplished. And now, her wrongdoings were going to rain Hell on her poor child and her tired mother. All she ever did was cause pain. She knew she had to figure out how to fix it.

Eve made them all sandwiches and lemonade and they sat around the plastic table in the back yard. It was a beautiful Spring day, so Amara kicked off her shoes and sat in the grass with her baby girl. Aiyanna immediately crawled into her lap, snuggling her mother's neck. Amara felt unworthy. She was afraid any part of her would rub off on the child, and she would never have wished that for her. Eve sat at the table with a cautious smile on her face.

"Eve," Amara started, high as Hell, and unsure how to begin. "Mother," she sighed, Eve's face showing surprise at her use of the word. "I've been in some trouble, and…" She sighed again, at a total loss for words. "You guys may be in danger." Amara shrugged. She had no clue how to begin to tell her mother everything. She had no idea where to even start. She should have planned what to say. She was drowning.

Eve's mouth had disappeared into a thin line. She was displeased. Amara was sure she assumed her address had been given in exchange for some drugs or whatever other depraved scenario she could drum up. It was not her fault, even, for thinking it. Amara had disappointed her so many times – she would be ignorant not to be wary of her doing it again. And there she was, doing it again.

"There's a man," Amara tried again. God, what was wrong with her? Why could she not just explain?! She was not helping the picture she knew was forming in her mother's mind.

Exasperated and obviously disappointed, Eve cut her off. "What do you need, Amara?" The crow's feet around her eyes had deepened since she had last seen her. Parenting takes its toll, apparently. Amara could not deny there was a trickle of relief that she was not the one paying that toll. Eve's hair had grayed some more, and there was a sadness in her eyes when she looked at her daughter. She was obviously under the assumption that Amara had come to her for money or something.

Frustrated, Amara replied, "I don't *need* anything but for you to listen to me." Aiyanna was picking fistfuls of grass from around them, her little feet kicking and her tiny soft body constantly wiggling. Amara gave her a squeeze and handed her to Eve.

Now facing her, the baby gave Amara a quizzical look, a small wrinkle on her otherwise perfect brow. Amara somehow managed even to disappoint a little child. Eve bounced her on her lap. It felt like she had fallen into a painting, some Norman Rockwell portrait of a happy family on a sunny day in a small town. Obviously, she did not belong in that picture. She belonged in the city, just another beautiful face in the crowd. She was not a real mother – she did not even know how to hold her own child. She was a terrible daughter. She was not even a decent person. She did not deserve sunshine. She belonged in the smothering smog and overbearing buildings of the city. She belonged amongst the apathetic. The frustrated. The climbers.

Eve was not hearing her. It was Amara's fault, really. After so many years of deceit and drama, she could understand why her mother no longer heard a word from her mouth.

Eve had tried. She really had done everything that anyone could have tried to make her daughter into a decent human being. It just didn't take. She had sheltered Amara and sung to her, hugged her and read her stories. Made her dresses and dolls and encouraged her to do the right thing. She had loved Amara. The truth was, Amara always knew she would disappoint her. There was no way she could ever have been even half the woman Eve was, and that knowledge poisoned Amara from the very beginning. She therefore chose a different path for herself.

Now, that life had caught up to her. She had been a terrible, selfish person for the span of her life. She used people and ran off when they started to get close. She ruined Ronnie, then she slipped up and told him about their daughter. That had only been a week and a half ago, and he was bound to catch up to Ai sometime soon if Amara did not intervene. She brought evil into the lives of the only people on the planet she truly loved.

And she did love. She realized that in the span of that visit — she loved her mother more than she could bear to see her disappointed. And she loved her daughter. It was love that had Amara placing her daughter on Eve's doorstep that fateful night. She could not incur any pain on them. Eve had had to put up with enough already, and her baby girl did not deserve any darkness because of her. That was why she had given her up to begin with - to avoid this.

No, Amara would have to handle it herself.

CHAPTER 44
Evelyn I

I was in Dr. Haney's office again. With Jamma's diagnosis and my uncertainty about the future and all it could contain, I felt I needed to find the answer somewhere in the past. I somehow just knew it was there. Whatever answer to whatever question was pinging around inside my mind, that intangible something that I needed to know or to understand, was to be found in one of the lives I have lived. I had no doubt, but I also knew Jamma had warned me not to keep returning. But I needed clarity more than anything. I was a thunderstorm, ravaged and miserable, washed out from all I thought I knew before. None of which was real.

Dr. Haney's smooth voice was glassy ice as I skated back, rewinding myself further and further. I slid across the timeline of my life and back in time. And when we broke through, into the frozen depths I plunged.

In this vignette of time, I was lithe and ladylike, my slender muscles tensed beneath my frilly dress, my long legs crossed at the ankle. I smoothed the lacy white fabric on my lap, bringing the dainty porcelain cup to my lips. I was clearly being entertained by a friend this afternoon. She was faintly familiar as Daisy in a distant way. No, her name was Rose in this life.

Rose...that name nagged me in the most infinitesimal whisper from many years later on a sofa in a therapist's office. My name... it was Evelyn. Evelyn... the name emerged through the fog on the other side, where I, as Aiyanna, was stretched out many years from now. Evelyn was Jamma's mother. Evelyn was me.

I sipped the steaming tea through my pursed lips. I had known from the start that my best friend, Rose, was my husband's lover. That first evening he came home, smelling of rose water, I knew. I met his mistress shortly thereafter, and the scent invaded my senses. I knew it was her. I saw the way they looked at each other beneath their lashes when Rose stopped by for a neighborly tea break one afternoon. Like they had a shared secret. And if none of that were enough, I was watching through the large paned window in the front room when he walked her out, kissing her hand and touching her fondly.

I had lived a thousand lives, and all of them had their fine points...and their flaws. There were ages of oppression, suffering, surrender. I had tasted the fruit of Eden and lived amongst the pharaohs. I have been kings and slaves and someone you happen to pass by when you are out shopping for produce. I am every man. Life, in all of its intricate weavings, was always the same, really. People were always the same. Consistently selfish and flawed, with moments of divine surrender to goodness and decency. I had had my heart broken, I had been disappointed, persecuted and prejudiced, praised and revered, so there were no surprises left. I knew what people were planning before they even knew themselves, sometimes.

Therefore, I never let on. I wanted to give my husband and my friend a chance for redemption through their own actions, by their own hands. I loved Randall, despite his deceit. I loved Rose, anyway, through her faults and falsehoods. God had put me on the planet to love and to show mercy, to be Light where there was none. Even a small candle can illuminate the darkness. All it takes is a touch of love and a ton of patience, and through all of time, those are things I certainly possessed.

A calmness and clarity covered the me who was stretched out on a sofa almost a century later, like wrapping that version of myself in a velvet cloud. I am here for you. For me. My ancestors and myself. Eons and decades of love trickled and wove like a river system to open into the ocean of Aiyanna.

I loved Rose, and I loved Randall. I laughed with them and supported them. I cared about their happiness and their souls. They were just people, doing what they thought was best for their own lives. I was ready to give them to each other, to remove myself and allow them that life, when Randall left for the war. But he never returned. I never had the opportunity to let him have Rose, if that was what he wanted. To tell him that I loved him, anyway, even though I no longer wanted to be his wife. To let him know that I was growing a child of God within my womb. My baby would be a beacon of Light and Love throughout his or her life, and of that, I was certain. That was my purpose and my plan. That was what Evelyn Elizabeth was born to create.

I had not realized that all of those lives I had lived deducted from my life as Evelyn. I traveled back almost daily, enthralled with the history and humanism of each life. The difficult lives taught me lessons, as did the easier ones. To see the world outlined in history books with my own eyes (or mind) was fascinating. It was rarely ever exactly what I had been taught. I thought that was interesting, as well: people always have to put their spin on it. There are always motives or rewrites with the "winners" in the best light.

I wanted my child to have the best chance he or she could. I caressed my belly, my baby kicking inside, and tried to tell it everything I knew, hoping it could somehow understand. It had to know that it had a life to live, here, in this era, and it mustn't keep returning to times gone by. I needed my baby to know that, but I would never get a chance to tell him or her.

I already knew I had spent my time in this particular tale, that it was once again time to take a turn elsewhere. I had seen it in a dream – it was almost my time to go. The dream was vivid and felt more like a warning than a fantasy. To have the chance to plan for it was a true gift. Most people never have such an opportunity.

Thus, I spilled my secret to Rose. I had to tell her everything. I placed my faith in my friendship with her. My parents had passed onto another journey already. I had no siblings, and now no spouse. Someone had to be able to guide my baby through this life, and many others, and to let them know they were going to be okay, to let them know they were loved. To teach them that they *are* love. That that is everything.

With that cognizance and a deep peace that penetrated my soul, I awoke as Aiyanna many years, and only moments, later. A rush of understanding of my Jamma, and of Ethan and Daisy, draped over my mind like a net. Love was not black or white, all or nothing. Someone didn't have to be perfect to deserve it – not Ethan, not Daisy, and not me. There were multitudes and variations and different levels of love. To show it was an active choice I had the power to make; I could forgive, and in doing so, I would free us all. And I could love, without needing to be a part of someone's life or in constant contact with them. I could love, even if it was never shown to me. It was my decision, and I was in control of that. I may not know what was going to happen in my life, and I may not have authority over the outcomes or circumstances getting there, but I always had the choice of when and whom and how to love. I had the choice over my own actions and reactions. It was an enlightening and serene epiphany. I felt control for the first time in many months. I was not helpless to the fates or whims of other people. I could navigate my own little boat through the tempests life tossed toward me.

I thanked Dr. Haney for his help and headed to my car to go home to my grandmother. I felt like an enormous stone had been lifted from my shoulders, and I could barely wait to tell her all about it. Jamma had been a priceless teacher with regards to my regressions. She understood me and my stories and how they correlated to this life. She could fill in gaps and help me analyze and understand the lessons to be learned from the lessons I learned in former lives.

"Aiyanna!" Dr. Haney called out, walking as rapidly as his limp would allow toward my car. "I just… could I have just a minute with you?" His face was troubled, his forward wrinkled, his glasses pushed down.

Concerned, I nodded. I tossed my bag into my car and leaned against the door.

His long, slender frame leaned against my car, too. He sighed. "I don't know the intricacies of what you're experiencing when you regress. It's not for me to know. I don't have that privilege – that's your journey to take. I just want to make sure you're okay."

I glanced back and forth, not sure what to say. What was he getting at? Why would he think I wasn't? While I was flattered that he seemed to care, I was apprehensive at what he saw that had him chasing me down in the parking lot to ask if I'm okay.

"What I'm trying to say," he explained, as if he were reading my mind, "if I may be so bold as to give you advice…is that therapy – regression - it is a tool. You should *use* it to improve your life, but you mustn't *rely* on it to live your life. If that makes sense." He had a look of genuine concern on his face, a slight crease between his shaggy eyebrows. "And while I look forward to your sessions, I have seen you quite a bit lately. It would be easy to get lost in memories, if you're not careful."

"Yes, sir. I do understand that now." I nodded. I felt a lucidity I hadn't had before the day's session. I was finally at peace. "But thank you for your advice. It's always welcome," I smiled. I offered my hand to shake. He took it in both of his and patted the outside of my palm. I felt a rush of appreciation for the person who had guided me through several lives.

Then I had an idea. Dr. Haney's house was empty every time I visited, despite the portrait of a pleasant-looking older lady in pearls mounted proudly on his mantel. He was alone, and I hated the thought of it. "Dr. Haney, I know Monday is New Year's, so you probably have plans, and I know it's little notice, but do you think you'd be interested in coming over for dinner tonight? My Jamma makes a mean pot of spaghetti." I laughed.

"Actually, Ai," he said slowly, seemingly surprising himself, "I would love nothing more."

"Excellent! Are you free around six-ish?" When he nodded, I opened my bag and found an old receipt. I scribbled Jamma's address on the back.

"See you then," he smiled. His face was lit up like a Christmas tree, and I felt delighted to be able to put that smile on his face. I slid into my car and pulled the keys from my messenger bag. I hoped Jamma would feel up to company.

CHAPTER 45
Ethan

His fingers danced across the keys, the piano humming with his mellow sound. He dressed up pretty nicely, if he did say so himself. The tuxedo looked impeccable on his tall frame, and he fit in well with the elite crowd. Of course, he was hired to play the gig as a hired worker, so he could not think of himself as one of them. Not yet, anyway. Maybe one day. He smiled at the thought of himself as a socialite, his wealth and influence raising his nose a few more millimeters every day. He could spoil Ai and himself. It would be awesome.

The crowd mingled and mostly ignored him, as usual. He was background noise. It did not matter to Ethan – he was getting paid either way. The occasional lonely housewife, bored by her husband's glad-handing would saunter over and sex him with her eyes, but that was not unusual, either. Not to toot his horn too loudly, but he attracted females pretty easily. He was just that sort of guy. He got better tips when he engaged with them, too, so he smiled and flirted back. It left him feeling like he needed a shower, but at least it paid the bills.

He did find it odd, however, for that man to stare unabashedly at him all evening. Most people had the courtesy to glance away or smile coyly. That guy just sat there, sipping his liquor, staring from one of the white linen-covered tables. Ethan would sneak glances between his sets, but it did not stop the man's intense stare. He did not fit the bill for that particular crowd, and Ethan wondered how he had gotten invited to such a fancy soiree. His hair was long, combed back, and he could see his wrists were tatted beneath his cufflinks. He would have assumed the guy was a musician or artist if it were not for his complete lack of social mores or manners.

"What's up, man?" Ethan inquired casually as the man finally made his way toward him at the end of his set. The stranger walked with purpose. Ethan's mind was searching for the best way to let him know he was not homosexual. He wanted to be as polite and politically correct as possible. The man had waited until most of the place was cleared out, the remainders gathering their coats and throwing back the rest of their champagne. Ethan figured, at this point, that he was looking for a hookup.

The man leaned in so close, Ethan could feel his breath on his neck. It was hot and smelled like whiskey.

"You will leave my daughter. Or else."

Ethan's eyes flicked back and forth, confused. Homeboy was definitely a bit touched, so to speak. Ethan had not messed with any girls since he started seeing Ai, and she did not have a father. The women who had approached his piano that evening were not young enough to be the dude's offspring.

Puzzled, Ethan replied, "Hey, I don't know who you're talking about, but—" he stood, his full height usually enough to deter a fight from some insecure male.

"Aiyanna Burns."

Ethan froze, his mouth gaped open. Had Ai been lying about her father? Was this guy just insane? He was unsure how to respond. The man just stared at Ethan as if he hated him. Before Ethan could make sense of any of it, he felt a sharp point in his back, at the kidney. He tried to wriggle away, but that made the tip of the knife sink into his flesh. He gasped. The man did not even try to hide the fact that he had a knife on Ethan and the stragglers were now gone. They were alone in the ballroom.

"I'm coming for her. She is spawn of evil. I am the light. If you want to live, you will leave the picture immediately. Otherwise," the man whispered menacingly, the sharp bite of his breath full of alcohol, "you will die. I will end you in the most excruciating ways I can think. And I'm very creative. If you contact the police or if you don't take me seriously, your family and all you love will die. I will ruin you. I will end you. You will beg for surrender." He twisted the tip of the knife before pulling it away and pocketing it discreetly. "And it will not be a peaceful ending," he added, before walking away casually, still talking to himself.

Deeply disturbed, Ethan packed up the rest of his things and rushed to his car. He thought about calling the police. Obviously, he should. The man had threatened his life, after all. But he was bold enough or psycho enough to confront Ethan at work in front of other people. What if the police couldn't nab him? What if he got to Ethan first? Or Aiyanna? Or his family? Ethan did not know what to do. He didn't know how to protect any of them.

Aiyanna would be waiting for him at home. He could not understand why she lied about her father. Was she ashamed that he was crazy? Was she worried she inherited it? Or did she even know? She told Ethan she had never known her father. It did not make any sense.

She had only been living with him for a few months, but Ethan had never been happier. She was so sweet, and she tried harder than any other girl he had ever dated. She, without fail, did what she thought would make him happy. She was considerate and thoughtful and she put him even before herself. What guy wouldn't love that? But how in the hell could he date a girl whose psycho father just threatened his life? Was he really going to have to break up with the only girl he had ever seen as wifey material? Should he tell her? Should they run away? Could he stop this at all?

Ethan knew Ai would fight for him, and for them. She would not just walk away without Ethan destroying her first. He would have to break any hope for her. How could he possibly destroy someone so perfect?

He was lost in his own thoughts, so he had unlocked his car and loaded his bag into the backseat (after ensuring it was empty) before he saw what looked like blood covering his windshield. Written in it, clear as day, *Leave Her.*

CHAPTER 46
Robert

He could not conceive of why he would be nervous, but nonetheless, Robert Haney was wiping sweat from his forehead as he locked his car and kept a deliberate slow pace up the flower-lined walkway to the front door. His footsteps felt like a performance, like he had forgotten how to walk. He had to consciously place his heel, then his toes, and ignore the wobbling in his knees.

He had not had any plans for New Year's. He just assumed he would be home to watch the ball drop on the television. Just as with Thanksgiving and Christmas, it would be another holiday alone at home with his cat, Casper, and a hot cup of cocoa. Just another day like any other. It was a lonely life as a widower.

He felt as nervous as a pre-teen going to his first dance. It was ridiculous. Social engagements were so common for so long, one would think he would be accustomed to them. But mingling with academics in his youth was a far cry from some old man showing up for dinner at a virtual stranger's house.

It was a red door with tall, slim panes of glass on each side. He spotted the curious face of a golden-red dog in the bottom of one of them, which made him smile as he rang the doorbell. The dog barked, as if to announce his arrival.

Robert had never fraternized with a patient. Well, only once before, quite a long while ago. It had been against his code during his licensed years, and he found it was much easier to treat someone with whom there was a distinct line between professional and personal life. But he was retired now, not even licensed anymore. This had all been a sort of experiment, and the experiences in which he had played a small part in Aiyanna's journey bonded the two of them in a way he had only ever known once before. That was a very different way, then, though. But a bond, nonetheless. And Aiyanna seemed to almost need him, which felt surprisingly nice since his wife had passed over a year ago. Robert had not realized how lonely he had been. Ai's sessions gave him purpose. He found himself looking forward to her visits.

Aiyanna whipped the door open, a smile spread across her face. "Thanks for coming, Dr. Haney." She stood aside to let him in.

"Please, call me Robert, under the circumstances," he smiled. He wiped his feet politely on the welcome mat and crossed the threshold. He held his car keys in one palm and the pie he purchased from a grocery store down the way balanced on the same arm so he could reach down and pet the dog dancing laps around his legs, tail wagging furiously.

"That's Cooper," Ai laughed and patted his head, his stand-up ears shaking slightly when she did so. His curly tail pitched this way and that, never a full circle but swinging with excitement. "The kitchen is right this way," she gestured. "We are finishing up in there."

Robert could have just followed the smell if he needed to. It was a deep, Italian scent of marinara, garlic, and other spices. His stomach emitted a low rumble.

"This is my Jamma," Ai introduced as the small frame turned from her stirring on the stove, "Evelyn Burns." The white-haired woman wiped her hands on a floral apron around her waist and raised her eyes to meet Robert's.

The pie crashed to the floor as every sentience in him was at once both alive and in a dreamlike state. In an instant, he was unaware of his limbs or his thoughts, even. He could not breathe.

"Eve," He could barely whisper, his lips trembling and his body frozen.

She studied Robert with steady eyes. Her crystal-blue eyes, those same eyes, were filled with tears, and she seemed stuck to the floor. "Red," she finally said, almost as if she expected him. She swallowed audibly. There was a childlike look of hope on her face, as if she did not really trust her own eyes. Robert could not believe the moment was real.

He was distantly aware of Aiyanna's head snapping back and forth between the two of them, confused. But Eve was all he could see. She was all he ever saw. He could not believe the white-haired woman in front of him was the same one he had loved all of those years before. The love of his life, God rest his wife. He supposed he was not the same, either. She had the same small stature and proud shoulders, the same sparkling blue eyes, and his heart pounded in the way that had only ever stirred for her. She was definitely his Eve. His entire life, all of those years, between knowing her and now, disappeared in that instant.

His thoughts swum and spun like a maypole.

"*The*...Red...?" Aiyanna gawked, her mouth fallen open and shock across her face.

Finally, he willed his legs to move. Whipped cream from the pie he dropped was splattered across his pants and the floor, but he carefully walked-glided through it to stand in front of her. Aiyanna moved from between them, backing away slowly in some instinctual move to let them have the moment. Red stood in front of the woman whose face was both strange and intimately familiar. He took her in. Breathing deeply, he abstractedly recognized how lucky he was to be near her, to share her air. He had wondered about her for so long. He had once, or really many times, kissed those cheeks, now wrinkled and delicate like crepe paper. Her lips, once full and moist and forever smiling, now thinned with age. Her shoulders, straight and strong, where he would kiss her collarbone, now slumped a little and were somehow more fragile. He had loved her then. And he loved her still. He had not seen her since she disappeared from the train window on his way to the War. Nothing was ever the same after that. He thought about her every day during, and every day since. God, how he loved her.

"Eve," he finally spoke, his voice now full, thick with all of his thoughts. He took her hand, so soft, so frail, and lifted it to his lips. With that, they both let go. He could hear Ai leave the room as they took each other in their arms and let the memories of love and loss and time lost rinse their eyes with tears.

They wept together, no words spoken. They wept for who they were and what they had, how they lived, their friendships and affections, themselves. They wept for all of those years apart. They wept for everything they would never be and all they had been.

***

"What on earth brought you back here?" Red inquired around a mouthful of spaghetti.

They were finally able to gather themselves and assimilate with Aiyanna for dinner. It took a bit of explanation, but they were all on the same page and acquainted enough with the series of events to be curious of the details.

Eve dabbed her mouth and replied, "You already know." Shyly, she peeped up at Red from under her lashes, a small smile on her pasta sauce-stained lips.

Him. She had come back to his hometown to find him.

"I thought you were gone," she continued, "and I wanted to be close to what was left of you."

A shiver scurried down his spine. He could not decipher if it was delight at the idea that she had not let go of him completely or the notion that she had been living just a couple of towns over from him and he never knew.

How different everything could have been. It made the life he had lived already seem so small. How had they not crossed paths?

"I thought you died over there. I had lost you. Then I saw you one day. I thought it was a dream, but it was you. My Red. At the market. You were alive! And then I saw your wife take your hand and kiss your cheek. You were married. I've seen you several times over the years, but I've kept my distance out of respect. And I am so very sorry to hear about your wife. Would you tell us about her?" She asked without malice or jealousy, her eyes like some kind of sparkling gemstone. She had always been inquisitive, non-judgmental. Robert loved that about her.

It would have almost been some sort of betrayal, to both parties, to mesh the two worlds. To speak of his wife of many years to a woman he had loved silently through all of them. They never had children – he and his wife. He was not able to after the war, due to the hip and spinal injury he sustained from being shot. So they dedicated themselves to each other, becoming the best friend and confidante and lover the other needed so desperately. The two of them were their own family, and it worked out well. However, since losing her, Robert felt the loss of being childless, as well. It was lonely without her and without any other family of his own.

His wife had been faithful and loving, and passive, which he had needed so badly after the war. He was broken when he came back from the war, only partially a man. His life after 'Nam was nothing like his life had been before it, with his wild and passionate romance with Eve. The only bridge between those two separate men, the two very different versions of himself, was his interest in psychiatry. And his memories.

Ignoring the question altogether, Robert opted to try to explain. "I never meant to abandon you. I was not the same man anymore, and you deserved more. That's what I thought then," he ducked his head in shame. "I am glad you had a family of your own." He smiled at Aiyanna.

"I understand. I figured you had moved on."

There was a long, awkward silence as they ate their meal. Aiyanna's eyes flicked back and forth between them.

Robert attempted to break the silence. "Did you...continue?"

He hoped that would be enough for Eve to know of which he was referring. He stole a glance at Aiyanna. It was a breach of confidence to mention her therapy and/or Aiyanna's, but he found the link fascinating. Grandmother and granddaughter, both with the ability to regress fully into past lives. Both coming to him suffering, feeling small and insignificant. Both finding themselves and their strength through therapy. He was privileged to be a part of it.

"Yes," she smiled, and with an inclination of her head toward Ai, she continued, "she knows about the gift. I knew you would have to be the one to help her find it." She looked at her granddaughter with as much love as with Red had been looking at Eve all evening.

Aiyanna grinned, her cheeks stuffed as full as a squirrel's. Gulping, she directed her question to him, "So you helped Jamma find out she could time travel, too?"

"Regression was something I was fascinated in when I met your grandmother." He stole another glance at her as she delicately tore apart a piece of bread. "It was relatively new at the time. We tried many different treatments before it, but the whole Bridey Murphy thing had come out a little while earlier and there was a lot of attention on that kind of therapy. So we tried it," he shrugged.

"I was as shocked as you were!" Eve laughed, nodding toward Ai. "But it helped me when I was broken," she continued seriously. "You saved me," she said softly, staring into Robert's eyes across the table. It stayed that way for several seconds. "So when you were so devastated," she continued, again turning her attention toward Ai, "I knew what needed to be done."

***

Eve, as elegant as ever she was, despite her overly thin frame and spats of coughing, gleefully pulled out an old record player and was setting it up. Smiling, she showed Red an old LP cover of Roy Orbison. Memories flooded his senses when the static broke to the song, *Love Hurts*. Smiling, Eve came to where he was sipping cocoa on the sofa. She took the cup from him and placed it on the side table.

"Dance with me, Red," she commanded, taking his hands in hers and tugging on his arms. Bashful, he peeped at Ai, who was in the armchair, feet tucked under her, laughing to herself from behind her mug. Changing his glance to implore Eve not to, she had such a sparkle in her eyes, he could not say no.

"Not sure I've got the same moves I once did," he said softly, lifting his pant leg to reveal his titanium leg.

A rush of understanding moved through Eve's face. "So that's what happened," she nodded. "I wondered why you never called."

"I wasn't a whole man again for a very long time," he sighed.

Eve took Robert's hands in hers and hugged her small frame against his. "You're the whole world to me," she whispered. They danced that way, slowly, unabashedly, right there in her living room in front of Aiyanna. Eve tucked her head beneath Red's chin, her cheek pressed against his chest. The song sang on:

Love hurts
Love scars
Love wounds and marks
Any heart not tough or strong enough
To take a lot of pain, take a lot of pain

Despite her thinning white hair and a hand that felt like bones in his palm, despite his lower body screaming in protest and his hips moving more like a zombie than a dancer, they were in their twenties again. He was teaching her how to dance, whispering jaunty encouragements. His fascinating love, raised an orphan, but so full of life, her feet fumbling around for the proper placement, and he, puffed up with confidence at finally knowing something she did not, proudly teaching her the moves.

Them, actually getting their own feet tangled together and tumbling to the floor with laughter. Him, kissing her, his heart full, her arms wrapped around him as the record player resonated in the background.

They spent several hours that way, Aiyanna joining them, the three of them dancing to oldies and Christmas music in their socks on the living room rug. Eve and Red taught Ai how to do the Twist and the Mashed Potato, and she taught them some line dances that were popular.

At last, all of them exhausted and filled to the brim with delight, they plopped themselves into the chair and sofa. Eve refilled their mugs of cocoa, adding marshmallows and playing Auld Lang Syne on the record player before joining them. She had turned off the lamps, leaving only the twinkle of the Christmas tree and lights hung around the room for ambience. They sat like that, silently, taking in the lyrics and the lights. It was one of the most perfect moments of Robert's life.

Should auld acquaintance be forgot, and never brought to mind?
Should auld acquaintance be forgot, and auld lang syne?

Shortly thereafter, Red hugged Aiyanna goodnight before she slipped off to her room. He felt a closeness to her that was not there before.

Arm in arm, Eve walked him to the door. It was so hard to say goodnight. He had not realized how lonely and desolate he had felt until his heart was full again. It had been a long time since he actually enjoyed himself and was not just going through the motions. Days were just habits. But just like that, after all these years, he had his Eve again. He wanted every second with her, but she looked completely exhausted. All of the energy in her earlier that evening had vanished.

He just had to tell her one more thing before he left, though. "I never stopped loving you, Evelyn. You stole my heart all those years ago, and you've had it ever since." With that, he leaned down and wrapped his arms around her waist. He kissed her. Deeply. He kissed her for all of the times he had not gotten to, for all of the times he wanted to. He felt alive again for the first time since his wife had died. After they kissed, he held her body close to his for just one more minute. Raising her hand to his lips once more, he bid her a good night.

"I'll be seeing you," she winked, with the warmest, most beautiful smile that ever graced the world.

CHAPTER 47
Daisy

Who the hell was this psycho?!, thought Daisy. He was lurking outside of Ethan's house when she stepped into the night and bumped right into him. He did not move or excuse himself. He didn't explain what the hell he had been doing at the window by the front door in the middle of the night.

Had he been there the whole time? Had he been watching when Ethan let Daisy in and closed the door behind her? Was he watching as they drank together, saying so much with their eyes as they peeked out over their bottles of beer? Or when she let him literally cry on her shoulder? Daisy had been so goddamned understanding. Was the psycho watching when Ethan slammed his fifth empty bottle on the coffee table scattered with mail and bottle caps and stained with rings of old beverages? When he stood abruptly, grabbed Daisy by her hips, lifting her lithe body effortlessly? Did he see her legs wrapped around Ethan's waist as he pulled her head back by her hair, wildly biting her neck and shoulders like an animal as he carried her back to his bedroom? She smiled at the thought of someone watching them. It was sort of thrilling.

The terrifying shadowed man just stared at Daisy, breathing hard. What a creep. She wanted to dismiss him as a drunk or a voyeur, but there was something about him that shook her to her core. Long hair shaded his eyes, the inky black night and weak yellow light over Ethan's front door yielding shadows across his face in a frightful way. Like how you hold a flashlight under your chin in summer camp while you tell scary stories. She tried to walk around him, but he blocked her way.

"You're just like her, aren't you?" he hissed, revulsion across his face as he skimmed Daisy's body up and down. Her hair was tousled, her makeup smudged or sweated off. She had not bothered to put any underpants back on, since she was just going to her car. She suddenly felt exposed and vulnerable. She held her heels in her hand and considered how she could use them as a weapon. He smelled like alcohol and unwashed clothes.

"Whatever, man," Daisy tried to say casually, though she was starting to feel seriously frightened. She could hear her heart beating in her ears. She attempted to move around him again, but he obstructed the way once more.

"You dirty little slut," he spat at her, his face just inches from hers. Flecks of spittle landed on her cheeks. His words were aggressive and filled with rage. His face contorted with all of the hatred in the world. Shit.

Daisy screamed out for Ethan and tried to knee the lunatic in the groin, now filled with terror, but he evaded her hit and grabbed her by the throat. She thrashed and fought to get free, but he was surprisingly strong and lightning fast for someone so thin.

The front door swung open behind them, and Ethan rushed out. In a fraction of a second, the man was on top of Ethan, drilling a long butcher knife into his chest over and over again, his screams of the Devil barely heard above Ethan's animal cries.

Daisy ran barefoot toward her car, screeching for help into the darkness of the night. Before she could open the door, the man had her by her hair, dragging her across the dark pavement.

She fought him as he forced her into the passenger seat, where he had put the seat down as far back as it would go. She fought back, as best she could, as he bound her wrists and ankles with zip ties, screaming and clawing at his face desperately. She shouted for someone to please help her before he could duct tape her mouth, but she assumed no one heard her in the stillness of the early hours. And if no one heard her then, they certainly could not hear her behind the muffling of the car's closed windows and the tight strip of duct tape across her lips. Weirdly, and in a way that managed to fill her with terror even further, he averted his eyes and politely rolled Daisy's dress back down, as it had ridden up over her waist in her struggle against him. It obviously was no priority to her to cover her exposed self, but he took the time to do so. It was disconcerting. If that was not what he wanted, why was he doing this!?

Daisy's eyes bulged with fear and trepidation as he climbed in the driver's seat and started the car. She spun to a sitting position in the bucket seat when they rolled out of the subdivision so she could try to recall every turn, to see where he was taking her. She lost her sense of direction at some point fairly early on, though. He drove on and on, out of town and into the countryside. She had the most peculiar and ill-timed thought that it was a beautiful night. The stars shone brightly in the sky, away from the street lights of town that dulled them down to a haze. Houses were farther and farther apart, the roadsides instead filled with fields and forests. She was not sure she had ever been out that way before, as the city was in the opposite direction. How would anyone know where she was?

What seemed like an eternity later, her captor pulled the car into one of those empty fields. There was a sort of driveway over the ditch, though it wasn't gravel or paved. It was a grassy pull-off that went to nowhere. Just flat field land. Perhaps it was where the farmer drove his tractor into the pasture. The blackness of the moonless night was just giving way to the dull gray of morning. It was that time of day/night when everyone slept because what was one to do in a time like this? Clubs were closed, but breakfast was not yet open. Business hours were well over, or had not begun yet, depending on how you saw it. Animals were sleeping, even the crickets, and the world around them was eerily silent. It was that purgatory of time, a blurred line between the night and morning, when you cannot tell the end of one day from the beginning of another.

The lunatic ran his bloodied hands through his long hair and began mumbling incoherent thoughts. It was as if he were lecturing or ranting like the nuts you see holding signs and preaching about the end of days. He gripped the steering wheel hard, his knuckles white in the places that were not caked in blood. He squeezed his forehead as though his very brain hurt. He rambled on as Daisy desperately looked for an escape of some kind, her eyes darting over every inch within sight. They sat there like that for God knows how long. The windows fogged as the psychopath alternately screamed and sobbed, occasionally bashing a fist against her face or pushing her head into the window. A trickle of blood or sweat or possibly tears tickled her face as it rolled across her temple. He went on and on about Evil and Darkness, about his birthright and his Descension because of a She-Devil. It made no sense, and he spoke so quickly Daisy could only catch every few words.

She blinked hard through the liquid combination of her tears and the blood from her cut forehead. She tried to keep her attention focused on some way to escape the torment. It was not the time for shock. She needed to stay aware and take notice of every little detail. She had to get out of there.

The doors were locked, and her hands were bound behind her back and her ankles strapped tightly with zip ties. So there was no hope of slamming open the door and making a run for it. She hoped her tears and blood would trickle down and loosen the tape over her mouth. If she could call for help, perhaps the sound would carry further in the country? Though there were fewer people to hear a cry for help, there was more open space over which it could carry? Is that how that even works? She had spotted a hint of a driveway in the distance while wildly looking for some way out of the mess she was in. There was a car parked in it, so people had to live there. Though it was still very early, didn't country folks wake up early, too? If she could just call out for help, maybe it would be enough for whomever lived at that blurry driveway in the distance to hear her and help her. Or at least maybe they would call for help. Someone had to help her. It could not be real. It could not be happening to her...

CHAPTER 48
Ronnie

To Whoever is Reading this—

I have left. I had to go.

I am nothing but a shadow. Just smoke.

I used to be somebody though.

It started many years ago

With a woman I used to know.

This is my manifesto.

She was the devil. Evil. Delicious and tempting. I wanted to eat her and own her. I was everywhere-inside her and all over. ~~I was so in love~~

SHE WAS EVIL!!!!!!!!!! I loved her**DARKNESS**

She didn't love me. I AM LIGHT

BUT I AM FIRE!

She never loved me. She hated me. She never loved me. OUR DAUHGTER 

We have a dauhgter. She can't be like her mother. Her mother. She never loved me. She never loved me. She never loved mesheneverlovedme

SHE was just like my mother. She left. She left all of us

NO DAUGHTER

GONE We are all gone…

~~The devil took my daughter~~

My daughter is the devil. The devil had her so now she is the devil. Devil gets devil… Am I the devil? Should I SAVE her??! Can I save her? Is she saveable?

I will find her. I will find out if she is the devil. I MUST RID THIS WORLD OF EVIL

I WAS BORN TO DESTROY DARKNESSSSSSS I AM LIGHT!!!!!

Evil. A M A R A She is evil. Did she make me evil or was I all ready? She caused my descent to HELL

If I canFIND her, I can talk to her. I have to find her. I have to find her. I have to find her. I have to find her.

CHAPTER 49
Daisy

He was still raving. Daisy's body was excruciatingly uncomfortable. She thought, for a moment, maybe the man was going to take her home when he finished what he wanted to say.

The crazy man blubbered on about his daughter or his lover or something. Adrenaline drowned out much of what he said, for Daisy's heart and her breathing had been seizing from terror for hours now. She was exhausted, and what must have been something akin to shock was starting to set in. She was so focused on other senses – sight, touch, even smell – that she scarcely heard the madman's ramblings. What she did hear made no sense. Tears ran from her eyes and mucus and/or blood gushed from her nose. She still hoped it would soak through the tape across her mouth enough to loosen it, though she supposed there would not be much she could do, even if it did. Even if her calls were heard, what could be done? Would the farmer shoot the man? If his aim was not perfect, the shot might hit her. Maybe she wanted that at this point. to just be done with the nightmare. She was at the mercy of a psychopath. Was that how she was going to die? How had this even happened to her?

Then the man said something that caught Daisy's attention. He had spoken a strange name that was very familiar to her: Aiyanna. Wait, what was he saying? Had she heard correctly? Yes! He said it again! How did he know Ai? His daughter?!? Wait, is that who he had been talking about?! She tuned into his rants, trying to decipher what he was saying.

"No," Daisy frantically attempted to explain from behind her sticky gag, but it came out as a grunt. "No!" she tried again, shaking her head violently. She kept on, despite the muffled mess of noise emanating from her. *No, you must understand. I'm not Ai! I can take you to her. I can get her in the car! I can trick her. I'll say I need help or something. You can have her, and I won't tell anyone. Just please let me go. You've got this all wrong! You've got the wrong person, god damn it!*

Daisy's hysterical mumblings drew the man from his own insane soliloquy. He looked at her for the first time since he started driving and a change spread across his face. His eyes, which had been glazed with his angry rants sharpened, and it were as if he noticed Daisy again and realized where he was. He seemed to snap out of whatever mind frame he had been in because he started the car once more. But he did not shift it into drive. He just sat there, staring at Daisy. With a quizzical, almost confused look on his face, he ripped the tape from her mouth. Her lips screamed in pain, matching the screams of pain from her wrists and ankles and skull and shoulders and probably-broken nose. Good. She had his attention. She had to make it count.

"I'm not Aiyanna," Daisy mumbled through swollen lips and foamy, bloody spit in her mouth. She spoke slowly, with measured words. The guy obviously had a screw loose, and she wanted him to hear her clearly. She swallowed a gulp of mucus blood, almost gagging on the wad as it went down the back of her dry throat. "I can take you to her." She nodded, a promise, as she met his gaze.

It was the first time she really saw his eyes, since they had been shadowed by his hair and the dark of night. Upon sight of them, though, it petrified and panicked her. They were dark green, hazel maybe, but they bore a look of hatred in the gray light of morning. She saw no soul in them whatsoever. Whatever this man had been before was gone, broken. It dawned on Daisy with a punch of realization that he was never going to let her go. He was going to kill her. Of that, she was certain. She could see the commitment in his eyes – he was going to kill them all.

She blinked the fat tears that immediately welled up in her swollen eyes. They were different tears than before. These were tears of surrender, instead of fear. She noted the sensation of a hot drop of sad saline as it rolled gently down her cheek and dripped from her jaw. She watched it disappear into the fabric of her dress. Just as she would soon disappear from the pages of time.

She could not take him to Ai.

He was going to kill her anyway. She knew it in her heart – she would die that day. The knowing of it, the certainty that fell upon her like a heavy blanket and was almost a relief. She now knew it did not matter how hard she fought or what she said, her path was laid out before her. Her immediate future would be the rest of her future, and this day would be the day she died. Therefore, she would surrender herself to that fate without dragging anyone else into it. She did love her friend, and while only moments before she was willing to sacrifice Aiyanna to save herself, knowing that would be pointless was a resolution in itself. She would not hand her over to some insane man claiming to be her father so that they both could be slaughtered. It was Daisy's choice, in that moment, as to how she wanted to spend the end of her life. She wanted to matter – that was all she ever wanted. To do so would require being brave and selfless, doing the right thing. She had squandered her short life on the bet that she could make it up later. She had one more chance to be remembered in a good light. Her bravery would be her memoriam.

She decided she would tell him they were going to get Aiyanna, and she would direct him back towards town. There, someone would at least be able to identify her body when he killed here. There, maybe someone would catch the man and make him pay for what he was about to do to her. But she would not let him get to Ai. She would fight him first and force him to just get it over with already, to kill her quickly. She would fight him before he could find her friend or hurt anyone else. She would fight.

CHAPTER 50
Amara

Amara hunted Ronnie for years. It became her objective and her obsession. She was a silent guardian in her daughter's life, her entire existence dedicated to protecting Ai. From every evil Amara created. From everything Amara was. From her own father. And from her own mother.

She could admit it was a bit self-indulgent. She wanted to be a part of Aiyanna's life, but without the ability to influence her. She wanted a way to contribute to bettering her daughter's life without necessarily having a relationship with her, for a relationship may have meant Aiyanna could learn to be anything like her. That was something Amara did not want to happen. Ai was better off, anyway, not knowing her. That did not mean, however, that Amara wanted to forgo knowing Ai or helping her. And the way she could protect her from a distance was Amara's penance for the life she had led before. That is why it was self-indulgent – because Amara wanted a way to "buy" her way into Heaven. She wanted to be a better person, without really knowing how. She was afraid to attempt to be good enough that she could be an active participant in her daughter's life. What if she failed? What if Ai came to care for her and she let her down? There were so many temptations in life, and it was just easier to be who she had always been. But to make up for her mistakes, to try to be the sort of person she could respect, Amara had to do something to right her wrongs. Instead of saying Hail Marys, she made sure Aiyanna's father could not hurt her.

Amara was able to get Ronnie taken to prison and locked away for years. After she left Eve's when Ai was but a toddler, she knew it was up to her alone to make something happen. To protect her daughter. Ronnie had a problem with drugs for as long as Amara had known him, so she just made sure he had enough of them on him at just the right time. He was caught, arrested, and sentenced to prison for several years. The immediate threat was averted.

Meanwhile, she got her life together. Once she knew Ronnie would not be a danger, she attempted to become the sort of person she would want around Aiyanna. She hoped to be a part of her life eventually. She wanted to make her proud. In the meantime, however, she had to keep her distance. She wanted to trust herself before she would allow her own entry into her daughter's life. Junkies always reverted back, in her experience.

Surprisingly, Amara actually led something close to an ordinary life for those couple of years Ronnie was imprisoned. She got herself a job and an apartment, on her own, with money she earned. It turned out she did not need a man after all.

Ronnie was released early, due to good behavior. They obviously did not know him. He immediately resumed his search for their daughter and, to a lesser degree, for Amara.

There were countless times Ronnie almost found Aiyanna, almost figured out who she was. It was then that Amara would intervene, seemingly random occurrences or encounters keeping him from that particular line of pursuit. She stayed in the shadows, like some secret crusader. She felt like she should wear a cape and whip it around whenever she turned a corner. It was sort of exciting, really. It was up to her to keep her family safe.

If Ronnie ever got ahold of Aiyanna's name, that would be it. It was not exactly a common name, thanks a lot Eve. If he linked Ai's name to his DNA, it would be game over. There was no birth certificate, so he had no starting point. That had worked in Amara's favor for a while. She was sure Eve had since applied for one, but she would have likely put her hometown as the birthplace, and there was no telling how she listed the parents. However, recently, with the internet and social media so loudly asserting every iota of everyone's lives, it was only a matter of time before Ronnie connected the dots. Social media knows more about whom we *might know* than we do. It's algorithms and databases of users could easily connect two souls who never would have known of each other's existence in another time.

Amara had no plan anymore for keeping Aiyanna safe if Ronnie found her. She had relied on diversion and distraction until that point. She had years to plan and to prepare. She was able to divert him a couple of times he got close to finding Ai, but he was stubbornly obsessed. The laser focus it had taken to abduct Amara those many years ago had been focused on finding their daughter. Having no notion of his intentions with Ai but having endured a sample of that particular focus herself, Amara was not going to wait to find out.

If he found her, Amara wondered, would she be old enough or strong enough to fight back? Would she know him? Would some familial instinct kick in? Could she calm him or talk him out of whatever horrible things she assumed he had planned? Or was she soft and good, like Eve, and immediately assume the best in him?

Amara had no idea what would happen if he actually found her, but she did intend to give him herself in lieu of her daughter. That was the last card she had to play. She hoped that would be enough. He had looked for Amara again, after she *discharged* herself from the hospital and after she warned her mother. She found out he was looking her up, but she had changed her name. She was Ann now. An easy name. She did not know if he still wanted her or if he thought he could use her to get to Ai, since he did not know she was never a part of Ai's life.

She wondered if Ai would even recognize her if she passed her daughter on the street. Ai looked just like her as an infant, but Amara no longer looked like herself. She let her gray hair grow out. It was now an ashen matte color, so different from the silky blonde it used to be. She also cut it very short in an efficient over-the-ear pixie. She stopped wearing makeup, and she ate whatever carbs she wanted. She put on a few pounds and started buying boring, non-descript mom clothes that she could afford on a budget of her own, legitimately-earned income. Her skin, once taut and smooth, hung heavy and loose with the weight of a lifetime of guilt and regret. Deep grooves cut themselves into the skin beside her eyes and mouth. She was sure years and years of cigarettes and drinking and drugs had not helped, either.

After Ronnie was released from prison, Amara had to be on him constantly. She watched, without being seen. After years of trailing and stalking, she had learned to be invisible. She was no longer the bombshell who stole the attention of everyone around. She could be any middle-aged housewife or soccer mom strolling the city. In its own way, it was still a form of disguising herself, as she so enjoyed in her younger years. It gave her purpose.

Ronnie had actually seen her several times over the ages, but there never was a flicker of recognition. She walked right past him once when he was passed out in an alleyway, high as ever, his eyes glazed and foggy, rolled toward the sky, mumbling something unintelligible. He bumped her elbow outside the grocery store once while he was aggressively panhandling. He asked her for change and moved along. She supposed he did not know the difference between reality or fantasy anymore, anyway. He could see her and recognize her as the one who broke him, but he would not know it was really her in front of him. She was everywhere, in everything. She consumed him. And he obviously could not distinguish the younger version of her in his daydreams from the older, understated version. After all, she had molded her life around his completely. She rented an apartment just a block from his and was often quite near him, watching his movements.

With everything she wanted to learn in tracking and researching, she obtained a private investigator's license. She needed an income, after all, and access to Ronnie. For the first time, she actually worked for what she had. She paid her own bills, and it felt good. Because of Ronnie, she was clean and had a steady job for the first time in her life - and a reason for living it. In a way, dedicating her life to stalking the dangerous man sort of saved it.

Ronnie had saved Amara in many of her lives, in fact, and in each one, she managed to destroy him. With each one, it was easier to do. His loving her, which he continued to do through every trial, was always what ended him. And in every life, with every existence, she had allowed it. Would she ever learn to be better?

He was admitted to the psych ward twice, but they eventually let him go both times. What difference was another drunken, delirious homeless man on the streets of the city? He was a burden, unable to pay his bills and unwilling to get better. In fact, he was getting worse every year. Amara honestly had thought he would give up the pursuit at some point. It was so many years ago that she had broken his heart. But when she broke his heart, it broke his mind and the rest of him along with it.

That glimmer of instability that had been so attractive to her cracked through his delicate shell like a piece of fine porcelain. And just like porcelain, once broken, it can never go back to what it was before. A tiny crack that once hinted at a glow from within had been pulled apart and broken open to expose a blinding fire of hatred that engulfed them all.

It was a shame – he could have been great. And happy. He was so creative and imaginative and he saw the beauty in things that were rotten and discarded and worthless, like Amara knew she had been.

If she were honest, there was a strand within her that was tugged at the sight of him, the man she destroyed. It pulled at her heart and hurt her to know she had a hand in damaging him so severely. She wondered if she was the impetus to push him over an edge he was already unsteadily standing on, or did she do it to him entirely on her own? Did she break him? Would he have gone on to live a very healthy, happy life if he had never met her? Would it have been with her? Would he have married her had it happened differently?

Amara could finally admit that she had loved Ronnie. It terrified her at the time, but she had loved him. That was why she left. In another life, he could have been her soul mate. In another life, he *had* been. It was tragic. they could have been together if he could have just held on a little longer. She might have changed who she was. She might have been able to love him back, properly. Especially after she saw her baby girl for the first time. But by then, he had already gone off the rails. Their cycle of love and madness continued into this life, too.

Maybe she needed him to break to be able to see the effects of her actions. Before him, for her entire life, it was easy enough to walk away from anyone who ever got too close. Even her own mother. She had learned many lives ago to love no one. Money was what she should chase – not love. She never let anyone in. No one had the power to hurt her because no one was given the opportunity to love her. But he had gotten in somehow. Whatever strand of humanity she inherited from her mother had twined its strings around her heart, and she loved him. She loved him in spite of herself. And he was the first person for whom her culpability was shoved in her face, down her throat, and inside herself so much it was no longer deniable. He had been kind, and good, and loving, and he took her in. He had shown her only love, and she had broken his heart because of it. So when he abducted her, and she could physically see the nuclear fallout from that moment when she had pushed the proverbial red button in her cold, cold heart, it cracked her and broke her open, too. He got his finger inside the splinter of goodness her mother had given her, and he ripped it open. She saw it in his drawings, in the photos he had taken of her. She could not look away and she could not ignore it. It was all Amara's fault.

That was another reason she made the decision to forever keep Ronnie within her sights. Not only was it to protect their daughter from him, but it was also to protect him from himself. From her. Because she cared. She was responsible for Ronnie now, too, for she was the one to make him that way. It was part of her penance to see that he could not hurt himself, nor anyone else. Otherwise, it may as well have been Amara hurting them, since she instigated his mental collapse.

There was a time he almost died. She wondered later if she should have interfered.

Amara had not spotted Ronnie for several days, and she had made it a habit not to let more than twenty-four hours go by without at least knowing where he was or what he was up to. Fearful that he had eluded her, she managed to convince the super to loan her a key to his apartment, on the down low, of course. By *convinced*, she means she handed the poor overworked, underpaid gentleman a twenty-dollar bill. When she slid into Ronnie's place, a similar shithole to the one in which he had held her hostage, he was sprawled on the floor, spread eagle, his eyes staring unblinking at the ceiling. He looked dead already.

She considered leaving him like that, knowing no one would be around to find him for a while. A younger Amara would have. It would certainly be easier. She would not have to hunt him anymore, and she would know that her daughter was safe. She could actually move on with her life and live again, instead of existing solely as a wall of protection against his actions. But there was something in that vacant stare of his, some kind of sadness in his eyes. She just did not have the fortitude to let him die that way, soaked in his own vomit and urine.

As mentioned before, he could have been great. He was truly gifted as a poet and musician, and it broke whatever was left of Amara's heart to see him that way. He was so...pitiful. With tears in her eyes, she scanned his apartment quickly. She grabbed a tattered, heavily used notebook from his night stand and let herself out of his apartment. She could not just let him stay that way, so she placed an anonymous call from a payphone blocks away.

It was not until she got back to her own apartment that she immediately regretted that decision. She settled into her cheap, overstuffed armchair and pulled the bent notebook from her bag to distract herself from the emotion she was experiencing after discovering Ronnie that way. The cover was a mess of scribbles and incoherent words mashed together in a nonsensical way. The notebook itself was filled from cover to back with what appeared to be some sort of rambling manifesto. Handwritten, scribbled in a frantic manner, the slant of the letters shooting out in every direction, the drawings done with so much pressure, they tore through to the next page. The text was not within the lined pages but fell and rose with no boundaries. Even the margins were completely filled with terrifying afterthoughts and imagery. None of it flowed or made perfect sense, but the ragged pages appeared to outline his plans to abduct and "educate" Aiyanna. He was going to force her to see the error of her ways, and then he was going to rid the world of her sin. He would wipe her from the earth, eliminating what is left of himself and Amara. He wanted to end the lineage. He saw it as his duty, as a child of God, to destroy the demon. Ai represented depravity and immorality and everything that was wrong with the world. He saw her as the origin of Sin. Amara had been the serpent, but Ai was the apple. She was the thing that would ruin them all. God, he had fallen so far. It was then that Amara understood she should have left him to die in his apartment that day.

She therefore felt more than responsible for the whole situation. She had created the problem, and she had kept it going. It was her error in loving him, and it was her fault for breaking him. It was she who told him about their daughter. It was she who saved the man intent on hurting her and her child. It was her problem, and therefore her responsibility to fix it. Whatever that entailed.

CHAPTER 51
Edan

The Highlands call us back again...

The scents were overwhelming. It was almost too much to bear. The smell of death was like a punch to the skull. Corpses. So many of them. Scents Edan recognized. People he knew. Hands that sneaked him scraps from the table or scratched behind his ears. He lowered himself closer to the ground and plowed on.

The chaos of the battle frightened him. He tucked his tail between his legs and scurried between the bare knees and flying kilts and swinging swords. He ran as fast as his paws would carry him, hoping his master was following. But he was not. Edan waited until the screams and the noise died out, cocking his ears on occasion to listen for his master's voice calling to him.

As Edan made his way down the hill, the smells of death began. That was where he found himself sniffing through the iron of blood and odor of mud and stench of death to recognize the man beneath. He was searching for the unique smell of Emrys. His was of coal and leather and wood burning smoke.

And then he found him.

His master was amongst a wad of men from both sides. He was stiff, his hands frozen half-open and his face stuck in a state of pain. His eyes were open and unblinking, reflecting a white cloud from the sky overhead. It broke Edan.

He howled a long, low, sad tone. He held the note until he felt like his lungs would give out. His eyes filled with tears. He whimpered and pressed his wet nose beneath his master's cold fingers. The fingers did not close around his fur as they always did before. They did not scratch that spot on Edan's chest that always caused him to kick his leg. His fingers did not move. Edan whimpered again and kissed his master's hand with a lick. He was Edan's best friend in the entire world. He lifted his stiff hand with his nose and put his shaggy head beneath it. He put his chin on his paws, the weight of his master's hand on his skull. He would never leave him like that. He would just die right there with him.

***

Edan would not be left alone to die like that, however. Scavengers in people form descended from the hilltops, seeking any loose coin or marketable weapons. Scavengers from the sky descended with their squawks to tear the eyeballs and flesh from the dead. Edan kept them all at bay with growls and bared teeth. He snapped at the overly aggressive ones with every intent to kill them if they were so determined to get to his master. His life would not be demeaned or disrespected by the abuse of his body afterward. Edan would see to that. They would have to get through him first.

Eventually, they showed up with the death carts. They piled the corpses high, but they treated his master with extra respect under his watchful eye. He plodded sadly beside the cart the entire way back home.

Edan would not leave Emrys. He refused to leave his side as a stray puppy until Emrys finally caved and took him home. Edan was by his side for all of the years between that and this, and he refused to leave his master as he marched toward the field where he would die. Edan could feel the fear in his heart, he sensed it. And he would not leave him now, even after his soul had departed elsewhere and there was an end date after the dash on the piece of wood they would carve up to represent his life, placed at the head of his grave. Edan would not leave him now, and he would not leave him ever.

CHAPTER 52
Amara

He found her. Dear God, it had finally happened.

Amara was panicked, her heart beating faster and her palms sweatier with each interstate exit closer to Aiyanna. Ronnie was in a rental car from the city, edging closer and closer, and Amara was following several car lengths behind in her unremarkable sedan. When she realized what direction he was headed, she almost had an anxiety attack. Her heart was beating hard against her chest, punching the air from her lungs.

Asinine as it was, she tried convincing herself it was a coincidence. She would keep following and find that he had an old uncle who happened to live in the same area. One whom he had never visited before in all the time she knew him. He would drive his car up to the curb at some nondescript ranch house where he would pull a brightly-wrapped birthday gift from his trunk. Or maybe he had found a dealer out in the country who grew his own weed, skipping the middle man. She should have known where he was headed, if she were doing a proper job. He had not found Aiyanna. He could not have. Amara tried to keep up with his internet searches and phone calls made, his daily routines and his social media movements. She dedicated the last two decades of her existence entirely to following his movements and keeping him away from the very direction in which he was headed. Had she missed something?

Okay, whew. He was not headed toward Eve's house. That wasn't the way. They were two hours away from Eve's. But where was he going? And then it dawned on her. He must have found Ethan. She still kicked herself for letting that happen without her knowledge, but he was behind on Ai's whereabouts. He obviously did not know Ethan and Aiyanna were no longer together and that she had moved back in with Eve. Amara could not be sure, but she hoped if her hunch turned out correctly, and Ronnie had found out about Ethan, he would get no further than that. However, she ruminated as her stomach dropped and a sense of dread sent spurs throughout her blood, if he were that close, it was only one step away to finding out about Ai. He was so close. How was she going to fix this?

Finally, Ronnie parked the car in the end of a cul-de-sac of small homes with little yards. He parked and waited. He did not step out of the vehicle. He just waited, staring at a discrete tan house with a black door and drinking from a bottle in a paper sack.

Eventually, Amara began dozing off, her head snapping forward and her eyes flying open. It was so late, or early, depending on how you looked at it. The night was still, well past the hours of activity. She directed her gaze once more toward the rental car, but it still sat there, and she had not heard Ronnie's door slam.

They had been there for hours. She watched neighbors come and go, a couple walking their giant black Newfoundland, singles slipping out of their cars with sack dinners from fast food restaurants, secret lovers sneaking in through back doors. But Ronnie's gaze never broke from the black door. They had both observed a woman in high heels stroll between their two cars hours ago, her curves bouncing with each stomp, the muscles in her legs tight from the teetering heels. Amara perked up at the sight of Ronnie's overhead light indicating his open door just as the woman rang the bell on the very house he had been stalking. Ethan's house.

Amara had not taken a proper breath since she watched Ronnie slither from his car and saunter right up to the door. Her heart was pounding so loudly she could hear it in her ears. She wondered if she should intervene or call the authorities. If she called the police, they would have to let him go. They had no proof he had done anything wrong...yet. And then he would know she was onto him. But before she had to decide, he moved to the side, peeping in the windows instead. What was he looking for? He must know this was not Eve's house. He stayed there, lurking and occasionally peeping, close to an hour.

Then, the outside light above the black door flicked on and the young woman emerged, clearly disheveled. The walk of shame. Amara had performed said walk a thousand times herself. Ronnie startled her. There was a disagreement. Dear God, what was he doing?!

Amara strained her eyes, but she could not make out what was happening. She had not seen Ronnie get back into his car, but he and the girl both were away from the doorway. Somewhere in the darkness. Ethan appeared, and he too darted into the dark. Amara panicked and began dialing the police, but Ronnie was moving again, and she could not afford to lose him.

He was shoving the girl into his car. Amara did not know what to do! The girl was not Aiyanna, but he must have thought it was. Of course! This was her boyfriend's house! But who was the girl?

Then they were moving. She had not seen Ethan go back into the house, but he was not in the car with them. She hoped he was okay. She was still uncertain on what to do, so she just followed. For miles and miles. She had to stay behind to make sure he was not headed toward Aiyanna's town. But perhaps Amara should take off and get there first? Would Eve take her seriously if she knocked on her door in the middle of the night? Would she even recognize her now?

Unsure of the right thing to do and her mind whirling, Amara just kept following Ronnie and that poor girl he had with him. She followed him to a field, where he parked conspicuously. It was increasingly difficult to keep pursuing unseen, as there was nowhere to hide and no one else on the roads. She parked in a driveway far enough away to avoid his attention, but close enough to keep his car in sight. She could make out the outline of the two bodies in the car, though she could not hear them or catch the finer, slighter movements.

She needed to call some law enforcement. She cupped her hand around the screen to hide the light. No signal. She would have to act if she saw him try to overtake the girl, even not knowing her. Amara's goal was to keep her daughter safe and stay with him until he was back home and Ai was safe, but she could not bear witness to the assault of some poor girl and just do nothing. However, it did not appear he intended to rape or otherwise truly hurt the girl. He just kept talking, it seemed, his hands gesticulating wildly. Perhaps the girl would explain to him that she was not Aiyanna. But if she did, he would set out to find the real Ai. Amara could not allow that.

Without being able to make a call, she just watched. She saw him hit the girl, and she opened her door to go help her, but by the time she started to jog that way, he was already back to ranting. He stopped even looking at the girl, seemingly talking to the empty field out of his front windshield.

No telling how long he was there, his mouth and hands both moving around rapidly. The girl sat in the passenger seat, mostly still, moving her head around slightly on occasion.

And then he was driving again, peeling out of the field, flipping mud up over the back of the rental car. He headed the opposite way he came – toward Ai. Amara did not know if he discovered he got the wrong girl. She did not know anything about what was going on or what she should do. Her mind was cluttered with a traffic jam of thoughts and panic. Ronnie was driving toward her Aiyanna, and she could only assume his captor had confessed that she was the wrong one. The way he peeled out indicated to Amara that he was pissed off. She could not - she would not - allow a mad Ronnie to get to her daughter.

The time had come. She needed to make her move – it was now or never. She spent years and years of her life planning for this very moment, and she was ready. It was time to end the nightmare.

Ronnie was speeding down the empty backroad, and Amara was racing to catch up. She was afraid – there was a very narrow shoulder on this rocky road, and there are places where tree roots grow below, pushing the asphalt into large speed bumps. He was flying, and so was she. She was no longer afraid of being seen. Faster, then faster. They were flying around bends, the back end of her sedan almost lifting from the ground when it rounded each curve. He knew he was being followed at that point, but she absolutely could not lose him. It was a matter of life or death.

She had to do it – it was time. She pressed the gas pedal until her toes touched the floorboard, gripping the wheel with white knuckles, praying an apology to the poor girl with mistaken identity riding shotgun in the rental car. And then she was plunging into the rear of the rental vehicle.

The moment might have been an eternity for how slowly it unfolded. But it was just a blink of an eye. A shower of scratches fell upon her face, twinkling shards of glass sprinkling and shooting like precarious confetti. It was a glittery rainfall of fear and failure and finality. The sound of tires screeching and metals contorting, scraping and bending in unimaginable ways. Screaming. Hot spikes of pain stabbed into her flesh. One second, one beat in time.

She thought of her name. Amara Astilbe Burns. Eve, her mama, chose that name specifically for her. What had she meant when she did? Amara in Sanskrit meant immortal, in German it meant eternal, and in Greek it meant unfading. That makes sense, given the family's ability to access past lives. In Latin and Italian, however, it meant bitter. But in Nigerian, it meant God's grace. Had Amara's mother been able to see that she would be all of those things? Or was Eve giving her the opportunity to decide her own fate in giving her a name that could mean almost anything?

When the world stopped spinning, Amara could hear shrieking. Perhaps it was her own. Maybe it was a siren. Maybe she had been blacked out while the whole thing unfolded around her. It was as if she heard the whole thing from the bottom of a swimming pool, far away and gurgled.

Maybe she was dead. But her body was burning and screaming in pain. She could not move her legs. She was drowning in her blood.

He was dead. Her Ronnie was finally dead. She was relieved and yet, saddened. He died on impact. The girl was critical. The police on the scene did not realize Amara was conscious, or even alive, and she heard them confirm the death of the man.

Thank God. Aiyanna was safe. Amara was so sorry for the sacrifice of life in order to be free. She was so sorry that girl had to be involved, the dear. But Amara was finally free from the madman she loved. They all were.

A paramedic in a black polo shirt leaned over Amara, checking her body, a look of consternation wrinkling his forehead. The young man with his beard and piercing brown eyes could not know she was already on her way out. Off to live another life. He urgently performed CPR. Those were the last breaths her body would breathe. She could barely make out a tattoo on his arm as he frantically worked to save her soul. *Love is life*. How incredibly true that was.

Amara rolled her eyes toward the sky, the first glimpses of sunlight beaming brightly across the horizon. A magnificent tourmaline sunrise.

She surveyed her mangled body from somewhere else. Somewhere afar, uninvolved. She was free of pain. Free of everything she had felt weighed her down. Her body, that body to which she no longer belonged, was in rough shape. It stared back at her, barely alive. The flame tattoo on the ankle was faded.

Maybe she would be better next time, in her next life. She finally learned what love was, after all. She could no longer understand why she fought it for so long. It wrapped its arms around her and comforted her in its velvet serenity. She squeezed the paramedic's hand and blinked a *thank you* into his soft eyes.

She sent forth a prayer, into the ether, into the world. To her Aiyanna, *I love you. Mama, I love you.*

It was the last thought to ever pass across her brain before she was no more.

CHAPTER 53
Aiyanna

All of the energy Jamma had had the day before was gone, plus more. She had spent herself, and I could see it in the deep lines on her face as she slept late into the day. That was so unlike her. Normally, Jamma was up with the sun, happy for another morning and another day to live.

Concerned, I pulled the rocking chair next to her bed, as she had done so many times for me. A ray of sun shone through the window in a shaft of light across the room, lighting her face with a soft glow. The air was glittered with particles of dust dancing in the illumination. I counted her white eyelashes as she slept, her eyes darting back and forth in a dream, her dry, wrinkled lips occasionally pursing. I patterned my breathing with hers, listening for the shallow rattle before beginning my own inhale. I have no idea how long I was there, watching over her.

Then her eyes fluttered open, a soft smile on her face when she noticed I was there. Her eyes were distant. "Aiyanna," she whispered, her voice thin and her breathing ragged, "my beautiful blossom."

I put my elbows on the side of the bed and wrapped her hand in my own. It was so small, which somehow surprised me. Those hands had rocked me and wiped my tears and cooked so many meals. They drove cars and tied shoelaces and brushed the knots out of my hair. The hands that held up the whole world, as far as I was concerned, were soft and fragile, the bones frail beneath my own fingers, the skin loose as I rubbed a thumb across them. I had to stop myself from squeezing, an urge surging through me to just drive more life back into her by force. If I could donate some of my own life and health, I would. I just needed her to be okay.

"I saw my father," Jamma spoke softly, her ragged voice like a child's. "And mother. It was the most glorious thing."

Her eyes were distant, somewhere far away, and peaceful. "And I saw your mother. My Amara," she whispered with a small smile. "She was happy. Surrounded by light."

I brushed a fine gray hair from my Jamma's forehead.

Her eyes focused on me. "Sweetie," Jamma choked out, "it's time." She had known, I could tell. She had made peace with it and was letting me know. She nodded ever so slightly and squeezed my hand.

I shook my head, tears pouring from my face in an unexpected rush. I suppose I had known it was time, as well.

No. I refused to accept what was happening. It couldn't be happening. It just could not.

I needed this woman. I always had. I could not do the whole life thing without her. She was my confidante, and my friend. She guided me and cared about me, as she did everyone around her. She loved with abandon. It never mattered how someone had hurt her or if they continued to disappoint. If she had two pennies to rub together, she would donate one to charity. I couldn't be without her, but the world needed her just as much as me.

"It's okay, my beautiful blossom," she whispered, always with some insight into my thought processes. Each word was an effort, but I listened intently, absorbing every syllable. "You will live on, as you must." She paused to take a rattling breath. "I want you to seek out your own happiness, for you have always been mine. Make your own life, Aiyanna, as you made mine — happy, warm, full of love. Life is love, my girl, and we will find each other in the next. Until then, don't ignore today. Don't take it for granted," she whispered, her eyes glistening. "It is a gift."

I blinked tears out of my eyelashes. I would not let go of Jamma's hand for anything. I could feel my own heart breaking, but I didn't want to miss one second of her. Not one second of life.

"I love you." She squeezed my hand.

Her sky-blue eyes rolled to the ceiling and widened with something resembling recognition, then joy. The sunlight from the window illuminated her face like an angel, lighting her sky-blue eyes. A small, tender and soft smile was the last thing my Jamma ever did before she closed her eyes. And then she was gone.

A sob escaped my chest before I could stop it. I let out a long, ragged shriek. Why?! Alone, there with what was my Jamma, I sobbed. For everything. For all that had happened. For the loss of the greatest woman I ever knew.

CHAPTER 54
Adelbert

He was in ruins. It is wrong and unnatural for a man to lose his child. Adelbert lost both of his in just one lifetime.

He lost his son to war and he lost his daughter to the sea.

He was German, and he was strong and proud. He immigrated when he was a boy. He was resilient. He learned the language, and he started his own business. He was successful and stoic. He never cried. Not until he lost his first child. A note was all he got. A standard-form letter from the army telling him his boy had died. He cried right then and there. It was not two years later he lost his girl. His sweet baby girl. She disappeared, without warning. They tried to tell him she took her own life. That was not who his daughter was. They would not listen.

"It's time to say goodbye now, love," Violet whispered gently, her hand on his arm. She had been a lifesaver.

She moved her long, dark tresses off of her shoulder. She was magnificent. Adelbert would be lost without her. She had taken over managing the business and paying their debts. She handled everything.

It felt as if a ton of bricks pressed down on his shoulders. How could he say goodbye? His girl had been so young. And how do you have any resolve without any answers?

It was still a mystery, what happened out there on the sea. The crewmen said she must have fallen overboard, but his Anastasia would not have been so careless. It was unlike her, as the sea had always made her nervous. Then they tried to tell Adelbert his daughter had taken her own life. That, too, was not his Anastasia. There was something about her death that haunted him and invaded his dreams and most of his thoughts.

Violet helped him stand and walked with him, arm in arm, across the lush carpeted hallway and up a long aisle, lined with flowers and sympathetic nods and darkly-dressed people. He pushed the thought from his mind that it would never be Anastasia to walk up an aisle, her hand on his arm, so he could give her away in marriage to some deserving gentleman.

At the front of the church, there were just flowers. There was no casket, for there was no body. There was no family left but Violet and himself.

They sat on a very hard pew and listened to words of some man who hardly knew her speak of the short-lived life of his Anastasia. The man did not mention the way her laugh sounded like music or how her curly hair often bothered her, and she would, with a puff of frustrated breath, push it out of her eyes. He did not speak of the way she always stopped to pet an animal or how she loved the colors in the twilight sky.

That man did not truly know her. Only Adelbert did. Only he, in that church full of people, knew the soul of his sweet girl. And he would be the only one who ever would. The thought of it stabbed through his heart and he felt like he, too, was dying. How could he alone bear the weight of all that was magnificent about his baby girl? How could he make them see they had lost something truly beautiful?

How could he say goodbye? It was not something he was prepared to do. It was not something he would ever be prepared to do.

CHAPTER 55
Robert

Red stared hard at the enlarged picture until the black and white portrait's pixels were all he saw. It sat on an easel, above a table with programs and a framed poem, in memoriam, just staring into the small crowd milling about. He had taken that picture many years ago. Eve wore red lipstick and a heart-shaped locket with a picture of him inside. He had to snap the shot between bouts of her singing love songs to him, changing the lyrics so he would laugh and forget to take her photo. Those eyes were looking through the lens then at a younger Red, full of love and promise. So how could those same eyes still slay his heart all of these years later?

She was dead. And all of those people were huddled together and chatting about the weather as if the world had not ended.

He had just found her again, and now she was gone. One night. It was not enough. Yet how could he complain when he had had a chance to say goodbye? How many people are given an opportunity to tell the person who meant the most to them in their whole life goodbye for good? Or at least…goodbye for now.

It was hard to let his wife go. He had not been ready, and it broke his heart. But this…losing Eve after just reconnecting…it was devastating.

Aiyanna had done a lovely job of arranging everything. At least, Red assumed it was her. He was not aware of any other family. There were white lilies and mixed bouquets as bright and vibrant as Eve herself. His heart ached for poor Aiyanna. He knew what Eve meant to her, and he did not know how she had been handling the whole thing.

He should have called. He should have offered help or his condolences or something, at least. Instead, he had been in a fog since he first read the obituary online. It was a blow for which he was wholly unprepared. He just knew they had gotten it wrong. It was a misprint. It was the wrong Evelyn Elizabeth Burns, the wrong dates, the wrong surviving granddaughter named Aiyanna. They had just shared their first kiss again. They had danced and laughed and she had been so...alive.

He stared at the photo with the dates of birth...and death. The end date, after the dash, glared at him from the page. How could that one date, a seemingly insignificant series of numbers, break a human being and stab through his heart like a knife? How could one small hyphen on a page filled with words encapsulate everything a person was? How could a dash tell the world that Eve was the sun, and they were all lucky to just be close to her? To feel her light upon them and give them life? The end date presented itself as so finite. No one could know that is so often just the beginning.

It could not be – the fates could not be so cruel as to steal her from him twice in a lifetime. But he could not deny the picture, the same picture that gazed lovingly from an easel at the funeral, stared out from the computer screen.

Selfishly, he felt more alone than ever.

"Robert," said a soft voice, interrupting him from his thoughts.

Aiyanna's face was swollen with grief, her eyelids puffy, her mascara running below her eyes. Red's heart broke all over again for her. They stood there like that for several seconds, silently, just understanding each other. Perhaps they were the only ones there who really comprehended the loss. Perhaps they were the only ones truly lost without their Eve.

She hung her head, tears visibly falling from her eyelashes. "You're the only family I've got now," she spoke softly, sadly.

Red was flattered that she would think of him in that way, but he was also thrown off by it. That must have been apparent in his bewildered expression because she gazed up and cocked her head.

"You… didn't know?" her shoulders slumped even more, rounded with the weight of everything, her bloodshot eyes showing surprise. "You're Red. The love of Jamma's life. She was pregnant when you left for Vietnam," she said gently, understanding spreading across her face that he had no idea before that moment.

Sparkles danced across his eyes and he thought he was going to pass out. It felt like someone had punched him in the gut and the shock of it exploded throughout his body. A tingle of goosebumps scattered down his arms. He stammered, not sure what to say or what to think. What was she talking about?

Observing his bewilderment and graciously giving him time to compose himself, Ai continued on. "She had a girl. You had a daughter," she corrected, "Amara. My mother."

Love and pride and surprise surged through him, washing out the years of loneliness and regret. He grabbed Aiyanna in a big bear hug, startling her. She let out a small grunt.

Red loved his wife. She was everything he needed then, and he had accepted all of her flaws, as she had accepted his. Though they never spoke of it, a part of him knew she understood that he always had love in his heart for another woman. But he was devoted to her for the remainder of her life. And he stayed true to that vow until her death. Therefore, he had long ago given up the notion of having children of his own. She was aware of his injury and his inability to father children. She had moments of sadness about it, but they became more infrequent as time passed. And Red had hidden his deep disappointment and regret about the matter from her, for that was not helpful, and he never would have hurt her by speaking those thoughts aloud.

He had been so deeply lonely since she had passed. He tried to pass the time by reading or gardening, but nothing could stop the idea that he was going to die alone. He had no family left, no one to notice or care if he keeled over one day. No one to spend Sundays with or tell stories to from times gone by.

And when he saw that the light that was Evelyn Burns had been snuffed out, in this lifetime at least, he was deeply saddened. It should have been their family, one they created together, that lasted past them in time. As the fates would have it, it would.

He squeezed Ai. "Thank you," he said, finally releasing her. He had been crying tears of pain and loss for days, but it was tears of joy that fell from his thin eyelashes. He really studied her face for the first time. She had his chin. She smiled gently, seeming to understand what he was thinking.

"We have each other now," she whispered before wandering around the room, absentmindedly shaking hands and accepting various murmured condolences.

CHAPTER 56
Aiyanna

I was in a daze the days since Jamma passed, aimless and alone. I don't recall how, now, but I somehow managed to arrange a funeral and present myself to all of the crying faces in attendance. But after that social obligation, I had fallen apart completely.

I had not heard the news or answered my phone or even gone to the door when Red stopped by, twice a day, to check on me. I had done nothing, really, but sleep and survive. I had not eaten for days, and I didn't want to have to brave the outside world. Alas, I was out of groceries, though. So when the girl at the drive-thru, whom I vaguely recalled as a classmate, babbled on about someone finally completing their physical therapy, I assumed it was idle classmate gossip. I had barely been paying attention, just willing her to hand over my burger and take my money and leave me to my grief. At least until she mentioned Daisy's name.

I drove next door to the supermarket and read the Sunday paper standing right there in the entrance way in the pajamas I had worn for three days.

It was a front-page story about Daisy's bounce back after her horrendous ordeal. I was numb as I read on. I knew I should feel guilty because the last time we spoke had been a fight, and that had been quite a while ago. I knew I should feel sorrow that she had stopped by several times to talk to me after Ethan died, but I had turned her away. I read about what she suffered and how she was finally back to living a normal life.

Intellectually, I was bewildered and concerned and horribly guilty. Emotionally, I had spent myself, and there was nothing left. It was like when too many people try to rush through the same doorway, it all gets jammed up and no one gets through. That was my brain and my emotions at the time – all jammed up.

I *was* sorry we had fought. I had been meaning to contact her since my last regression, but with Jamma getting worse and all that had been going on, I just hadn't. Daisy had inadvertently shifted further and further down the totem pole, until I had forgotten my duties to her as a friend. I would never forgive myself for that. I just did not know what to say or how to explain to her everything that happened.

I wanted to forgive her for our fighting, though I could never phrase it in such a way to someone like Daisy. I wanted to forgive her for the times she had hurt me without ever intending to, just by being herself. I wanted to forgive her for the times she made me feel like I was lucky to be her friend, instead of gratitude for a shared friendship. I wanted to forgive her for our pasts – all of them. And I wanted to ask her forgiveness of me. I was self-conscious and indecisive. I had not made her friendship the priority I should have. I had not recognized that she needed me.

I wanted her to know I loved her, just as she was. I loved her for being a friend to me and for wanting to make a mark on the world and for trying so hard to be memorable when she really needn't try at all.

The next morning, I put on some clothes and drove myself toward Daisy's house. Stopped at a red light, I heard the Sunday morning sermon blasted from the same church that hosted Jamma's funeral. Something was said about forgiveness. I was compelled to pull in. As quietly as I could, I let myself in and shuffled silently to the back row.

Once I settled in a pew in the back corner of the church, I finally allowed myself to feel it. The light of the massive stained glass cross shone upon me as I crossed my arms over the back of the pew in front of me and buried my face in them. I let myself remember. I allowed my memories to wash over me and to flood through my mind.

From our first meeting through the last fight, through every regression in which Daisy was a part, even the bad ones. I cried for those memories, forgave her for what she had been, sorrowful for what she could have been. I cried for my Jamma. I cried for Ethan.

I did not hear the rest of the sermon that morning – I just sat there, silently sobbing for all that was lost. I could not keep it inside any longer, and the light of the cross shining down on me felt like permission to let it all go. I wept at the feet of the stained glass God and gave myself to His will. I forgave Him, too, for taking my Jamma. I had hated God for some time for what I believed to be cruelty toward me, but in that pew with the light of the late afternoon sun filtering through the reds and purples and teals of the glass, my anger was purged. I was blessed.

I was vaguely aware of folks filing past me and the jostling and shuffles of the crowd leaving. The sermon was over, but my mourning wasn't. So I stayed there just like that, with my head buried in my arms. They could kick me out if they needed the space, but I just couldn't make myself leave.

The acoustics and illumination of the church were comforting and encouraging. I felt less alone and not as lost in the place of worship. I wanted to prolong that feeling just a few more minutes before heading into the unknown at Daisy's house or back home to an empty house with a forlorn dog and a lifetime without Jamma.

I felt a warm hand press my back, and I finally broke free of my little cage of lamentation, face wet with hot tears. It was like a scene in some movie, Daisy's face illuminated in the light of the church, framing her features like the hero who saves the day. Without a word, she sat beside me. I could feel the warmth of her leg as it brushed against mine. She was very much alive. *I* was alive. I had another day to do right and be good, to honor my grandmother by living.

I had lost the best part of myself, but I was still alive. Jamma would want me to carry on and to live a life of which I could be proud. One which would make her proud.

I objectively analyzed the face of my friend. The friend I thought I needed to be a part of society. The friend I thought I could not live without. And yet, there I was, living without her. I realized I did not need her at all. My love for her had framed her in a sort of resplendent light, and perhaps that had been my problem all along. I raised my friend to the highest of pedestals, and perhaps that was unfair. Perfection was my expectation of her, and I was therefore always bound to be disappointed. Perhaps the lesson was to raise my eyes even further, to something truly majestic. Perhaps I had unfairly been using Daisy as a crutch in order not to have to stand on my own. She was not a bad person. She was just a person. I did not need her. I did, however, want her in my life.

"Aiyanna," she started, "I…" She seemed uncertain of what to say, starting and stopping several sentences. "I'm sorry," she finally conceded, her shoulders slumping with the words. Her eyes searched mine for forgiveness.

"I'm sorry, too," I confessed.

"So you forgive me?" she asked almost sheepishly.

"What on Earth is there to forgive?"

Daisy blinked in confusion. "Have you not read up on any news stories?" She began to realize that my access to information was limited. I did not know the full story.

"If a few things had happened differently, you and Ethan would have been married."

"What things?" I asked, genuinely curious and to that day not knowing what caused him to break it off with me. I had not realized how desperately I still wanted that closure.

"Circumstances, things," she said vaguely. "Okay, let me start at the beginning." And so she did.

When she was done telling me what happened with Ethan and her kidnapping, she pulled a neatly folded news printout from her handbag. She opened and folded it to frame the photo of a mangled car wreck.

"Aiyanna, you need to read that." She had a strange look on her face. As I opened out the paper to read the article, she put her arm around my shoulder.

That's when I saw it. Her photo. The name beneath it said she was a lady named Ann, but I recognized the face instantly. It was my mother. Her eyes beamed from the pixelated newspaper. She caused the wreck! I felt sick to my stomach. My mother was alive?

Daisy patted my shoulder to let me know she was still there. "Keep reading," she encouraged.

My mother *had* caused the wreck, but authorities believed, based on evidence found in her home and Ronald Proctor's apartment, that she was acting in a way to try to save the kidnapped girl. The rest of the article was a glowing review of my mother's work as a private investigator and her vigilante attempts to keep that Ronnie character off of the streets. Goosebumps prickled throughout my body. I ran my finger over the headshot of her. She was different from the picture I had, older. Still beautiful. She had been just a few miles away. I felt the loss of not knowing her, but the way she lived her life made me proud. I knew Jamma would have been proud, too.

Daisy pointed to the mugshot of the intense Ronald Proctor. He was her abductor. He was Ethan's murderer. And he was my father.

"Ai, Ethan did love you. You were the love of his life. If circumstances had been different, he would have given you this," she said, presenting a stunning single diamond ring with a purple Forget-Me-Not tied around the stem. "He gave it to me that night to give to you, and I finally got it back after... Anyway, he was a mess without you. His house looked like a hoarder's house! I stayed for hours helping him clean it up."

Stunned, I started laughing at the nonsense of it all. Then I cried again. A while later, when I was good and ready, I wiped my eyes and set my shoulders. I slid the ring onto my right hand and clenched the emotion I was feeling into a fist. It was time to get busy living.

"Daisy, I wouldn't undo any of it." I placed my hand over hers to let her know I didn't mean that in a harsh way toward her. I knew she had experienced some serious trauma. "If things hadn't happened exactly as they did, I would have missed these last few months with Jamma. I wouldn't trade that time for anything in the world. And you, just look at you," I smiled. Daisy was as fresh as...well, a daisy. She glowed from within. There was soul in her eyes, where before she had kept it hidden away.

She said she understood, and we both fell silent. One of the panes of stained glass was an image of Joseph and Mary, with baby Jesus. It was the portrait of a loving family. And in that second, I had an epiphany. I realized Ethan was never the love of my life. He never even had a chance. That position had already been, and would always be, filled already. By my Jamma.

Romantic love wasn't the only kind that existed, and it wasn't even the strongest kind. The bond between the soul that was, that still is, Evelyn Burns and myself would always mean the most to me. It is a union deeper than marriage and greater than any event – even death. It was a promise and a choice. It was a pledge and a pull toward each other that would live throughout eternity. That is what Jamma had been trying to tell me. The love doesn't go away. We would always be soul mates in some way, and even after this lifetime was over, we would love each other through many more. Heaven or Hell would never break our bond. We were more than that. We existed because of each other and for each other, and our stories would always intertwine.

I had no idea what to make of all of the things Daisy told me that morning. But something had certainly changed within her. Probably within me, as well. We sat there for quite a while, staring ahead at the Lord in the vivid stained glass mural, tears in His eyes. Finally, we said our apologies and acknowledged our new association. We forgave each other, and we gave ourselves permission to move on. There in that church pew, shoulder to shoulder, Daisy and I absolved ourselves.

CHAPTER 57
Beatha

I had informed Dr. Haney that it was going to be my last session. It had been a month since Jamma passed, and I had thought about her ceaselessly. I pondered the things of which she spoke, considering her stance on time. She had wanted me to live my life, this life, and stop seeking answers from my past. I could find love in my memories, and I could live a sort of limited existence by seeking out other lives, but it would be detrimental to this one. I had to keep moving.

I relaxed my body and allowed Red to guide me back. His steady voice lulled me out of my body, which was prone and extremely relaxed on his leather sofa. I was headed somewhere very specific, with a particular purpose in mind. I needed his help to navigate it.

And then…

Emrys paced, tapping his thumbnail against his front teeth.

"I wilna disappoint my clansmen, Beatha. I canna let them go alone."

"You canna leave *me* alone!" I pleaded. I placed a protective palm across my belly. It was flat now, but it wouldn't be for long. "You canna leave us. We're to have a bairn, Emrys," I reminded him. Edan rose from the floor and licked the hand not touching my belly. I petted his shaggy ears, grateful for him.

Emrys covered my hand with his, warm and strong. In this life, and in my heart years from then as I lay on the couch in Dr. Haney's office, I felt loved. Emrys, or my Ethan, as I'd known him, embraced me with all of the love in his body. I could feel it engulf me, then and now.

"'Tis true, I've no notion of how this will turn oot," he admitted as he pulled me away so he could see my face. "But I am a man, and a warrior. And if it be ill-fated, you'll always have my love, Beatha. My beautiful wife," he smiled, and lightly kissed my lips, brushing my cheek with his fingertips. "Our love will never die. I will find you again, if not in this life, then the next."

A cloud of sadness hung around the woman on the sofa so many years and miles away, a tear sliding out of my closed eyes and rolling down my cheek.

However, a stern resilience set Beatha's shoulders straight, my green eyes narrowed as I set myself to it. Emrys and I both knew he would not be returning, and I didn't want to spend our last evening arguing about it.

Edan sniffed around as I pulled out the gift I had for Emrys. I wanted him to know that I supported him, even when we disagreed. I tied the leather bracelet to his wrist, the inscription of my clan stamped onto it: Ne Obliviscaris. Never Forget. It was a promise between us - we would never forget. We would always remember who we are and where we came from. Our heritage. Our dreams. What we wanted. Who we were. I would teach our child about his father and his heritage, and they would teach theirs. We would never forget the love between us.

Emrys wrapped his arms around me, holding tightly. I thought I could feel him shaking with sobs, but I did not say a word. We both understood implicitly that this was goodbye. I breathed him in. His smell, his love. I let it wrap around me in a memory I would never forget. Silently, I said goodbye.

Goodbye, Ethan. ...Goodbye, Jamma. I love you, and that love will never die. Ne Obliviscaris.

CHAPTER 58
Aiyanna

Red sipped his tea and smiled at me over his cup.

"What?" I laughed. The sunlight twinkled in his eyes. We had arranged this weekly lunch date to keep up with each other. We were all we had now. I stopped going to him after that last regression – I didn't need his help as a therapist anymore. I needed him much more as my grandfather. My family.

We spent hours during that first lunch just catching up. I showed him the picture I had of my mother and told him everything I knew about her. He wept for not knowing her. She had his chin, too. I let him have the photo, and he placed it delicately in his shirt pocket with a very sincere thank you.

"You look so much like Eve," he said, rather out of the blue.

"Really?" I smiled. I knew I was a spitting image of my mother, but I had never made the leap to resemble my Jamma. There had been no pictures of her from when she was younger except the one displayed at her funeral. Some part of me ignorantly only ever imagined her in her older years, when she had led an entire life before I came to know her. Many lives, actually.

He ducked his head and stared at some imaginary crack in the pavement of the café area. "I wasted so much time." He sighed. "I loved her for my whole life, and I'm not sure she ever knew."

"She knew." I believe Jamma knew so much more than any of the rest of us could understand. It would take several lifetimes. She knew I would need family, and so would my grandfather. She had found Red before she left us, and she made sure to put me in his capable hands. She knew Ethan wasn't the end of my story. She knew how much I loved her, too. "Love will always find its way back to us. You two will be together again, I think. In some way."

As I reached across the table to pat his arm, I knocked over my cup of coffee. It spilled all over the table and my shirt and the floor. I scolded myself for my clumsiness, but I still couldn't help but laugh. It was the first time I had truly laughed since losing Jamma. It felt good, like an old friend I hadn't seen in a very long time.

"I've got you," a handsome man smiled as he furnished me a handful of napkins. He was sitting directly behind me, and I had not noticed him before. He wore a black EMT polo shirt, and he had dimples beneath his beard and twinkling brown eyes. My heart gripped with recognition, but I had never met him in my life. Not this one, anyway. Adsila. My perfect wedding in the grove of trees.

"Hey, have we met somewhere before?" he asked curiously.

I could not conceal my laughter. It was just too much.

The man knelt down and helped me wipe the mess on the floor. As he shifted the wad of napkins to sop up more of the coffee, I caught a glimpse of a tattoo on his forearm in unpretentious black scroll. It said simply, "Love is life." I laughed again and sent up a silent prayer to Jamma for sending me a reminder. I was not always the best with subtleties.

I then proceeded to live out the rest of whatever this life had to hold for me.

It was not a goodbye. It was goodbye for now.

EPILOGUE

Time is fluid. We think of it as a thing, something tangible we can create or waste or manage. But it folds back upon itself, with layers of recognition entwined with the unfamiliar. It is not a straight line of chronological occurrences. It is twisted and malleable. At this very moment, you can make a decision that could change your future or someone else's. It would only be natural, then, that there might be times when one could be exposed to another period of time, whether cognizant of it or not, when the different layers of time touch, overlapping and intermingling.

So I ask you this, reader: what are you doing with yours? Are you a prisoner of your own memories, as I was? Trapped in a loop of replaying what already was, until that spinning wheel of the past rolls right over the present? That is a dangerous cycle, indeed – stuck in an endless rotation of what ifs. Are you trying to better yourself and those around you, or will you be doomed to start over again in the next life? Are you actively pursuing the very best you can be, or have you given in to the temptations that keep us imprisoned? Many lives were led, and many lives were lost, to bring us to the point where we are today, to the people we are today. We are creating history every day. What will be your story?

ABOUT THE AUTHOR

Lynda Abernathy lives in Georgia and works as a freelance writer and editor. She has been writing since she was old enough to hold a pencil. Her words are her courage, strengthened by her Celtic heritage of pride and poetry. She adores her dogs, coffee, family, and planning her next travel excursion.

NOTE FROM THE AUTHOR

Word-of-mouth is crucial for any author to succeed. If you enjoyed the book, please leave a review online—anywhere you are able. Even if it's just a sentence or two. It would make all the difference and would be very much appreciated. Thank you for your readership. Follow me via social media links below.

Thanks!
Lynda

www.facebook.com/authorlabernathy/
www.instagram.com/authorlabernathy/